THE ABBEY

Studies in Austrian Literature, Culture, and Thought

Translation Series

Alois Brandstetter

The Abbey
A Novel

Foreword by Alois Brandstetter

Afterword by Peter Firchow

Translated by

Peter and Evelyn Firchow

ARIADNE PRESS
Riverside, California

Ariadne Press would like to express its appreciation to the Austrian Cultural Institute, New York and the Bundeskanzleramt - Sektion Kunstangelegenheiten, Vienna, for their assistance in publishing this book.

Translated from the German *Die Abtei*
©1977 by Residenz Verlag, Salzburg and Vienna

Library of Congress Cataloging-in-Publication Data

Brandstetter, Alois.
  [Abtei, English]
  The abbey : a novel / Alois Brandstetter : translated by Peter and Evelyn Firchow.
      p.   cm. -- (Studies in Austrian literature, culture, and thought. Translation series)
  ISBN 0-57241-045-0
  I. Firchow, Peter Edgerly, 1937   . II. Firchow, Evelyn Scherabon.
  III. Title. III. Series
      PT2662.R258A6413   1998
      833'.914--dc21
                              97-16849
                              CIP

Cover Design:
Art Director, Designer: George McGinnis

Copyright ©1998
by Ariadne Press
270 Goins Court
Riverside, CA 92507

Foreword to the American Edition

Inspector Einberger, the "hero" of this novel, who addresses his report on the theft of a famous chalice from the Abbey of "Freimünster" to its Abbot, is not only a detective but also an accomplished complainer, a grumbler who finds fault with God and just about everything else. Among other things he complains about America.

Not long after the novel was first published, I received a letter from Professor Otmar Drekonja of the Department of Modern and Classical Languages at Saint John's University in Collegeville, Minnesota. In this letter, the grossest errors in my protagonist's image of America were addressed and (in full awareness of the fictionality of fiction) "corrected." Fiction and reality, poetry and truth...I have never been to America, but as far as I'm concerned, the best book about the New World was written by Franz Kafka, who likewise had never been "over there." He simply and plainly, and yet compellingly, called his book *Amerika*, thereby doing justice to the power and profundity of his book.

And so it was made clear to me that in America there is a vast Abbey which not even my fictional "Freimünster" can measure up to, at least not in terms of the number of its monks. Nor, for that matter, can the Abbey of Kremsmünster, which lies close to me in more than one sense and which possesses the most famous chalice in Austria, the Duke Tassilo Chalice. Incidentally, as chance would have it, the Abbey of St. John's was also robbed – really robbed and not just in the imagination. In this instance a whole collection of chalices was stolen and not just a single one, as in the case of the "Arnulf Chalice." In Europe, it would appear, everything is smaller and of more modest proportions, even crime...

Alois Brandstetter
Klagenfurt, Austria, July 1, 1996

P.S. I would particularly like to thank my translators, Peter and Evelyn Firchow. Intimately acquainted as they are with both the Old World and the New – the American and the German – they've been a rare and genuine stroke of good fortune for me.

Let's start again at the gate. From the word go I've started at the gate. I didn't just get praised for doing that. I got a lot more ridicule than praise for starting at the gate right from the beginning, and also for coming back to the gate. Today it's different; today naturally nobody has a problem with the gate anymore, even the gentlemen from Headquarters claim – now that the case has been solved – to have had the main gate in mind from the very beginning. In fact for a long time nobody went along with me about my gate. Remember, my dear Abbot, just remember back half a year ago, when the Viennese would say mockingly that Dr. Einberger always starts at the gate. They thought I was just a simple country cop and a dimwitted detective who couldn't make head or tail of this case in any other way. "Are you still trying to make it through that big gate?" the Chiefmost Viennese Inspector asked me at the time with his forked tongue in his cheek. "Inspector Einberger is of the opinion," the Viennese specialists added with amusement, "that the person who stole the Arnulf Chalice left Our Dear Lady of Freimünster via the main gate." And I actually was of that opinion, my dear Abbot, and in the end it turned out I was right. Later on the Federal Police came to believe in my gate too. It finally dawned on them too and a gate opened wide for them which they had been standing in front of like oxen at a new barn gate. It's not so long ago, my dear Abbot; only half a year ago my gate was still too big for everybody. They didn't "gate" it, so to speak. Even as late as September – yes, even far into October – my gate theory struck the Viennese as being too simple and too primitive. As late as the middle of October the Viennese were still saying that Frei- münster has 17 gates, but Einberger has this fixation on the main gate. There are 760 windows in Our Dear Lady, not counting the swallow holes, roof vents and basement shafts, but Dr. Einberger keeps standing and waiting for everything to happen at the main gate. You have no idea how many sermons I had to suffer through at the time. A camel will sooner pass through the eye of a needle, they said in Vienna, than a thief through the main gate. But I can tell you, my dear Abbot, a camel will sooner pass through a needle's eye than an idea through the heads of our Viennese bureaucrats.

Back to the gate, my dear Abbot. High above the main door of the main gate there is a Latin inscription chiseled into the stone in capital letters: ORA ET LABORA. Or, translated into the vernacular, "pray and work." Whoever sees and reads it, and surely the man from Regensburg also saw and read it, knows, and surely the man from Regensburg knew it too, that in this Monastery there aren't any Trappists, Carthusians and Zealots, or any stylites, mendicants and minorites. Nobody sleeps in coffins here and there isn't any absolute ban on talking either. In Freimünster we have the strict and yet so supple and flexible rule of Benedict of Nursia. To be sure, there is rather more in Benedict's *Rule* than just ORA ET LABORA, even though some folks may think otherwise. If you ask anyone these days about the Benedictines, then you don't hear anything for a long time and then you hear, if you hear anything at all, ORA ET LABORA. People nowadays don't know anything anymore; people nowadays can't even tell a Benedictine and a Jesuit apart. And there is a difference, as you well know, my dear Abbot. The two orders resemble each other as much as the names Ignatius and Benedict resemble each other. That's to say, they're like two different religions. In the *Rule* of St. Benedict there is of course a bit more than just ORA ET LABORA. For example, there's the Saint's description of what he expects and imagines the gates and gatekeepers of his monasteries to be like, to wit his description in Chapter LXVI *de hostiariis monasterii*. In this sixty-sixth chapter I read: "The gatekeeper should be an old and wise brother who knows how to take messages and provide information, and who, in consideration of his age and experience, should not be kept running around all the time." My translation is a little free. In the original it says: *cuius maturitas eum non sinat vacari; maturitas*, it says in the original, and *vacari*. But in one of the so-called "Consuetudo," that is, one of those additional instructions that continue Benedict's *Rule* in his spirit and also make it more specific, it says: "Let the Abbot take care that the gate, through which all and sundry in the monastery enter and leave, be guarded by a man who is watchful and careful but also friendly and reliable, so that everything harmful and detrimental to the monastery will be kept out but everything good, helpful and serviceable to the salvation of souls will find entry." The gatekeeper should be *vigilax* and *sobrius*. *Vigilantia* and *sobrietas*, Watchfulness, Alertness, Caution and Sobriety are the most essential characteristics of a gatekeeper. Hence the gatekeeper is not only called *hostiarius*, but also *vigilator* and *ostiarius*, that is to say, keeper of the gate, sentinel and watchman. Watchman, my dear Abbot, comes from "watch." Watching, watching wide- awake is what Benedict wants from his gatekeeper. The *Rule* doesn't say anything about a gatesleeper. Benedict differentiates between the gatekeeper's lodge, which he calls a watchpost, and the dormitory, the sleeping room or sleeping hall; for Benedict there's a certain difference between these two places. As for some sleepyhead or dreamer or drunkard, since it is the custom to sleep, dream and drink in our Freimünster porter's lodge, well, Benedict would never have dreamt about anyone like that in all the sleeping hours of his life.

In the old days, my dear Abbot, that's to say, during the early period of Benedictine monasticism when the Order didn't as yet possess such large-scale houses, such fortified, palatial castles and castle-like palaces as now, in the old days when the gatekeeper was really still a watchman and an unlodged sentinel who did his duty indefatigably out on the bridge and was exposed to wind and weather and continuous drafts, in those old days, my dear Abbot, a sleepy sluggard would certainly not have lasted long at this job, this exposed and hazardous job. After all, who can manage to sleep on his feet? But nowadays, gatekeepers and sentries aren't sentries and definitely aren't watchmen anymore, aren't ostiaries in the old Benedictine sense, aren't monks anymore, but laymen, in every sense of the word, that is secularized porters, masters of splendid and comfortable and luxuriously appointed porter's lodges with soft, deep stuffed chairs into which not only porters of moderate physical proportions plunge, sink and disappear almost to the point of vanishing completely.

Nowadays they are surrounded by every imaginable kind of convenience and technical aid; nowadays, my dear Abbot, the morale of porters has unfortunately suffered a great deal in comparison to former times. A tired watchman can hardly keep himself awake in his vastly overheated lodge, while a stream of virtually uninterrupted traffic passes through the gate. In the meantime the heat from the central heating system keeps on lowering the porter's threshold of attention and concentration, and a rush of traffic in goods and people surges and breaks through the gate. But all who pass through the gate aren't in a state that, according to Benedict, would have qualified them as being *idoneum*, that is fit for and conducive to the salvation of souls. The devil himself could walk in and out of the gate and the porter wouldn't recognize him. He would merely greet him negligently, the way porters at the entrances of factories nonchalantly greet everybody walking past them who doesn't look like the boss. Our porter here in Freimünster always operates according to the dictum of "open the door, open the gate wide." But observe: it isn't always the Lord who comes hither in splendor. I've watched lots of sleaze sneaking through the door. In the summertime girls stroll unabashedly through the inner courtyards, yes even into the churches, girls where you have to look twice to catch sight of a saving remnant of clothing, not to mention the utter absence of head-covering, female creatures whose appearance is, in Benedict's view, on the whole surely *unsuitable* for the spiritual salvation of monks and not only of monks; *idoneum*, *apt* and *suit*-able, though unfortunately not with suitable dresses and clothing, but suited only to transform life in the monastery into a state of disorder and unholy turmoil. My dear Abbot, one really doesn't have to be a monk, and one certainly doesn't have to be a fogey or a prude to want to preserve a distinction between a public swimming pool and an abbey church. Anyway, if it were up to me these ladies in miniskirts and hotpants would be kept waiting for a long time. If I were the gatekeeper I wouldn't raise my toll-bar for them. But, alas, nowadays all the barriers have fallen, or are barely standing, or have been barred. There isn't even an electric eye there, so that suspicious characters could at least be kept at bay or at a minimum be registered and counted. The Benedictines – so say the Benedictines along with everybody else whom they allow into their abbeys and into their cloistered cells, or in other words everybody – the Benedictines are open and tolerant. Everybody says the same: "The Benedictines are open and tolerant." That's a dubious reputation to have, my dear Abbot, because nothing worthwhile emerges from this opening, and nothing worthwhile comes into the monastery either, by virtue of such openmindedness and openness. That's not only evident from the fact that suddenly a valuable chalice vanishes.

My dear Abbot, along with a more profound understanding of what once actually constituted a house there has vanished the concept of what a gate should be. In other words, once upon a time it wasn't just a matter of protecting objects of material value which may have been contained in the house. In the old days there still existed something called "domestic peace." Just as, in the larger context, there used to be a "public peace." The gatekeepers of the Benedictine monasteries kept the peace, the so-called holy peace *intra muros* – they were peace-keepers. We who live in one-family houses probably don't have a real conception of that venerable and sacred peace any longer. Moreover, houses used to be almost like individuals; houses had a special spirit about them. One could justifiably speak of the genius of a house. Of course, our row houses have yielded up whatever genius they might have had long ago. There aren't even any spirits or ghosts haunting our mass-produced houses, not to mention geniuses. The old Romans, my dear Abbot, whose tradition the monks carried on so brilliantly, would really be astonished at the way we live now. They worshipped their own special house gods in their houses. Every house had its Lar, and next to the Lar near the fire they set up a little altar. These good spirits have left us to our own devices, not to mention the Manes, the deceased sometime owners of the house who kept on shaping the spirit and spirituality of a house long after they had passed on. We, on the other hand, can't stand having a dead body in the house for even an hour, and there's simply no question of holding a wake. The houses themselves have lost the capacity for mourning; nowadays there are no more houses of mourning.

There aren't any more houses of mourning, my dear Abbot, but instead there are lots of mournful houses. Not just architecture itself, but life within this architecture has grown melancholy and desolate. Usually, my dear Abbot, it's not just the dead who are hauled unceremoniously out of their houses but also old people. This is not conducive to bringing blessings down on these houses. People nowadays select their fellow lodgers according to completely new criteria; they assume that the wife and children have to be color-coordinated with the furniture. Grandfather, however, conflicts with the decor. According to the young people, he seems like a stranger in his residential environment. Grandfather is a fitting candidate for a nursing home, they say, and they put Grandfather into a nursing home. What I want to say, my dear Abbot, is this: there is too much that is wrecked and broken in our houses, viewed both from the outside and the inside; and that is the reason why we see in a house-door and a gate only a wooden board with hinges on it and a doorhandle, and nothing else. And what I don't want to say, my dear Abbot, is this: that perhaps we ought to go back to closing ourselves off, to segregating and excluding others. On the contrary, I'm a declared enemy of all clubs, coteries, lodges, cliques, claques and cartels. The mental and spiritual chaos in many houses derives precisely from their having closed themselves off. Encapsulating yourself leads to misery. What's important is to find the right rhythm for opening and closing – to keep the house open at the right time to the right people but to close it off to the wrong people and when the time is wrong. Even flowers and plants know when they should open their petals, because it's daylight, and when they should close them, because it's the onset of evening and nightfall. My plea is for a gatekeeper who has instincts, nothing more and nothing less.

Vigilax, my dear Abbot, is not the right word for the porter here in Freimünster. Unfortunately he isn't watchful but rather, I'm sorry to say, very often drunk. Since he is a layman I don't want to subject him to Benedict's code and measure him according to Chapter 40 of the *Rule*, which treats of *mensura potus*. Even though it's precisely this chapter that provides lots of food – and even drink – for thought concerning the appropriate quantity of nourishment and drink. Benedict introduces this chapter with a Biblical quotation: *Unusquisque proprium habet donum ex Deo, alius sic, alius vero sic*. Every man hath his proper gift of God, one after this manner, and another after that.... Benedict continues: *Et ideo cum aliqua scrupulositate a nobis mensura victus aliorum constituitur*, and therefore it is only with a certain reserve (*scrupulositate*) that we prescribe the quantity of food for others. The other day I tried to interpret this passage for your porter. "This means," I said, "that Benedict recognizes that each Brother's gift for being ascetic or anything else is variable and individual. And it would be wrong," I told your porter, "to interpret Benedict in the way you apparently do, namely to mean that he assigns it to the correspondingly different gifts given by God to humanity, in the hypothetical case of some individual's being able to eat and drink and digest more than another. It would be an exaggeration if I, basing myself on this passage, were to understand Benedict in the following manner: everyone has received his own special gift from God, this person the gift of science, this other the gift of prophecy – the former therefore is good at research, the latter at foretelling the future – and a third has a good appetite and is a voracious eater or drinker. That's not how it's meant," I said. Benedict's *scrupulositas* in limiting food and drink certainly didn't derive from that kind of outlook. Benedict's *Rule* is flexible and supple but it's not that flexible and supple. Moreover, Benedict in his *Rule* places a *non plus ultra* limitation on drinking. He says that one hemina of wine daily ought to be enough. About Coca-Cola which, to judge by the empty bottles under the staircase leading up to your office, you're in the habit of drinking, nothing is said in the Benedictine *Rule*.

One hemina of wine per day, my dear Abbot. But how much is that? In connection with my researches into the vanished Arnulf Chalice, I've had the latest literature concerning the hemina question ordered for me and I've studied it. I've found everything in it, my dear Abbot, except for unanimity. The hemina question is in fact answered in very different ways, and hemina research is the most controversial area of research you can possibly imagine. One hemina scholar says that a hemina is, according to present standards, a quarter of a liter, and another maintains that two liters wouldn't be far off the mark. One claims that in establishing this measure Benedict was thinking of the Umbrian hemina; another thinks he meant the Tuscan hemina. In the so-called *Inventarium instrumentorum* of 1123, it says of our Arnulf Chalice that it contains three heminas (*continens heminas tres*). That would therefore seem to provide us with a point of reference, except that now there's a new dispute within the Umbrian and Tuscan contingents as to how full the chalice would have been filled in the first place. How full is full? The Trier school of hemina research takes the view that the water level – or rather the wine level – was never allowed to exceed the height of the hammered gold image of the seated Pope on the outside of the chalice. The Beuron school, on the other hand, takes no cognizance of the Pope; they declare that this argument is untenable and invalid, and consequently they are pleased to see the pontifex maximus beneath the water table or, more precisely, beneath the wine table. It goes back and forth like this.

Initially I had the vague impression that the demonstrative zeal of the Benedictine hemina-scholars was not entirely innocent and did not always correspond to the first principle of Western science, namely to proceed *sine ira et studio*. I rather suspected that among the heminists who argue for the small quarter-liter hemina, there must be several teetotallers, and among those who speak of double liters and other astronomical numbers, several potent drinkers. *Cum ira et studio*, my dear Abbot, *cum studio*. For there is hardly a problem in moral theology which is debated with greater zeal by historians of the Church and the Benedictine

Order than this hemina problem. But later I changed my mind. Anybody who does research on a problem that is so marginal and does it with such persistence and zeal must have, as it were, a personal and vital stake in it. Then I realized that this was simply an inadmissible rationalization on my part. And I started to take joy in the *pure* passion of research. I found myself being invigorated by the idea of doing scholarship for its own sake. It's really an indication, I thought, of how a problem has been misconceived if some scholar devotes himself to one of humanity's great and eternally insoluble questions, whereas if he limits himself and doesn't overextend himself in the selection of his subject, it's a sure sign of the scholar's thoughtfulness and insight. The universities are half full of people who are working on the problem of squaring the circle, and most researchers, my dear Abbot, are still building away at the Tower of Babel. Others are still – or again – busy proving the existence of God instead of praying to him. In contrast, despite its contradictions, how cheerful and amusing is the field of hemina research! For it's better to know a great deal about a little subject than to waste a lot of effort on one of life's great questions and then in the end discover nothing at all. My dear Abbot, I could have told Faust right off that we not only don't know anything about the profoundest mystery of the universe, but that we also are unable to know anything about it. He could have saved himself the trouble. Then he wouldn't have had to hang around and complain that his heart was about to break from disappointment.

My dear Abbot, I'm not a minimalist. I'm all for geniuses trying to solve big problems, but wherever I look around in the academic world I only see dwarfs and lilliputians who, of all things, are determined to take up weight-lifting or highjumping. People should know what they're capable of thinking, and then they should think about their subject and think deeply about it, no more and no less. If somebody's no good at systematic thought, then, for God's sake, they should stick to the history of philosophy and not insist in the face of all reason on trying to tack some system together. And there's no reason either to look down with disdain and contempt on other people who aren't fiddling around with discovering the Synthesis of Being.

For example, consider the contempt with which our hardy friend Ernst Radinger is treated, even though he's a teacher and far and away the best authority around on Alpine Nativity Art. And what immense breadth and depth of knowledge he possesses in this neglected area of Art History and Folk Art! I could listen to him for hours on end when he guides people, as he does every year at Christmas, through the Schwanthaler Nativity in the Abbey Church. In one corner of this Nativity there is a figure, a double figure, a man with a boy hanging onto his coat, which in the field of Nativity Art is called the *Fatherletmecomealongtoo*. When I see this man, this teacher, walking through town during Christmas on the way to giving his tour at the Abbey, I step out of my office and say: "Radinger, let me come along too!"

Every year I listen to his tour, and from year to year I marvel at how his knowledge of the subject has grown broader and more subtle. It's simply not true what those who dislike and envy him say about Radinger: that he only knows and talks about trivia, or what they happen to think is trivia, such as whether Joseph used to stand to the right or the left, or when and where the Wise Men from the East were placed, etcetera. Radinger is able to extract an entire history of culture, morals and religion out of your Nativity in the Abbey Church, a whole science of folk dress, folklore, etcetera, etcetera. Whenever I listen to him and watch him teach, I always think to myself that Radinger should be appointed to some Chair at a university. One of those many wasted Chairs of Philosophy should be turned into a Chair of Nativity Studies, thereby replacing some frustrating and frustrated ontologist or metaphysician – some Unwiseman from the West – with the Nativityist Ernst Radinger.

My dear Abbot, I also provided the gentlemen from Headquarters with the benefit of my experience in hemina research and Nativity Studies – and in scholarship and science generally. Unfortunately, however, the Federal Police showed no interest whatever in following up on this complex set of interrelations.

The Viennese adopted the point of view that all of this had nothing whatever to do with the theft in question. I myself take a fundamentally different view. "Without history and without taking into consideration the historical perspective," I said to the Viennese, "we will certainly not be able to understand or explain either the Chalice nor, most likely, its disappearance. We have to dig deeply into history, Gentlemen," I said. Now, my dear Abbot, was I or was I not proven right?

Back to the porter! *Vigilax*, my dear Abbot, is what the Freimünster gatekeeper is not. Unfortunately this guardian of the threshold is not watchful; he is, on the contrary, very often drunk. However, a porter is a kind of signpost, because many people form their impressions of a place according to the image of the porter at the gate. The porter is in a certain sense a representative of the institution one is entering, yes, indeed he is the chief representative. In other words, he becomes typical and emblematical of the place from the newcomer's point of view. And I can tell you lots of people come in through the Freimünster gate! Not all of them, however, are amiably disposed; quite a few of them in fact are rather suspicious or even hostile or at least not benevolent. Above all, nowadays lots of unbelievers visit the Abbey. The place is crawling with people who don't believe or don't care or simply can't be bothered about religion. You can find them in all the courtyards, hallways, churches, in the cloister colonnade, in the garden, in the Museum, in the Mathematical Tower – everywhere. Entire chartered trainfulls and busfulls of unbelievers roll up to the monastery, and the monastery is overwhelmed by people without belief and without reverence. But a person lacking in reverence not only does not understand anything about religion, he also doesn't understand art and definitely not Christian art. In former centuries, if an unbeliever approached the monastery, one could be sure that he meant to do it some harm. In former times unbelievers either avoided monasteries or else they burned, looted and desecrated them. At least one knew what to expect. Particularly robbing and stealing seems now to have come back into fashion, but today the motives are completely different. The motives of our contemporary thieves and plunderers are purely materialistic; here, as everywhere else, the dominant factor is the most unabashedly naked materialism. The thieves are either businessmen and entrepreneurs or else possessive, greedy amateurs. In every case the motive is materialistic. Compared with the materialists of today, the iconoclasts of the Middle Ages were out and out idealists. The motive behind the devastation committed by the historical iconoclasts and plunderers was a purely spiritual and philosophical one. The iconoclasts were adversely motivated against any kind of materialization, fetishism and idolatry. That's where the difference lies, my dear Abbot. Nowadays even crime has become hollow and contemptible. Today not even crime is what it used to be.

On the whole, however, the unbelievers who visit Freimünster today are uninterested and harmless. It's my belief that the unbelievers who visit monasteries today are really indifferent to them; they're not interested in monasteries, they merely visit them. Visiting and touring monasteries or gaping at churches, are, in the final analysis, simply expressions of an immense apathy and indifference. Marvelling at monuments is a sign and indication of essential indifference, of the inner barrenness and emptiness of humanity. Because people are no longer interested in monasteries, or in what is characteristic and essential about monasteries, they visit them. Nowadays the unbelievers merely visit monasteries, whereas in former times they visited them with destruction. Perhaps it's only the contemptible nature of modern disbelief – not consisting of disbelief but merely of a stale lack of belief – that continually enfeebles not only the porters and gatekeepers of our monasteries but also the Church itself. And suddenly, my dear Abbot, the Arnulf Chalice is missing...

My dear Abbot, I still have a few words to say regarding the Abbey's material and artistic treasures which nowadays elicit such awe and stupefaction among so many unbelievers and so-called believers alike. And another word about the vanity and arrogance of our contemporary artists, who constitute the obverse side of this admiration. Nowadays people don't just gape and marvel at some old, conventional and traditional work of art, but also at new works of so-called art. Even if that new work turns out to be nothing special, the artist is nevertheless immediately gaped and marvelled at by the masses. And so the person being gaped and marvelled at gives himself airs because he's being gaped and marvelled at. *He gives himself airs* is much too friendly and elevated an expression for the undignified and nonsensical and shameless boastfulness of our artists. They give themselves *arse* is how it actually ought to be put; that would sound a lot better. Both artist and audience, my dear Abbot, nowadays have a completely perverted, because godless, relationship to art. Benedict tested everything according to whether it served *Ad maiorem Dei gloriam* or the greater glory of God. Today on the other hand it's merely *Ad maiorem artificis gloriam* – to the greater glory of the artist. Members of the various Academies of Art should be made to learn by heart the 57th Chapter of Benedict's *Rule*, or at least the following passage from it: *If there are any artists in the monastery, then they should exercise their art, when the Abbot permits, with all due modesty and humility. When, however, some individual is proud of his art because he imagines that he is serving the monastery with it, while in reality he is only serving himself, then he should be suspended from practicing his art and only be allowed to return to it when he shows himself contrite.*

Be that as it may, it's certainly not a good idea for visitors to Freimünster, even unbelievers, to be received and welcomed at the gate by a drunken gatekeeper, or, more accurately, not received and not welcomed because the gatekeeper is counting sheep in his comfortable lodge. The unbelievers especially should be properly received, and it is unfortunate if the gatekeeper of the institution makes no effort to ensure a proper reception. People these days, especially the unbelievers, have the craziest ideas; they run in circles and crosswise, mostly unwise, and there's nothing more shortcircuited than the mind, or rather non-mind, of an unbeliever. If the gatekeeper at Freimünster doesn't act properly, then probably the Pope in Rome isn't altogether infallible either. Unbelievers unhesitatingly make the logical leap from a drunken gatekeeper in an Austrian monastery to the Pope in Rome, or they even make the leap right away to the existence or nonexistence of God. If they don't see any sign of life in the porter's lodge, they say: "God is dead." That, my dear Abbot, is the way most of mankind's philosophical, but not only philosophical, conclusions have been arrived at.

Most university faculties of philosophy, including the Benedictine Educational Institute in your Bavarian home abbey, still teach logic and the strict art of judgment and deduction by means of the syllogism. This is an utterly unwordly enterprise. All human beings are mortal; Socrates was a human being, ergo and etcetera. Premise, minor premise, conclusion, condition etcetera, etcetera. Please, my dear Abbot, that's how judgments are arrived at in seminars on logic in universities and in their philosophical and theological faculties, but certainly not in real everyday life. It's about time that universities got around to teaching practical logic, that is, illogic. That's where the real need lies, to instruct students in illogic, in the recognition of false logic, to make it possible for them to see through the mischief and absurdity of the whole thing. A critique of the power of reason, my dear Abbot, is all well and good, but what is primarily needed is a critique of the weakness of reason, a critique of the lack of reason.

I don't want to commit a sin, my dear Abbot, but sometimes I think, as I'm listening to some unbeliever and considering the utter dimwittedness of what he's saying in all its length and breadth, and no bolt of lightning falls from heaven and punishes him on the spot for his stupidity, that perhaps there really is no God in heaven. Then I have to take hold of myself, so as not to become an unbeliever myself and lose my faith. But, as the proverb has it, even the gods can't cure stupidity. That's a saying one shouldn't just mutter to oneself but should take to heart. It's a truth that is thousands of years old, an incontrovertible truth that strikes terror into one's heart. God's omnipotence reaches an end when it comes to mankind's stupidity. Even God's Church, God forgive me, is not composed entirely of intelligent people, my dear Abbot.

Perhaps not all unbelievers make the logical leap from our porter in Freimünster to the Holy Father or to merciful God. But they certainly make the leap to you, Monsignor Abbot, and to the Prior and to the staff of the Abbey, and certainly not without reason. If the Monsignor Abbot doesn't call his gatekeeper to order, then the discipline of his House must be in a sorry state. Or they conclude *a priori* that if the porter drinks, then the Prior most likely drinks too. If the porter has a liking for alcohol, then the whole Abbey probably isn't averse to it either. Or their process of deduction leads them to the conclusion that if even the porter, who is located at the very periphery of the Abbey, drinks, then how much more must those be drinking who are hidden away deep inside the furthest cloister. The porter isn't even a monk, they say. The porter is only a layman, they say, and in so saying they mean that the porter is a mere babe in the woods when it comes to drinking. The porter hasn't taken orders, they say, apparently confusing taking holy orders with taking orders for drinks. And the unbelievers drive home and tell their amazed and unbelieving family about Freimünster. We've seen everything, they say; we've seen enough.

Oh my God, what are they seeking in Our Dear Lady of Freimünster, this multitude of unbelievers? Are these multifarious unbelievers perhaps seeking their lost belief in this place of pilgrimage, Our Dear Lady of Freimünster? I can't believe it. But let's assume, just for the sake of argument, that some unbeliever really comes along who is seeking his lost belief here in Freimünster, and immediately on entering he finds an empty gate or a full gatekeeper. Now he will probably turn back and think to himself, "Here I've lost my belief and also my way." Another seeker may hope to experience a spiritual awakening in this place of pilgrimage and then he finds right at the entrance a sleeping porter. It wouldn't be the first time that the Church had stood in the way of religion. Sometimes, instead of a spiritual awakening, there's simply a nasty wake-up call. Spiritual awakenings, my dear Abbot, aren't always easy to come by in your Abbey;

sobering-ups are easier. This is a place where many people have sobered up.

You know that often, after midday or in the evening, depending on when I get out of work, I like to take a walk through your grounds. At other times too I gladly make the rounds of your gardens. I'm always delighted by their vegetation, by the rank growth of the shrubs and the age-old trees, the stout oaks and the birches, the knobbly nut trees and the supple willows. And I delight not only in Nature but also in the Art that I find there, the statues of saints, and the figures out of Greek and Roman mythology that line the paths, the magnificently athletic men and, above all, the marvellously and beautifully formed women. What an occasion it must have been when Venus and Dido took up residence in the monasteries and when the Rape of the Sabine Women was erected in the Laurenz Garden – all of this no doubt not intended for the sole purpose of deterring sins. I can envision in my mind's eye how the Abbot Floridus Rheinsperger and his monks must have reacted when the sculptor Gabriel Reich in 1633 exposed his new work to them, exposed it in every sense of the word, mounted as it was on a horse-drawn wagon and hauled down from Linz, where he had chiselled these beautiful women. The monks must have clasped their hands over their heads in disbelief, just like the Sabine women. But then, after all, it was they who had put in the order for them. And still today, after more than 300 years, the ladies sit on the horses of the Romans and struggle and struggle in a vain effort to free themselves. It's a bit pharisaical of Abbot Rheinsperger when he writes evasively to Inspector Carlo Avena – who seems to have been puzzled by the whole affair himself – that the primary function of the statues was to provide materials for demonstration and display, so as to instruct the pupils of the Abbey Preparatory School. Perhaps they were meant to serve much the same purpose as the plaster of Paris casts in the school collection? No, of course behind all of this there's a feeling, a feeling for life, a remnant of the old Renaissance feeling for life, and that wasn't the worst of feelings. It bears witness to our ancestors' stupendous power for adaptation, to their capacity for relational change, their liberality and tolerance.

When I'm perambulating about like this in your heathen – or should I rather say, pre-Christian? – Laurenz Garden and I'm pondering its importance in the life of these sometime monks, it occasionally occurs to me that these monks must have felt their sojourn here as a form of relaxation, a short vacation from Christianity, a kind of release and recreation. I also often stand near the Laurenz Fountain and reflect on the people who may have stood here during all those preceding centuries. I look down into the black mouth of the fountain and tell myself that the fountain of the past is deep. Maybe even unfathomable?

The first families of the land sent their most gifted sons to Freimünster, entrusting them to the care of the patres. How many young people have studied in Freimünster, have been happy or unhappy in this Abbey! Who hasn't sought, perhaps in these very gardens, peace of mind in this peace of Nature, and found it or perhaps despaired of it – sought for it after profound disillusion and self-doubt, something from which pupils too, or novices and monks, are not exempt. On the contrary, these are feelings that shouldn't surprise us, considering the great impact on their lives of the decisions they have to make here. Their lives were and still are simply overflowing with crises. And I'm forced to look across towards the Mathematical Tower, from which more than thirty years ago, when I was myself a pupil in the Abbey school, my fellow classmate, Isidor Seitenstettner, the best student of our year, plunged to his death.

And now as the evening bell begins to toll, I imagine how the monks are readying themselves to go to vespers in the Oratory, and how your cook, Katherina Schindler, and her female helpers are beginning to bustle about in the kitchen, preparing the table and putting the House in proper order. And I continue rambling along in this westering mood, over to the Mosque, up the stone steps, taking Benedict's Way over to the stables and the dairy. And always I'm reminded of books, always at the same places of the same books, books about abbeys and boarding schools and seminaries, books written for novices and monks, such as in the old days I used to read with pleasure and even today I still reread often with pleasure. That's why every time I pass Maiwöger's Pavillon I always have the same powerful experience of Nature and of Art. The Pavillion is an archetectonically hybrid and oddly unserious edifice which everybody calls the Little Hall. It is a structure which causes me to feel profound melancholy.

But then again there's always and suddenly this coming back to earth, this return to reality. I might be thinking of Hermann Hesse's Narziss and Goldmund and while I'm thinking of Hermann Hesse's Narziss and Goldmund, suddenly up pops the sacristan near the fish pond and crosses my path, leaving a disgusting stench of alcohol in his wake.

Or another time I'm walking up and down the cloister colonnade and reflecting on some problem in the history of Western Monasticism. Why is it, I'm wondering, that Benedict of Nursia should have been in favor of, should have preferred so markedly, the so-called Coenobites to the Anachorites? And in Chapter I of his *Rule* he even goes so far as to call the Sarabaites a wholly disgusting kind of monk, *monachorum deterrimum genus*, and, to top it all off, he calls the fourth category of monks, the Gyrovages, *semper vagi et numquam stabiles*, or freely translated: *always on the move, never constant, worse in every way than even the Sarabaites.*

A fourth type of monk is that of the so-called Gyrovages. They waste time loitering about in various parts of the world, abiding in cells of other, reclusive monks for three or four days; always restless, never constant, they are slaves to their whims and their gluttony, and they are in every respect more depraved even than the Sarabaites. How averse this holy man must have been to travelling and to any kind of change of place! "Is the Benedictine *stabilitas loci*," inquires a Church historian who has apparently been corrupted by modern psychology or psychoanalysis; "is the rigorous insistence on stability of place which distinguishes the Benedictine Order from other monastic orders, merely the legalized and codified expression of its founder's neurosis, his phobia or fear of open spaces and motion?" But, as I do my rounds in the cloister colonnade, the thought may cross my mind that this idea is utterly absurd and untenable. Wouldn't it be, to put it in Biblical terms, just like driving out the Devil with Beelzebub, if a person were to wall himself up out of xenophobia and fear of change? Isn't a person who does this merely exchanging one phobia for another? Instead of a fear of open spaces or agoraphobia, he gets claustrophobia, a fear of enclosed places, such as cloisters; instead of motion neurosis, a catatonic syndrome; instead of enclosure anxiety, a mania against staying put? In short, let's say that while I'm lost in thought over this problem and am steadily plodding along, that is, while I'm courageously striding forward and putting myself in motion, philosophizing about the nature of the Benedictine need for stability of place or perhaps psychologizing or reflecting on some other problem of Divinity – Original Sin, let's say, or the Virgin Birth, the Trinity or some other mystery – suddenly the Porter crosses my path in the cloister colonnade, obviously hurrying from the gate to the Tavern, slips past me and asks if I haven't managed to catch the thief of the Arnulf Chalice yet, thereby rudely wrenching me out of my train of thought and then vanishing through one of the side doors, without bothering to stay for an answer.

My dear Abbot, there was no doubt in my mind from the very beginning that the weak spot at the gate must have played a role in the planning of the thieves. The thieves naturally knew about the disposition of the gate and of the gatekeeper. The moment I was notified of the theft I thought to myself that the thieves of the Arnulf Chalice must for a long time already have been unobtrusively studying the gate and the gatekeeper. They must have had a pretty good idea of what was going on at the gate and what the habits of the gatekeeper were, and they must have thought to themselves, "Let this cup pass from him!"

As for what kinds of people should be considered likely suspects, I told the people from Vienna straight away that we needed to check up not only on the large number of unbelievers entering and leaving Freimünster. I told them that we shouldn't just be looking for the unknown perpetrator or perpetrators among the inquistive unbelievers and tourists who come to visit Freimünster purely for artistic, so-called artistic or aesthetic reasons, but that we should also examine – perhaps even give absolute priority to examining – the so-called believers, the pilgrims or, rather, the pilgrims hypocritically disguised as pilgrims who, in the final analysis, are really to be viewed as elements alien to the Church and to its Faith. Let's look too at the friends of the Abbey, I said to the Viennese, let's look, I told these central and capital criminalists, let's look for the wolves in sheep's clothing, and I provided the Viennese with important background information about precisely this category of suspects, which of course in their usual arrogant and know-it-all manner they simply disregarded. And it was precisely in this body of material that the clue leading us to Regensburg turned up in the end!

For years, my dear Abbot, I've been watching the faithful, the pilgrims and the wayfarers, who come to Our Dear Lady of Freimünster. Some, even many of them, no doubt consider themselves to be pilgrims. In fact, they even identify themselves as pilgrims and say they are making a pilgrimage to Freimünster, but they are not making a pilgrimage; and they are not what they claim to be, nor do they by any means do what they claim to do. In fact, they are merely making an excursion, not really a pilgrimage, or not at any rate a pilgrimage according to the ecclesiastical definition, but an excursion, simply an excursion. Some of them say, "We're combining the two things, we're making an excursion and a pilgrimage too." As if that were possible, as if those two things were compatible! That strikes me like somebody saying that he's taking a holiday for his health while making use of the extra free time to indulge even more vilely in his habitual vices, such as gorging himself, abusing alcohol and nicotine, etcetera. Many of the people who come to Freimünster consider an excursion to some lovely Abbey to be a good and pious deed, one that is pleasing to God; for them an excursion to a place of grace will always and by definition be a pilgrimage.

Anyway, nobody arrives on foot anymore. Walking or any real *per pedem* locomotion is something that simply isn't done any longer. Since the last great migration of the Germanic peoples, nobody in our country walks anymore. In former times pilgrims made great sacrifices in this respect. Many a pilgrim, it says in the old texts, only managed to reach this hospice by making an immense final effort; and so as not to make it too easy for themselves along the way, they would put peas that were as hard as pebbles into their shoes or lug a rucksack full of granite stones on their backs. You can still find them, these heavy stones, lying behind the Gethsemane Chapel, bearing witness to the great power of faith which our ancestors possessed. People like us can hardly lift some of those stones off the ground... And nowadays visitors to Freimünster stand in front of this pile of stones, smiling pitifully, thinking themselves terribly modern and enlightened in the face of this weird and atrophied tradition. "Why did these people do it?" they ask uncomprehendingly. And they have no idea what weights our ancestors unloaded and rid themselves of behind the Gethsemane Chapel – not just physical loads but also spiritual ones, along with all sorts of burdens and worries and difficulties. *Come unto me, all ye that labor and are heavy laden, and I will give you rest,* says Christ. In Freimünster a load fell from the hearts of our ancestors, and they returned home relieved, renewed and full of confidence. Our ancestors brought stones and made sacrifices. And they had, my dear Abbot, a success experience, as I think people call it these days.

Their simple piety and their fondness for going on pilgrimages strikes us today as too obvious and crude; even the theologians – yes, especially the theologians – are always preaching spiritualization. Everything is supposed to be conceived of only in spiritual and pneumatic terms, and no longer as anything immediate and direct and naive. "There's nothing at all to be gained," they say, "by fasting and mortifying the flesh or maybe hauling stones around." We are supposed to concentrate on essentials, on the inner and the real, not on externals. But because it's so hard to make out what the essential, the inner and the real is, we mostly fail to concentrate on it and in the end we wind up with frustrations instead of success experiences. To me, my dear Abbot, the explanation for all this is simple. Behind our doubts about the value of crude sacrificial practices and physical actions there lies a false interpretation of the Bible, an abridged understanding of the Holy Writ – that is, of the New Testament. Of course, Christ says that now there should be an end of smoke and burnt offerings, along with an end to the whole of the Levitic Old Testament – in short, that we should no longer stand *sub lege* but *sub gratia*, no longer *under the old law* but *under grace*. But I don't believe that by this he meant that he wanted to deliver us up to the mushy, nebulous, ill-defined and deceitful spiritualization advocated by many theologians. The Lord simply thought too well of us to want to do that to us, my dear Abbot; Christ loved humanity too much for that. That's why the Gospel too is simple, so simple that anybody can understand it, whereas theology is complicated, so complicated that even the theologians themselves can't understand it.

There was a monk, my dear Abbot, an Augustinian monk in Erfurt and Wittenberg, whose name was Martin. I won't mention his surname because you probably wouldn't like hearing it, although its bearer was, to begin with anyway, not a bad monk; and he struggled more desperately and earnestly for the salvation of his soul than anyone else. This monk Martin, my dear Abbot, subsumed all his thinking and doing under a single heading: how do I get a merciful God? This question always crosses my mind when I see the stones behind the Gethsemane Chapel. Is there anybody today who still asks this question? How do I get a merciful God? That's a question nobody asks anymore. How do I get a raise in salary is more likely to be the question; or how do I get my insurance discount for not having had any accidents; or how do I get the title of Professor or Monsignor. That's what we ask for these days in our ignorance. My dear Abbot, it's unfortunate that Theology these days concerns itself far too little with sins. There's no Indulgence and Penitence Theology anymore; and *Confessio* and *Satisfactio* Theology has virtually died out. And nobody talks about hell and temporal and eternal punishments for sins anymore either. Instead the number one topic in theology is God's humane – *humane* – way of administering punishment. And what about the remission of sins, my dear Abbot? That's something one doesn't hear about either anymore. I praise the remission of sins and consider it something eminently good and practical; in this respect I differ from Father Martin. In the matter of indulgences and the remission of sins, among other things, Father Martin erred. After all, he was only human, even though he was a religious genius.

Making pilgrimages on foot to Freimünster – or, for that matter, making sacrifices of any sort – is just as much a thing of the past as hauling around stones for the sake of atonement. Nobody makes sacrifices on bus and train pilgrimages nowadays. The pilgrims slouch around in seats equipped with armrests and headrests, and if at times somebody gets up or walks up and down the aisle, it's only because he can't stand sitting anymore. The greatest sacrifice that these pilgrims make is to remain seated for a long time. If you sit a long time your circulation is affected, and your legs grow numb and start to fall asleep. When in the old days pilgrims used to come to visit the Queen of Heaven in Freimünster from all points of the compass and from all parts of the country to celebrate the Feast of the Most Holy Name of Mary, their legs certainly did not grow numb. Can you possibly imagine some Andalusian shepherd's feet growing numb as he crossed on foot the whole of the Iberian peninsula on his way to Santiago de Compostela? Once in a while some pilgrim gets sick from the continuous rocking to and fro of the bus and has to vomit, but that isn't a meaningful sacrifice. On the contrary, if anything it's the person sitting next to him who is making a sacrifice if he accepts the offering with Christian charity and humility, as duly noted by the lady sitting next to him. In any event, nowadays buses are completely air-conditioned; there's always a constant temperature, something that's very pleasant. We're familiar these days with the phenomenon of the well-tempered bus. And the latest models even have toilets, so that now stops to relieve the call of nature have become outmoded. In former times these stops slowed down and delayed bus pilgrimages considerably.

Pilgrims are driving further and further afield these days; the idea of increased performance has even invaded the field of Pilgrimage Tourism. Many people aren't satisfied with Freimünster anymore; they've got to go to Fatima or Czestochowa or Montecassino. My dear Abbot, of course these people could stay at home and pray, but then they don't make these trips in order to pray. When thou prayest, enter into thy closet and shut thy door. Sit yourself on a bus is, in any event, not what it says. That's not why these pilgrims drive such infernally long distances, not in order to pray a lot; that's not why they make these brutal bus journeys. Formerly, on pilgrimages people used to pray all the time. Only when people were walking uphill, when they had difficulty catching their breath, was there a pause in the praying, but otherwise they prayed all the time. Formerly, people only stopped praying when they were going uphill; nowadays they don't even pray when they are going downhill, downhill all the way.

Whole chartered trains and two-storey buses nowadays drive to Lourdes and still don't manage to finish saying a single rosary. Lots of people think prayer isn't modern anymore, including lots of pilgrims, so-called pilgrims. Prayer isn't in tune with the times anymore. Now people discuss, even in churches people are already discussing. And more and more often do I hear even in churches the hideous word "Communication." Do me the favor of counting along with me, my dear Abbot; you'll hear the word "Communication" more often than the word "Communion." Formerly, if somebody used the word *to communicate*, then he meant to say *to receive communion*; but according to contemporary usage *to communicate* means no more than *to talk to each other*, to spout words at each other. And this communication has to take place in a completely spontaneous and unplanned way, without any kind of form and full of mistakes. Grammar and literacy are definitely out. You're supposed to use only the most vulgar kind of slang – that is, Viennese dialect – otherwise it isn't communication. There are radio programs specializing in this kind of communication twenty-four hours every day. How long will it take until people are finally fed up with this unceasing extemporized chatter of idiots and illiterates? It's called communication when incompetent ignoramuses stammer at each other. Unfortunately, my dear Abbot, this absurd fad for adlibbing and improvising has also invaded the Church, which was once a bulwark of rituals, ceremonies and established forms. And this infantile ideology of spontaneity is even affecting the habit of prayer. We're moving away from set formulas, so they say, but where are we moving to? I tell you, my dear Abbot, we're moving away from set formulas but we're also moving towards speechlessness or stammering. Of course, God doesn't need our grammar, and it's true that there is a grammar of the heart too. But nowhere is it written that we have to make a *Rule* out of un-ruliness for that reason; certainly it is not written in the Holy Scriptures.

Quite different truths are written in the Holy Scriptures. With what incomparable thoroughness and clarity does Benedict's *Rule* regulate the prayer of monks! Chapters 8 through 20 leave no question unanswered in this respect, whether it's a question of singing the Psalms, the Vigils, Morning Prayer, the singing of Hallelujahs or whatever. And Benedict even addresses the issue of *lapsus linguae*, slips of the tongue made while praying in the Oratory. He censures them and demands restitution because, after all, they are the result of a failure of concentration, that is, of inadequate reflection: *De his qui falluntur in oratorio; Of those who make mistakes in the Oratory: Whoever, while reciting a psalm, a responsory, an antiphon or during a reading, makes a mistake and does not humble himself there and then and make restitution, is subject to severe punishment. For he did not wish to make good again in humility what he had committed through negligence. When children err in this way they receive a whipping.* It's the old problem of freedom and necessity that's posed here – not, I hasten to add, the problem of freedom and compulsion.

I'm not for compulsion, my dear Abbot, but for insight into necessity. And whoever renounces freedom out of insight into necessity has made the right use of freedom. Of course, first I have to reflect on where and to whom I wish to attach myself, and whom I should believe in. But in the case of Benedict I wouldn't hesitate. I'm glad that you continue to pray in the way he taught you to pray.

But back to the bus, where things are really hopping. During the whole trip to Lourdes scarcely a single rosary! Even the accompanying priest isn't bothered in any way if the group prays only one rosary during the trip from Linz to Einsiedeln, between the Mondsee and Salzburg, while the rest of the time they persist in singing a variety of songs ranging from the funny to the frolicsome. One joyous rosary between Linz and Lourdes but 150 improvised yodeling ryhmes and 200 improvised yodeling stanzas, 50 travel songs dating from the Nazi period, together with their refrains, etcetera.

There's always somebody along on the pilgrimage who is the life of the party. On a long pilgrimage this funnyman is more important than the tour guide and more important than the priest. Sometimes the funnyman and the tour guide, or even the funnyman and the priest, are one and the same person. Joke after joke comes popping out of the funnyman, and every three minutes there's so much shouting and laughter that the bus starts to lurch to one side and almost threatens to swerve out of its lane. Suddenly a pair of panties is handed round which supposedly fell out of the luggage rack. Laughter springs up along with the question as to whom this item of clothing might belong. When none of those present admits to owning the panties, the funnyman says that, such being the case, we now have to try them on and, by a process of elimination, find out whom they belong to. Of course, my dear Abbot, the funnyman brought his *corpus delicti* along himself, and it's not just on this particular pilgrimage that the play "Pants" is performed; it is also performed on other pilgrimages and tours. It's a standard item in the funnyman's repertory. I often see people climbing out of buses in

Freimünster who are so shaken with roars of laughter that only after many attempts by the priest to pacify them, do they become aware that they've already arrived at the goal of their spiritual quest.

My dear Abbot, I really do enjoy seeing happy people, for it is common knowledge that every Christian should take joy in the fact of being saved. It's a sign of having inadequate faith in God if people keep running around with long faces all their lives long. It was during the Christian Middle Ages, after all, that people considered melancholy to be a sin, always excepting sadness at one's own sins, a sadness which wasn't merely permitted but enjoined. Only a sinner, that is to say a melancholic person, had a right to melancholy.

If I examine the ecclesiastic doctrine regarding sadness and attempt to describe it with the aid of the nomenclature devised by modern psychiatric specialists in clinical depression, then I could and even would have to say that the Church has only sanctioned so-called *reactive depressions* but not *endogenic depressions*. Indeed, to be reactively *depressed*, that is reacting with sadness against anything bad, evil and sinful, was a requirement of the Church. The sinner had to know, in other words, what it meant when he felt so sad. Psychiatrists nowadays, my dear Abbot, are given to explaining everything somatically and chemically, though a few actually do employ psychoanalytic explanations; still, in my view the Christian explanation was not really so far off the mark. Christianity is better than Chemistry, my dear Abbot. And of course there is also guilt and not just guilt *feelings*. The psychiatrists say that there are only guilt *feelings*, only feelings, and the guilt in guilt feelings isn't objective guilt but only a subjective feeling, something acquired and conditioned. Psychiatrists take a positivistic view and consider guilt to be a result of social acculturation sanctioned by historical tradition. In their view, illness is a punishment for social nonconformity, whereas health is a reward for adaptation. What is more, health and illness are supposedly mere matters of definition, depending ultimately on what has been established as the norm and what as the deviation. So, my dear Abbot, if sadness were the norm and happiness the deviation, then I would be more than happy to be merrily mad, and, if it had to be, all by myself against the rest of the world. Naturally, my dear Abbot, there is so-called *guilt* and there are guilt *feelings*, but there is also *guilt* plain and simple. After all, there is also inferiority and not just an inferiority complex. Sometimes I secretly wonder why it is that more psychiatrists don't suffer from inferiority complexes.

I don't want to say anything against happiness or Freudian psychiatrists. But the happiness which is shown by the pilgrims who come to Freimünster is certainly not the happiness of which the Bible or St. Benedict's *Rule* speak. I must admit, however, that it makes me suspicious how little Benedict has to say about happiness. He speaks more often about how the Abbot should punish infractions in his monastery, how he should not only admonish his Brothers but also discipline them physically; and it gives me pause when I reflect that in Chapter 27, Verse 3, he writes – specifically in connection with corporeal discipline, with bracchial sanctions and penitences – that fellow Brothers should *speak in a friendly manner* to the Brother who has been reprimanded, *so that he should not lapse into immoderate sadness (et consolentur eum, ne abundantiori tristitia absorbetur)*. On the evidence of the index, my dear Abbot, Benedict writes about happiness only three times, whereas he writes about sadness on seven occasions. That's not a particularly cheerful item of news. Bonjour tristesse, my dear Abbot.

Benedict writes as follows about how pilgrims should be welcomed: *All new guests should be received like Christ. And all should be treated with the honor that is due them...As soon as a guest has been announced, the Superior and a few Brothers should go out to meet him with the love that they owe him. First they should pray together and then they should enter into communion with one other by means of a kiss of peace.*

Oh, my dear Abbot, if you had to give the "Pax" or Kiss of Peace to everybody whom your porter lets in through the gate, you would be occupied full-time just with the kissing part. And you wouldn't be able to extricate yourself from the praying part either. You would only be able to *orare* and not *laborare* anymore; you would have to labor at praying. The sainted author of the *Rule* never had the faintest idea of what it meant to cope with the volume of visitors that an Austrian Benedictine monastery has to put up with nowadays. On the occasion of the one-thousand two-hundredth anniversary of the Abbey, 160,000 people came to Freimünster; but even in normal years when there is no big anniversary, there are some 50,000 visitors. And it goes without saying that our Saint had no premonition about the appearance and state of many of the visitors and pilgrims who come to Freimünster these days. There are people who stumble stiffly out of their vehicles after long hours of driving, unwashed and sweaty. Others have already made watering stops on the way in restaurants or have imbibed spirits out of the communal bottle inside their multi-passenger public conveyances and therefore don't smell of violets but of brandy. And now the abbot is supposed to give them the Pax or Kiss of Peace, right, Benedict? Nobody, not even a saint, has a right to expect anybody to do that, or if he does, then only from another saint. But that's just what an abbot necessarily isn't. The abbot is no sainted martyr, my dear Abbot.

I can understand very well why you make only very rare appearances at the gate, even though I don't approve of it and have always urged you – even before the great Incognito relieved the Abbey of its Arnulf Chalice – to reform matters at the gate and change them for the better. That's a different issue, however. But what else can you do with all those people who arrive at the wrong side of the gate? The Pope in Rome can't shake every single person's hand in St. Peter's Square either. I can appreciate the demands of your office. And I too would refrain from giving the Kiss of Peace to a person who has declared war on hygiene and sobriety.

Year after year I observe you on Maundy Thursday when, in conjunction with the Holy Week liturgy, you follow Christ's example and wash the feet of twelve old men selected from among the residents in our Old Folks Home in Billroth Street. In the first place, my dear Abbot, you do the job in a very impersonal and ceremonial way, merely symbolically; and secondly, the old gents are delivered into your hands in an already pre-washed condition. And thirdly, my dear Abbot, the senior citizens selected by the Manager of the Adenauer Home in Billroth Street are in any case the cleanest of the bunch. I have reason to know because we often have to respond to emergency police calls in Billroth Street. I could tell you things about some of the people there that would put your humility to a greater test. The Manager wants to curry favor with you; he only sends you genuine candidates for washing. Candidate, my dear Abbot, comes from *candidus, candida, candidum*, which means white and clean and pure.

When Peter refused to allow Our Lord to wash his feet, then he surely did so mainly because he was aware of their condition. He himself no doubt knew best what sort of task Christ had set himself in this regard. Imagine, my dear Abbot, a fisherman, a workman in other words, who had gone barefoot or in sandals his whole life long, and not, mind you, on asphalt but in the dust of the ancient Orient.

In ancient times people had something different, that is something better – please don't misunderstand me – something more important and more useful to do than to wash themselves all the time like we do. Nowadays people spend whole lifetimes lying around in their bathtubs. The time that people waste in so-called hygienic and cosmetic activity! Of course, my dear Abbot, if a person is hollow and empty inside and incapable of doing anything good or worthwhile, then, as far as I'm concerned, he might as well spend half the day in the bathroom, splashing about in foam and cream baths and rubbing and scrubbing himself. As far as I am concerned, he is already dead, he is no longer part of the human race; the only thing left is, as it were, for him to embalm himself. Of course, a person like that isn't worth the hot water and the energy that he consumes, but I won't make an issue of it. A person like that apparently thinks to himself, "My body may be of no use for anything but at least I bother to take care of it." His body has no other function except to be taken care of by him.

I am by no means advocating pollution, my dear Abbot; I am no friend of scurviness and scabbiness, no lover of dandruff and pimples and yellow teeth. On the contrary, I am a wholehearted supporter of cleanliness. Of course, I do oppose going to extremes and exaggerating; I am against the misuse of bath water, against the torture of bathtubs. If people would devote the time they waste in so-called hygienic and cosmetic activity, the time, in other words, which they spend standing in front of mirrors and hanging around swimming pools and saunas, wallowing about and getting tanned – and I'm not merely referring to women whose mania for cleanliness I can at least partly understand or sympathize with, for after all society has condemned them to compulsory washing, has trained them to become, as it were, cleaning ladies from whom it expects so-called refinement – if, in short, people would devote their plentiful but squandered, dissipated and murdered time to their fellow human beings instead and make use of that time in socially responsible ways, then, my dear Abbot, we would surely have fewer problems.

Nobody loved Christ more than Peter, and when he said: *Thou shalt never wash my feet*, then this statement has, aside from its exemplary spiritual character, also a physical-bodily and hygienic character.

Nowadays any theologian interpreting Scripture in this way would most likely elicit a faint smile of ridicule from the progressive – the so-called progressive – theologians. This kind of interpretation is dismisssed by them as instrumentalistic. Nowadays the greatest theologian is the one who can make do with the fewest facts. Theologians no longer pay any attention to texts, they no longer think of the text or about it, they simply think it out of existence. They think whatever they like out of the text, they disregard and overlook the facts. They dispense with everything, including Christ. They propagate a Theology without God. That is why it is the declared mission of Christology or

Life-of-Jesus-Research not to do research into the life of Jesus but to use research so as to do away with the Lord Jesus. As far as Life-of-Jesus-Research is concerned, my dear Abbot, progress exists only in desearch, unsearch and dissearch. Progress lies in moving crabwise. Modern theology is a science of evaporation; our theologians proceed by evaporation and rarification; they have no intention whatever of leaving the village church standing in the village. But as Father Martin said: *You must let stand the word.* And also the Regulator of your Order knew the reason why, in Chapter 35, Versicle 9, he specifically prescribed the washing of feet as a weekly exercise in humility. In the end Peter too permitted his feet to be washed. When Christ said to him: *If I wash thee not, thou hast no part with me*, Peter replied: *Lord, not my feet only, but also my hands and my head.* Peter no doubt said *noggin* or something like that, something unceremonious. In a similarly critical situation Peter once said to the Lord: *Lord, thou knowest all things; thou knowest that I love thee.*

Back to our pilgrims. No sooner have they entered the Church than they feel an irresistible urge to go to the Tavern. Once there they resume the conversation that was forcibly interrupted because of their visit to the Church. The funnyman has gotten his second wind and immediately goes into action again. If one of the men happens to take a seat in a group made up exclusively of ladies, the joker says of him that he is blessed among women. Suddenly things are jumping again. "*Sursum corda*," says the priest. Thereupon they unanimously sing the well-known hymn: "We will all go to heaven." "*Ite missa est*," says the priest. The bus driver is already waiting.

In this connection, there is a remarkable sentence in Chapter 53 of the *Rule* to which I would like to draw your attention: *One should welcome poor people and pilgrims with the utmost conscientiousness because in the truest sense Christ dwells in them; as for the rich, their peremptory behavior enforces deference of its own accord.* But one really has to hear the last sentence in Latin, since *the peremptory behavior of the rich* is actually an imprecise and flattering translation of what the Latin original says: *nam divitum terror ipse se exigit honorem. Divitum terror*, it says, *terror*! I'm always reminded of this passage when we're told at the Police Station that some VIP is expected at the Abbey, and we're supposed to provide police protection and an escort. And then when I have to watch how everyone in the Abbey – from the porter on up to the monks and their Abbot, and down again to the gardener and the cook – how they all get nervous and excited as if Saint Benedict himself had personally announced his impending arrival. Already days in advance everybody is running around like stuck pigs. Everything that might conceivably pose a hazard is lugged away or covered up and disguised. Flags are dragged out of every nook and cranny, national flags, provincial flags, city flags and abbey flags. The gardener and his helper crawl around on all fours through the flower beds and weed them until their fingers bleed. For days the Preparatory School boys' choir has been practicing indefatigably the chorale *Locus iste*, and likewise Katherina the cook has been conferring incessantly with the Father Cellerar about the menu and the wines that are supposed to be served at table. Telephone calls are being continually made to the VIP's office to elicit information about the various habits of the VIP, about his favorite food and whether or not he suffers from diabetes, and what the state of his gall bladder is, and of his liver and his wife, and whether she would like to sit to the right or the left of her very important husband, and wether they should count on her wearing a hat and, if so, whether it will be large or small, green or yellow, so that the table can be set and decorated accordingly. Benedictus autem dixit:...*nam divitum ipse se exigit honorem*! It does not seem to have been any different during the early Middle Ages compared with the way it is today. It certainly can't have been any worse. Back then the High and Mighty had first and foremost to terrorize people in a personal, unmediated and direct fashion. Today, however, that's a job left up to their staffs, secretaries, receptionists, right hand men, adjutants and subordinates, among whose number I also count myself, along with the rest of the personnel at the Police Station.

Gregory of Tours recounts in his *History of the Franks* that the Merovingian King Clovis not only handed down his own judgments at trials but also carried them out with his very own hands. Nowadays, however, people with power have all degenerated into paper-pushers ensconced at their desks. They all hide behind their mahogany desks; they barricade themselves behind their teak desks. From there orders are conveyed to us in the Police Station *per telephonem*, no matter if it's a question of getting the Abbey ready for a reception or if we're supposed to use all available forces to break up a demonstration against some idiocy that they've perpetrated.

My dear Abbot, during the Middle Ages the consumptive weaklings who nowadays feebly try to *Rule* the world would certainly not have had an opportunity to exert their authority over anything. In those days a *Rule*r also had to be dominant physically, as was, for instance, the case with Charlemagne. Kings couldn't just let themselves be carried in sedan-chairs over the Alps or the Apennines on their way to Rome to mollify (or was it to maulify?) the Pope. *Rule*rs were simply tougher than they are today; they swam across raging streams, climbed over immense mountains and rode for days on horseback. They not only made demands on others, but on themselves too. And how many *Rule*rs died while fighting wars! Nowadays, if there's a war, you hardly ever hear of a politician being a casualty.

Please don't get me wrong, my dear Abbot, I'm not arguing for some kind of biological superiority. I'm not exalting or glorifying the Life Force, or at any rate not the Life Force in the guise of flesh and bone. Quite the contrary, I'm pleading for reason and political common sense, but unfortunately many of our politicians are sorely lacking in these qualities too. As a *Rule*, alas, our *Rule*rs are not *Rule*d by the *Rule* of reason. There is simply no other explanation for the criminal feeblemindedness of getting involved in so many wars. It seems to me that while our leaders may no longer be particularly strong physically, they make up for it by being either outstandingly stupid or morally corrupt. A nice example of compensation.

Oh, my dear Abbot, when I think of Germany in the night, of her Charleses – a name which in the old days had not yet lost its etymological kinship with *churl* – her Ottos, Louises, Henrys (specifically the fourth), or even of her Fredericks: then I wish it were day and they would return. Or for that matter the Bavarian Dukes, above all Arnulf the Founder, who established our Abbey and endowed it with the Arnulf Chalice. In 776 the Abbey of Our Dear Lady of Freimünster was given the Chalice; in 1976 it was stolen on the occasion of the Abbey's 1200th anniversary. That's the difference between the two ages. And why have we been groping around in the dark for so long looking for it? Because we who are in the business of carrying out the law have been hindered in carrying it out by those who make the law, because we've been continually prevented from doing our duty by the paper-pushers and technocrats in Vienna. The politicians are continually demanding a large supply of police. First the politicians devise an execrable policy directed against the people, and then they get scared of the people and demand police protection. That's the relation which the legislative and executive branches have to each other. In the final analysis, our job is to protect the politicians from themselves, namely from the disastrous impact and consequences of their disastrous policies. For not only do they systematically and methodically organize their war against crime, they also methodically incite crime. My dear Abbot, there has been a lot of talk recently about job creation and above all about job retention and job security. The fact that politicians devise such miserable policies against the people and so actually incite people to commit crimes is probably from their point of view primarily a way of fighting unemployment, a constructive contribution to retaining jobs in the areas of administration and law-enforcement. My dear Abbot, it's impossible to overlook the rise in the crime rate. Still, I'm not impressed by the hysterical outcry of the so-called silent majority and its associated gutter press about the increase in crime. Often the only thing I hear is: "Grab that thief!" I can't say, however, that this idea grabs me. But I also don't quite understand why anybody, no matter how level-headed, who points to the increase in crime and favors a little more in the way of order and security, has to be denounced as a fascist. It ought to be possible to establish order in such a way that it doesn't lead to despotism through some new disorder. But in view of the experiences we've had so far, there's probably not much reason to expect improvement.

My dear Abbot, nowadays our politicians are continually in need of police protection and bodyguards. Again I explain the fact that so many politicians nowadays need bodyguards by examining the make-up of the relevant political bodies according to scholastic psychophysics, that is, by distinguishing sharply between spirit and matter, body and soul. Schiller, who was an idealist, claimed that it was the spirit that nourished the body, but wherever I look I see the exact opposite. Nevertheless, what I see actually confirms Schiller's hypothesis by a process of negation: it's the body that starves the mind.

In a year when we celebrated not only the Preservation of National Monuments but also the Anniversary of the Abbey, it was simply impossible even to think of systematically pursuing the thief of the Chalice. That's why the trail leading to Regensburg was allowed to grow cold, especially by the Viennese – a circumstance which cost us dearly later on. But we were being continually hampered by requests for police escorts and protection. If during the Year of the Preservation of National Monuments any part of a building happened to have been refurbished – even if it was only the Tavern toilet – you could be sure that some Provincial Governor or State Representative or perhaps even some big federal politico was already on the way to preside solemnly over its reopening. Politicians don't miss a thing when it comes to public ceremonies; they don't even miss a toilet, especially not during election years. "That's the way to get publicity and popularity," they say. Opening a toilet, my dear Abbot, really appeals to the people. And on every occasion of this sort, there are always calls for assistance from the police. When it comes to preserving monuments, my dear Abbot, the specialists ask themselves in each instance whether the object in question is really worthy of preservation. In future we ought to make the same principle apply to questions of police protection as well. Here too we should raise the question as to whether the person is worthy of protection. There have been times when we've placed ourselves protectively around some gigantic pygmy, and the thought has crossed my mind: "Ah, you puny little fellow, nobody is going to touch you anyway. Who would want to bother with you?"

Long live Father Theodor! Three cheers for Father Theodor! He seems to be the only person in your whole monastery who doesn't let himself be bamboozled by any old VIP who happens to visit the Abbey. It's with great pleasure that I recall the visit of the Minister of Education three years ago, that is, not so much the visit itself as the special program arranged for us at lunch by Father Theodor. It was like this: we're all seated, including my own humble self, around the big table in the Marble Hall. We've finally managed to get done with the main course and we're starting to attack Katherina's splendid dessert. Father Theodor, the first to finish, unabashedly pulls out his pipe and makes preparations for putting it into operation. He cleans it according to the well-known abbreviated method of simply blowing into the stem so that the stale remnants are propelled out of the bowl. Generally speaking, this is a procedure which responsible pipe-smokers use only when they're out in the open. Either as a result of his carelessness or intentionally – knowing him, I would tend to assume the latter – Theodor let fly the residual lump diagonally across the table and over the head of our eminent guest. Suddenly dead silence fell over the room and everybody looked painfully embarrassed, whereupon Father Theodor said to the Minister: "If you can find it, Your Excellency, it's yours." It's very much to the credit of the Minister that, after pausing for a terrifying second, he replied, "Fire away!" and laughed.

What would St. Benedict have done with somebody like Father Theodor, seeing as how he had already stipulated a whipping in cases of simple slips of the tongue in the Oratory? If a mere mistake in saying one's prayers was enough to make the

Saint threaten a thrashing, then what kind of punishment would he have provided for monks who commit serious errors of protocol during visits from Ministers of Education? In connection with my investigation into the disappearance of the Arnulf Chalice, I have also had occasion to examine the Benedictine code of punishment and, in the process, my dear Abbot, I have discovered that in this respect you conform only very imperfectly to the *Rule* of your Order. This is quite in contrast to your predecessors both here in Freimünster and elsewhere, who, while themselves no sadists or lovers of the whip, nevertheless not only were dead serious about issuing warnings to offenders but didn't hesitate to exact punishment. That is also something recounted of the great Apostle of the Germans, the Anglo-Saxon Winfrid. The Pope, the second Gregory, awarded him the honorary name of Boniface, that is "doer of good deeds." And he did do good deeds, a fact which is in nowise contradictory with his having taken, according to tradition, the words of Benedict 2, 28 very literally: *The Abbot should punish the insincere, the recalcitrant, the proud and the disobedient forthwith at their first infraction with lashes and physical force. For he knows full well the proverb: Fools don't learn from words. And further: Take the rod to your son and you will save him from death.*

In this connection Boniface writes: *Let us not be silent dogs, not mute look-outs, not mercenaries who flee before the wolf, but faithful shepherds, watchful over Christ's flock, preaching every decree of God to the extent God has given us the strength, to the high as well as to the low, to the rich as well as the poor, to every station and age, whether the occasion be suitable or not.* My dear Abbot, God *has* given him the strength, not only to pardon and forgive.

Furthermore, my dear Abbot, in Benedict's view, the office of a Benedictine Abbot also makes physical demands on the person who occupies it. Benedict himself personified this fact. I myself would not have liked to have been slapped on the cheek by Saint Boniface or had my ear boxed by Saint Benedict if their statues are at all true to life. And we shouldn't let our minds be tainted by improper thoughts when we read with pleasure – with saintly pleasure, as it were – the old accounts of how he left an enduring impression, as a man and not just as a saint, on abbesses, nuns and other women of his time. For Boniface's sainthood was in no way the result of incapacity. And when he showed restraint, then it was with regard to an action that he really had the capacity to carry out. Boniface was no impotent saint but a mighty saint, a man like a tree. And one beautiful February day in 724 at Geismar near Fritzlar this man like a tree stepped up to Thor's Oak in front of a lot of frightened Germans and felled that oak with his strong hand and an axe. Without intending any offense, my dear Abbot, I'm not sure if you would be able to fell one of the trees on the 3600 hectars of woods – deeded by Duke Arnulf to the Abbey of Our Dear Lady of Freimünster in wise foresight of the material constraints and needs of the Church as well as of the price of lumber – to repeat, I'm not sure if you would have the strength to transfer one of those trees from a vertical to a horizontal position. Well, perhaps you might be able to do it in the case of some sorry specimen growing out there near the Rinnhof ponds on the Christmas Tree Farm run by Forester Father Simon. But a thousand year-old oak? Or the linden tree in the Prior's Courtyard?

In order for a man like Winfrid to get to be a martyr he really had to head up far into the north to the savage, heathen Frisians. In order to martyrize a man like Winfrid, they needed a heavy axe. And as the many holes in the Bible now preserved in the Cathedral Treasure Room at Fulda so unambiguously testify, it required several strokes of the axe, while the saint was holding this very Bible over his head. Only then were they able to do away with this hale and hearty 71 year-old greybeard and saint. The Frisians felled Boniface. And they played a dirty trick on him too. He was waiting for some people who were supposed to come to be confirmed, and instead murderers came. In the end not even Charles Martell's – that is, in German, Charles the Hammer's – letter of safe conduct which Boniface carried on his person proved to be of any help. But Boniface must have known that he was about to die. For on his last mission he had asked for his books and a shroud to be packed...

It may be that questions of discipline are no longer so urgent in monasteries today, since the number of monks has unfortunately declined. But just think of the personnel in a monastery like Hirsau in Württemberg which at various times in its history had more than 1000 monks living in it and where the liturgy was celebrated round the clock, night and day. I don't believe, my dear Abbot, that you could have been lord and abbot of such an army of monks, not with your soothing personality, and not by always trying to achieve peace and compromise. It's not a question simply of physical punishment, a practice which has rightly been abolished in our monasteries. But you need to act more decisively in all respects, give clearer orders, be stricter and grasp the reins more firmly. As it is you're only intent on playing the good shepherd. You take Chapter 27 of the *Rule* a little too literally: *The Abbot should also imitate the good shepherd, who is the example of faithful love.* Sometimes you don't even play the good shepherd but just the lamb, and once you were even the ass, if you don't mind my speaking plainly. Besides, I'm only using biblical and liturgical animals, so as not to offend you.

But you should not take only the Good Shepherd as your model, but sometimes also the Wrathful Lord, as for instance when he cleansed the temple of capitalists and dealmakers. Your gentleness often strikes me as being nothing more than a lack of get-up and go. In the interest of the Freimünster Abbey, I strongly advise you to skip over the New Testament and reach for the shining examples and heroes of the Old Testament. Moses, my dear Abbot, was no tactful and obliging and ingratiating person. How could he have been the leader of God's people otherwise? He is always falling into some rage, some holy rage; he acts emotionally and aggressively. There are many figures in the Old Testament who act like this, Jehovah included. Maybe the example of Moses is too extreme. That's why I want to provide you in what follows with an opportunity to identify with a more accessible personage. I won't offer you some saint's legend but only provide you with a straightforward, gripping account, drawn from the files of the police station here in Freimünster, of a resolute woman of the people. I have here before me the protocol, submitted by my Deputy Chief, of an accident involving Katherina Schindler, cook at the Abbey of Our Dear Lady of Freimünster, and Mr. Richard Kronawitter, unskilled laborer at the Hermann Stritz Sawmill in Rach, said accident having taken place and occurring on the Ides of July in the year of Our Lord 1975. I am adhering strictly to the original wording of the protocol drawn up by my deputy Erwin Hatzenbühler, who has in the meantime retired from the force. The report may strike you as a little longwinded but precisely for that reason it clearly does not exaggerate, but actually understates the role played in this case by the exemplary resolution of Katherina Schindler. I think it's only fair to say that a clear picture of her admirable aggressiveness emerges from this almost improbably articulate report. But enough of self-interpretation by the police. *Historia incipit. Exemplum docet.* Let the report speak for itself:

"On 16 July at 8:30 AM an incident occurred at Kilometer 23 of Federal Highway 14, halfway between the municipalities of Freimünster and Rach. Richard Kronawitter, driving a scooter from the direction of Rach, collided with Katherina Schindler, proceeding on a bicycle from the direction of Freimünster. As a result of the collision both of the aforementioned persons were thrown to the ground. At once, as was reported to me upon my arrival at the scene of the accident, Richard Kronawitter literally referred to Katherina Schindler as a blind cow. Thereupon Katherina Schindler seized the opportunity to reply and never relinquished it again. She was inspired to deliver a tirade whose equal in acerbity and offensiveness may be sought for in vain in the files of the Freimünster Police. Above all Katherina Schindler termed it the act of vile cowardice to use a motor scooter to cause a noiseless bicycle like her own to deviate from the lane and prevent it from continuing straight onward to Rach. In addition she repeatedly called her opponent a man, whereas she referred to herself as a female woman, which being the case didn't exactly in her view make the collision into a great work of art. Katherina

Schindler said that Richard Kronawitter really didn't have any reason to be proud of this ridiculous accident. In her time she had seen many more deserving of the name. One could only observe with shame how a fully grown man, propelled by the power of ten horses, drove straight into an unprotected female bicyclist. Katherina Schindler wanted to know whether Richard Kronawitter would go so far as to consider himself a Knight of the Road? As for herself, she could only consider Richard Kronawitter (who at this time was reposing in the ditch at the side of the road) as a highwayman and a fiend who tried to waylay innocent women on his absurd scooter, so as to deflect them from the path of virtue. It was a dirty trick, she said, but certainly not customary in this part of the world, to attempt to wage the war of the sexes out in the open or here on the highway. She was completely and utterly in the dark as to why Richard Kronawitter should have aimed himself straight at her instead of getting out of the way, especially since she was not aware of exercising any great sexual magnetism. In no way had she encouraged or animated him to produce this horrible accident. In a voice filled with outrage and coming from deep within her breast, she remarked that Richard Kronawitter showed cool impudence by throwing himself in the middle of July on her, Katherina Schindler's, breast. He had hurled himself on her with his machine like a wild man, like a beast in the shape of a scooter. It was evident, in her view, that Richard Kronawitter had apparently travelled the 15 kilometers from Rach with the sole and deliberate intent of crashing into her, so she said. Katherina Schindler did not even call a halt at Kronawitter's scooter. She referred to the vehicle as a wretched gas-powered ass. It was a sorry sight, she said, to see Richard Kronawitter having to seek recourse to a two-cycle engine, a mechanical slowpoke. Underneath there's an abused scooter gasping for air, and on top there's a lazy overweight bum turning on the gas, turning out a hideous stink and turning into a ridiculous sight. With his fifty years – at which she estimated his age – Richard Kronawitter was surely old enough (and on the other hand not yet too old) to be able to move about on his own power while making use of his own means of locomotion. It was enough to make one feel sorry for the two-cycle engine; it made one want to come to its aid. Blue smoke was coming out of the exhaust pipe because Richard Kronawitter hadn't adjusted the engine properly. 'You're a real gas,' Schindler said to Kronawitter. 'You pollute the atmosphere,' said Katherina Schindler. There was a noise, however, that went with the stink. As for the noise that Richard Kronawitter produced with his scooter, it could hold its own with any machine coming straight from hell. Under such circumstances, she, Schindler, could have started ringing her bicycle bell while she was still in Freimünster, 15 kilometers away from the scene of the accident, and it wouldn't have been any use against a maniacal, unhinged scooterist running amok at full throttle. Under such conditions, she said, she could ring her bell like it was Christmas. In order to warn an absent-minded dork like Richard Kronawitter you needed an alarm bell rather than a bicycle-bell. For such a purpose you needed bells to be tolling like those in the tower of the Basilica of Our Dear Lady of Freimünster. Bells like that, however, Katherina Schindler said, unfortuately cannot be attached to a small ladies bike. As a consequence thereof, Katherina Schindler drew our attention repeatedly and in a shrill voice to the loud noise of 10 phons which, in her underestimation rather than overestimation, was being emitted by Kronawitter's vehicle. 'Ten phons are certainly much too low an estimate," said Schindler. She termed Richard Kronawitter a phonetician and his scooter a grammophone. In her view, Richard Kronawitter must have come originally from the town of Fohnsdorf, she said loudly and distinctly. People like him could never hear a bell ring. Katherina Schindler sang a horrible song on Richard Kronawitter's grammophone, employing every imaginable linguistic dissonance. She even resorted to allusions and ambiguities. She said that Richard Kronawitter's scooter was bewitched and possessed of the devil. In former times, the arch-fiend used to be depicted as wearing exactly the kind of leather clothing that Richard Kronawitter had on now.

In Freimünster, where she was in charge of the kitchen of the Abbey of Our Dear Lady, there was a picture hanging over the left-side altar in the main church where the devil was shown wearing a jacket and boots similar to those which Richard Kronawitter had on. The resemblance was unmistakable, she said. Richard Kronawitter, she suspected, was trying to hide his horns under his big helmet. His scooter didn't just produce horsepower but also had a horse's hoof. Besides, anybody who took the trouble to wear a crash helmet like that was clearly planning on causing an accident to begin with, because a crash helmet without a crash didn't make any sense.

Mrs. Schindler, it should be noted, spoke very quickly, so that I sometimes had difficulty noting everything down in my report. Therefore I asked her to speak slowly and distinctly. My request, however, distracted her from her real antagonist and made her turn reproachfully towards me with the question as to whether police officers nowadays were only able to write block letters and no longer knew how to use shorthand. She couldn't spell everything out for me, she said. It's very unfortunate, she said, that at a time when vehicles were getting faster and faster in speed, the police was getting slower and slower in writing. She was afraid that of late illiteracy was spreading widely among the police. She was unable to explain otherwise how it should be that the police was relying so heavily on photography these days. Whenever she saw a policeman with a camera, she knew that here was a person who was unable to write. Furthermore, she was continually observing how at the entrance to the dairy in Freimünster, where it was forbidden to park, more and more police officers were not writing down the numbers of the illegally parked cars, but rather copying or tracing them, probably in order to have them deciphered later on in the station by Dr. Einberger. The copyists, she suspected, were made up of that segment of the police department staff who, due a technical and general ineptitude, were unable to learn how to use a camera. Finally, Katherina Schindler asked me indignantly where she had left off in connection with Richard Kronawitter, and when I told her she latched on to his clothing again. She not only ridiculed his helmet but also his pants. In the end, however, she turned her attention to technical details. She termed it gross negligence that he, Richard Kronawitter, had made no use whatever of the backpedal brake which the designer Sachs in Braunschweig had invented and developed for precisely this kind of situation. It wasn't just negligence, she said, but recklessness to let oneself go in the way that Mr. Kronawitter had. She vigorously urged Kronawitter to step back. Richard Kronawitter, however, was evidently committed to unrestrained freewheeling. Naturally, she suspected that the failure to brake was not merely the result of some technical defect or break-down, but of a damaged character and a failed code of behavior. Katherina Schindler beseeched me to record and note down in my report, for the benefit of future generations, the absence of any trace of a skidmark behind Kronawitter's scooter. After all, she said, Richard Kronawitter had had 15 kilometers' time from Rach to here to think about braking – even emergency braking – as well as to take the necessary steps and make the necessary adjustments to get ready for, begin and actually undertake the act of braking. Instead, he just let the thing run on.

My dear Abbot, why have I read out to you this report written by my now retired assistant, Erwin Hatzenbühler? I've read it out to you because one can learn a great deal from it. To begin with, one can learn from this report how not to make reports. Naturally, I would write a report like this completely differently, namely shorter: *Causa* Schindler *contra* Kronawitter. Then answer the following questions but only using keywords: *quis, quid, ubi, quibus auxiliis, cur, quomodo, quando.* Severe verbal injuries by Katherina Schindler *contra* Richard Kronawitter *pleno titulo,* and the investigating officer. *Finis, punctum, amen, explicit.* But that isn't the essential problem here: that's a matter for the police administration and doesn't need to concern you. What you can learn from this story is the quality of resoluteness that finds expression in it. It's important for everybody, it's important – vitally important, I maintain – to recognize clearly one's opponent and enemy for what he is – an opponent and an enemy; and it is important not only recognize one's opponent and enemy as an opponent and enemy but also to treat him accordingly as an opponent, enemy and adversary. All humanitarianism and philanthropy are utterly beside the point here. Of course, my dear Abbot, it's easier to identify and judge an opponent in the case of a traffic accident than to discern the real enemy in the routine of social and political life in a monastery or in the Church as a whole, especially in view of the multitudes of people and parties and groups that have managed to insinuate themselves pharisaically into the Church. The Church these days sorely lacks the gift of discriminating among people; she lets herself be embraced by her enemies for so long until she finally suffocates. The love of humanity and the so-called love of one's neighbor are often nothing more than lack of instinct and weakness. A neurotic weakness, that's what this stupid spirit of compromise is. One often gets the impression that the Church is a patient suffering from a comatose syndrome – too weak to engage in conflict. Everybody's right as far as she is concerned. She blesses and sanctions even what's contradictory. A spirit is abroad, my dear Abbot, and not just in Europe. The name of this spirit is "inability to discriminate among different kinds of intellects." *Let us not be silent dogs, not mute look-outs, but faithful shepherds, watchful over Christ's flock*...as Boniface wrote.

My dear Abbot, you have to look danger in the eye, not crawl into the...well, you know where...of those from whom danger threatens. That means you have to attack them from the front and in this way also keep your own backside covered. There is a theological proposition according to which Christians should be unyielding in defiance of heresy but yielding and amiable to heretics. This is a very dangerous, sophistical, scholastic/Thomistic distinction, my dear Abbot, which you must not take too literally, unless, that is, you are a proponent of suicide. But, as you know, the Church is particularly strict on the subject of suicide. To be sure, when I consider some of the biographies in the Catholic *Martyrologium Romanum*, then in certain cases the borderline between martyrdom and suicide strikes me as being rather fluid. Some martyrs really did comport themselves in a very clumsy fashion. A lot of Spaniards especially, so it seems to me, didn't simply meet death but actually seem to have been driven by their own peculiar *sacro egoismo* to seek it out. One man is shoved underground on the wrong side of the cemetary walls and the other is elevated with high honors at the altar. In the former case, it is said: "No priest accompanied him;" and in the latter hymns are sung. But I do not want to talk about suicide now, since how the Church manages to underestimate or wrongly estimate its true enemies has nothing to do, surely, with suicide as such, even though in the final analysis the verdict may result in negligent suicide.

I am specifically pleading, my dear Abbot, for a realistic conception of the enemy. I know that this is a very unmodern point of view, because nowadays everybody is talking about dismantling stereotypes of the enemy. But it's my opinion that when you've dismantled the stereotype of the enemy, you still haven't gotten rid of the enemy. In order to get rid of the enemy, you still have to go through the process of dismantling the enemy. By this I do not mean the destruction but the elimination of the enemy, something that might happen through convincing or converting him. To be sure, one shouldn't be unduly optimistic about getting this done, since a simple treatment of diet and exercise doesn't always help; sometimes you have to reach for the knife or even the horse doctor. When, for example, I'm depressed and tortured by some deep trouble, then I can act in one of two ways: I can either remove the trouble at the root, that is, clear it away radically; or I can resort to calming myself artificially, perhaps by means of sedatives. In the latter case, of course, I've not really accomplished anything. Let me get down to specifics, my dear Abbot: we are not going to rid ourselves of the great plagues of mankind, such as Materialism, Communism and Atheism, by means of self-appeasement. I am certainly not going to alter or diminish the aggressiveness of the opposite camp by handing out sedatives to people in my own camp. That's only making it easier for my enemy to eat me and easier for me to get eaten. If we are to reach a real balance of interests or achieve genuine coexistence, then our esteemed enemy has likewise to make up his mind to swallow an appetite suppressant. If it comes to that, deliberate suicide is preferable to a process of deadening your senses and instincts that amounts to the same thing anyway. At least then I'm more fully aware of what I'm doing to myself.

My dear Abbot, I can only hint at a variety of things here, but there is so much that simply needs to be said outright once and for all. However, an icy silence reigns. Such an infinite amount of trivia is uttered but the needful word is never spoken; the needful word is suppressed. The patient is suffering from a serious disease, but no one tells him. The patient is terminally ill but the doctors tell him he has a cold or some minor ailment.

This timid and halfhearted habit of speech really has its origin in the sermons preached in your Abbey Church. My dear Abbot, the sermons one hears these days in your Abbey Church don't fit anymore into its architecture; there is a great discrepancy between this bold baroque building and the timid sermons that are heard in it. I still find the building up-to-date and timelessly beautiful, but I can't say the same for the sermons. For the beautiful is always up-to-date; but the plain – I won't say the ugly because, naturally, that too can attain to a high aesthetic level – the plain may be the order of the day but it is nevertheless actually an anachronism, an eternal irritant.

Most of the time I don't even really bother to listen anymore. I stand there and look up at the ceiling, and I always find something new again in Adam Prenwöger's frescoes. I look out into the sky. Or I look at the magnificent pulpit and imagine that the preacher isn't there, that is, if he actually has mounted the pulpit and hasn't already reached the conclusion that climbing up isn't worth the trouble he's taken in preparing his sermon. Most of the time the preachers stay put right in front of the altar; it's a rare one who makes use of the chancel. Apparently they themselves have realized that, for the purposes of what they have to say, the trip up to the pulpit is hardly worthwhile. Sometimes I

leave the church during the sermon and make my way to the
Gethsemane Chapel. There I await the passing of the sermon.

I have, moreover, the impression that Pater Adalbert, your
Sunday preacher, is fully aware that this pulpit no longer suits the
style of his sermons; or the other way around, as I see it, that his
sermons don't suit the style of this pulpit. This fascinating
chancel, situated high above the heads of the faithful, simply
turns today's sermons into a mockery. Nowadays your young
patres all preach at ground level, quite low and quite flat, without
any elevation. The pulpit is too high for them. The pathetic
downplaying and false modesty that informs these sermons
preached from the bottom up! Or, rather, they aren't really
sermons anymore, but only petty observations and speeches.
Simply a little morsel to think about. They certainly provide me
with food for reflection, especially with respect to their quality.
Of course, these so-called stimulating speeches have nothing
whatever in common with a real sermon, either in the form of a
homily or an old-fashioned declamation; that is, they have
nothing in common with an edifying or a theologically sophisticated sermon. Nowadays the preachers in your church preach
like actors speaking their asides in the theater; they merely mutter a little incoherently to themselves.

Whenever I see one of your young patres in the pulpit, I
don't need to make any effort at all to imagine him away; on the
contrary, I have to exert myself and make a great effort in order
to become aware of his presence at all. He only seems like a small
foreign body attached to the great pulpit. After all, even the
liturgical vestments aren't up to snuff anymore, and the Church
has the worst imaginable tailors. The priests all look like laymen;
at most they possess a tinge or semblance of the Church about
their dress – they almost look like priests. You see a priest and
you think to yourself: he looks a little like a priest. I'm referring
to what they wear in Church, my dear Abbot, not to civilian
clothes. Nowadays when they're out in public, you can't tell
anyway who is a priest anymore. Nowadays priests routinely
wear ties. The first time modern priests wore ties they thought it

was a revolutionary act of liberation; at first the post-Vatican II clergy thought of themselves as very daring with their cravats, almost a little decadent. As a result you can't tell a clergyman by his tie anymore, or at best only because he's still a little awkward when he ties the knot. Nowadays, however, people have grown a little more sensible again; in any event, people have come to realize that the necktie wasn't the Gordian Knot of the Church. My dear Abbot, both within the Church and outside it, there's a lack of boldness regarding the use of traditional dress. In former times, even when they were outside the Church the clergy wore clothing that was more striking and more fashionably daring than priests do now when they say Mass.

That is not to say that I'm arguing here for keeping up with the fashion; I know the difference between a clothes horse and a servant of the Lord. Very much to the contrary. In former times priests used to distinguish themselves from the mass of the laiety precisely by not participating in the perennially changing idiocies of fashion; instead, they wore attire which was essentially identical with that established by the old Roman habit of late Antiquity, that is, not only in the names used to designate the various items of clothing but also in the choice of material and the way it was cut. Viewed in this way, they always attracted attention. But they did not attract attention because they were vain and wanted to attract attention. No, they attracted attention because the reasonable, the practical, the enduringly good and the genuine inevitably attract attention to themselves in a world of fashionable unreason, irritation and hectic mindlessness – because what's solid simply distinguishes itself automatically from what's hollow. And nowadays the servants of the Lord are so embarrassed about distinguishing themselves outwardly from all those other gentlemen. They no longer wear gowns, caps, sashes, stoles, collars, buckled shoes, sandals. There's hardly any difference anymore between a so-called lay priest and a monk. How splendidly both used to be clothed and attired, each after his own kind – the so-called lay priest, the priest who belonged to an order, and the monk! My mother, my dear Abbot, used always to say to me, *they look like something.* We would talk about the clergy in our dialect and in the idiom of our village, and say that they looked like something. In former times, priests looked like something; nowadays they only look like anything.

What impressive and lucid language Saint Benedict uses in Chapter 55, *De vestiario vel calciario fratrum, Of the Clothing and Footwear of the Brothers: Brothers should be provided with clothing that corresponds to the conditions and climate of the place where they reside, since in cold regions one needs more clothing, in warm regions less. It is the duty of the abbot to take cognizance of this fact. In our view, however, in a region with a temperate climate, it is sufficient for each monk to have one cowl and one tunic, a thick woollen one in winter and a lightweight or a worn one in summer, together with a scapular for work, as well as shoes and sandals for the feet.*

"Pragmatic" is the word for the spiritual outlook that's behind this dress code, or else "flexible," but flexible in a sense where flexibility or readiness to change has nothing in common with changeability or fashion or any other kind of fickleness. It's a flexibility, on the contrary, that results from a realistic estimate of variable climatic and geographical conditions. That means that this kind of fashion doesn't change every year or twice every year. At most it changes according to the rhythm of terrestrial change. There is no spring or autumn fashion, but only one fashion for the Ice Age, another for the transitional period after the Ice Age, and so on. Liturgical vestments, my dear Abbot, are a different matter. If a clergyman, no matter what religion he belongs to, makes himself handsome in connection with some divine service, then that happens for God's sake, for God's sake, not for the sake of pleasing oneself or mankind. For God, it used to be said, the best is barely good enough. Only in this way can the immense expenditure – immense, that is, from a worldly point of view – be justified that churches make in decorating themselves and their altars with gold and with works of art, or the heavy metalwork on the religious books that are used in the Mass, along with the general pomp in instruments, vestments, furniture and gestures, etcetera that accompany it.

It's from this perspective, too, that we have to evaluate the importance of the Arnulf Chalice and its loss. But the Viennese detectives wanted to deal with the case, as it were, divorced from religion. Detached from its spiritual/religious background. "That's not only ahistorical," I said from the very outset to the Viennese, "it's also the wrong way to go about investigating a crime." "How right you were, Dr. Einberger," one of the leading members of the Department told me just yesterday. "We should have listened to you from the very beginning." "Look," I said. "You should have followed my reasoning, which in your view was too subtle and too farfetched, with more patience, more endurance and more attention. That way you would have saved yourself a lot of useless effort." "Once you pass through the gates of City Hall," the gentleman from the Department said, "you get to be a lot smarter."

My dear Abbot, when I was young, the investiture of a priest before Mass was an event of major importance. I remember how the sacristan would always first consult a book before Mass, and even before the priest would enter the sacristy of the Church in Andach, where I come from. It was a book which listed not only the color of the liturgical vestments along with detailed directions relating to relevant liturgical matters, but also quite obviously contained secret information which the sacristan did not share with us ministrants. There was something mysterious about this book. After the priest had finally put in his appearance and had been greeted with "The Lord be praised," he would reply, "For ever and ever. Amen." Then we would get busy with getting him dressed. To begin with, the sacristan proffered the umeral, which the priest attached to his neck much as he would a scarf or a barber's apron, worn, however, not in front but in the back. Next the sacristan slipped the huge, bunched-up alb over his honorable head. If, however, the sacristan didn't carry out the procedure in just the right way and let go of the bunches and folds of cloth before the priest's head had reached the upper opening – the end of a vast white tunnel –, and before his arms had reached the sleeves of the alb, then the gentleman of the cloth could be assigned to the category of missing persons for some time. Then there would follow a struggle like that with the Hydra, with everybody taking part. The ministrants looked into the various openings, searching for their missing master, while the sacristan tried, by grabbing heartily and pulling at various places, to undo the tangle somehow; and in the process he would often manage to mix up the priest's robes or his suit in the general mess as well. Sometimes the sacristan and the chief ministrant would confer regarding this dire emergency, with the result that their critical summit meeting was also plagued by disagreements and differences of opinion as to how to proceed further. Once there even was a down and out Battle of the Investiture. When at last the priest would emerge into the light of day, a sigh of relief would be heaved all round. Epiphany, the appearance of the lord. He was among us again, although a bit the worse for wear. The lord is risen and revealed to his people. Then the priest would smooth his hair and wait to be given his cingulum or girdle. I was often permitted, my dear Abbot, to hold one end of the twisted rope and hand it to the priest to tie around his waist. As the cord was wound around the expansive alb – which had room not just for the priest but for a whole convent – it began to take shape; everything became tight and straight and puffed out. Then the priest placed the maniple on his arm, an item of clothing whose function I never really understood as a child and which I thought of as resembling a small jibsail on a boat. By way of culmination the sacristan lowered the heavy chasuble, the main-sail as it were, over the head of the bowed and kneeling figure of the priest. I always found this ceremony of dressing the priest very dramatic and exciting; and the subsequent undressing too. I felt as if we had returned into the sacristy from doing a great and mighty deed and now would be allowed to unpack the priest again.

As a child, of course, I only had a childish conception of what was going on. I had no real understanding of the cult signi-ficance of priestly clothing and liturgical vestments. But even so

I did have a sense of the worldwide and profound meaning of the Mass. And because the mysterious essence of the divine service and the Mass made intuitive sense to me, it also made sense to me that one had to prepare oneself properly for it. I understood perfectly well that whoever wants to say Mass has to dress warmly for it, and not just in winter, because the churches were still unheated back then. The manifold variety of vestment and cloth was rather the textile consequence of the sacred mystery. Today I might perhaps prefer to call it instrumentalization. I had often heard country folk singing about how people who wanted to go to Heaven had to take along mittens and had to dress warmly. Because, they sang, it's cold in Heaven, they sang, because the snow, they sang, falls from Heaven, they sang.

In Andach, when the flock of ministrants had left the sacristy with the priest after the investiture, then this exodus was always like going forth on a great adventure. This impression of adventurousness was heightened by the fact that saying high mass on important feast days didn't always go off without a hitch. On the contrary, often some unpleasantness or mishap intervened. Sometimes all of the participants would be left with the unhappy feeling that something had gone wrong. The chief cause of this feeling was the tightness and narrowness of the space in front of the altar in our village church. There wasn't enough room for any grand liturgical gestures or movements. When you witnessed the throng of ministrants and priests on the other side of the communion rail during the so-called troika high masses, you could only feel sympathy for this people without room to expand in. It was also a breeding ground for aggression. Everybody kicked and shoved, even if only furtively, everybody made room for himself at others' expense. There were a lot of hidden fouls. And not everybody used the holy vessels and instruments in accordance with their holy function. Especially the incense pot enjoyed great esteem as a weapon among the ministrants. The turifer too was always able to make his influence felt. It was also at this time that I realized that a bell can be used for other purposes than just ringing.

But the absolutely most dangerous part of saying Mass on

high holidays was the transfer of the Most Holy Sacrament of the Altar from the tabernacle to a sparkling gold niche located high above the altar. The priest, handicapped and impeded as he was almost to the point of immobility by his heavy Vesper robes, climbed up the five steps of the stepladder that a ministrant had lugged through the crowd to the altar. When this happened. everybody in the church held their breath until, balancing the heavy monstrance precariously in his hands, the priest finally put it away in its proper place. *Tantum ergo sacramentum, Honor, praise, thanks and splendor be to the Father and to the Son, seated together with the Holy Ghost on the Highest Throne: one Power and one Essence. Sing loudly and joyfully to the divine Trinity. Amen.*

Benedict of Nursia understood full well that the priesthood demands a strong character if the priest is to exercise his office properly and not succumb to arrogance, personal ambition and personal vanity, or, as he puts it, to eternal damnation. That is why he writes in Chapter 62 of the *Rule* that the abbot should select with care and with a due sense of responsibility the worthiest Brother from among his community of monks, who was then to be groomed for the priesthood or for the deaconate. Benedict goes on to say that the abbot should observe this person with the utmost care, guide him, and, as the case may be and as the need may arise, punish him. The Saint knew that in this office and in this calling it was not enough for pretty clothes to fit or for a black Florentine hat to look good. He wasn't satisfied if a cleric succeeded in looking like something, as my mother used to say. *The priest should be wary of arrogance and pride. He should take care not to do anything which the Abbot has not commanded him to do. He should rather know that now he stands even more completely under the discipline of the Rule. Being a priest should not be an occasion for him to neglect his obedience of the Rule and its discipline; on the contrary, he should strive all the more to be ever closer to God.* That's what Benedict says.

I myself, my dear Abbot, was about 15 years old and a pupil in the Abbey Preparatory School in Freimünster – you weren't Abbot yet, but only a novice – when I came to the conclusion that I probably would not make a good monk or priest. Of course, I wasn't aware either at the time that one day I would study law and wind up as a policeman. But by then I had come to realize that my earlier decision to become a priest had not been based on essentials but rather on mere atmosphere and aesthetics. In the final analysis, my decision was not rooted in the heart of my belief but at the periphery. Nevertheless, my boundless admiration for the cultural aspects of the Church has, as you see, survived; so too has my respect, though not my boundless respect – but still my aesthetic respect – for the hierarchy or political order of the Church, an order which derives, or at least should derive, from the spiritual order.

Well, at that time I also took stock of what my family thought about my clerical calling. Here too – in their ideas and hopes for me – I discovered a kind of predilection for secondary things and for the second-rate, even though I thought I recognized signs of genuine piety in the taciturn clumsiness with which they expressed it. My mother often said, "Franz [that's me], Franz has a voice that's as nice as the priest's," she said. And even today I can still hear my father saying: "Franz has a good memory. Franz," he said, "has a memory good enough to study for a priest." My parents always saw the real difficulty in studying – any kind of study, but especially theology. It was the act of memorizing and the need for a good memory that struck them as problematic. As far as the priesthood was concerned, they saw the main difficulty in the fact that the priest had to learn to say the Mass by heart, a difficulty caused at least in part by the brats who were the ministrants and who couldn't be relied on to bring the missal to the right place at the right time.

This view of the primacy of memory is not really so naive, my dear Abbot. Especially when I got around to studying law I learned in hindsight to respect and esteem my parents' views on the subject. *Repetitio est mater studiorum*; repetition is the mother of every kind of study. Whoever possesses a good memory doesn't need to repeat so often. Memory isn't everything when you study; but without memory there's nothing. That's something that's not affected even by the kind of intellectual vanity that flatters itself by despising and underestimating the importance of feats of memory, of *mere* feats of memory. Especially among politically active students, or among those who are only politically active – among such students, in other words, who would rather be politically than academically active – it's no longer advisable to learn anything by heart. They have put a cancellation on memorization. To a certain extent they are even right to do so, for in former times memorizing was sometimes exaggerated. But after all you can't exclude learning from learning altogether. And only to learn how and where to look for something and what to consult strikes me as being a rather pathetic and contemptible culmination of long years of study. Is it really enough to be versed only in the knowledge of how to find and use reference works? According to this line of thinking, anybody who knows the ABC and can tell the difference between the bottom and top ends of dictionaries and grammar books, has a command of all the languages in the world. But that doesn't mean he's a competent speaker of those languages, at least not in my unprofessional, commonsensical book, and not a listener either, if you don't believe that the act of hearing is confined merely to the ability to hear. That is, to the acoustic and physiological facts.

Learning vocabulary by heart, so I hear, my dear Abbot, is no longer customary with us. Now they're already carrying out experiments in the language laboratory of your Abbey Preparatory School, although pedagogical experts have discovered by now that the language laboratory can't replace old-fashioned learning entirely. Only Father Dr. Engelbert, your English teacher in the Abbey Preparatory School doesn't seem to have realized that yet. He strikes me as being excessively reluctant to ask for and require real performance from his students. But that's just how, my dear Abbot, laxity spreads from the Abbot down to the Fathers, and from there on down to the gatekeeper. That's the curse of the good deed, that it's doomed to breed yet further goodness. Birth control, I say, family planning. Sometimes I think you're so gentle with your pupils and don't make them learn vocabulary anymore because you're afraid that these boys might then even go so far as to lose their faith in God. You would rather place the boys in the language laboratory and let them play with their earphones. The boys don't have anything anymore in their heads except the language laboratory; the boys, my dear Abbot, have absolutely nothing in their heads anymore, but only on their heads, namely the earphones.

Every week, my dear Abbot, at the request of my sister I supervise the educational progress of my nephew, Werner, and week after week I grow more disheartened. In my day students possessed a living knowledge of the dead languages, the so-called dead languages. As far as the present generation is concerned, not only have the dead languages died, but these boys also understand very little of the living foreign languages, unless you count a couple of lines from English or French popular songs. Whenever I see Father Engelbert, I draw his attention to this worrisome deficit of knowledge. "Professor," I say, "your pupils' knowledge of foreign languages is utterly unsatisfactory," so I say. "It's not enough," I tell Father Engelbert, "it's not enough, Professor, to lead your pupils into the language laboratory and to put earphones on their heads." Father Engelbert listens to my objections and complaints with impressive calm and angelic patience, but never changes anything. The very next day already you'll find him sitting with his charges in the language laboratory again. Perhaps, my dear Abbot, this preference of your Father Engelbert for the language laboratory derives from his understanding of the Benedictine *Rule*. I believe it may be connected with the Benedictine motto ORA ET LABORA.

My father always said, "Franz has a good memory; Franz has a memory that's good enough to study for a priest." The word "memory" plays a big role in the dialect of my home town. In Andach they say of a madman that he "lacks memory." My father never referred verbally to any human being's madness except by using the sentence: "He lacks memory." He always said: "He or she lacks or lacked memory, has lacked memory." Whoever possessed a good memory, could study; but whoever studied had to be careful not to start lacking memory. In this way, more was meant by the word "memory" than we mean when we use the standard dic- tionary-word "memory" today, that is, possibly nothing more than simply some technique for memorizing or some knack for remembering things, or else short-term or long-term memory. They, on the other hand, meant by it our whole rational faculty, along with our feelings. If somebody was hopelessly mad, people in Andach said that he had "lost his memory." To be sure, my dear Abbot, I grant that my father must have conceived of the process of going mad in a rather mechanistic way. At any rate, after listening to the grown-ups, I imagined the onset of madness as a disease that broke out suddenly and without any warning symptoms, somehow or anyhow, because of an act of negligence or mere carelessness while studying. My father always considered studying to be a dangerous thing, even though he encouraged me to study for a priest or at least didn't discourage me. There were too many examples of people in our surroundings – yes, even among our relations – who lacked memory or, as it was called, had "disstudied." After a while there were so many in our surroundings whom I knew, who lacked memory and had disstudied, that I was forced to consider the outcome of study as uncertain and risky. The people who had really studied and those who had disstudied were about equal in number. For every one who had studied, I could think of at least one person who lacked memory and had disstudied. And, my dear Abbot, how many people did I later get to know or know about, during my time at the Abbey Preparatory School or while studying at the University in Vienna, who went mad while poring over their books!

As you know, my dear Abbot, it's not my style to wax senti-mental in view of this unfortunate and lamentable situation, or even to pretend to move you – or even me – to pity or terror, the way the great tragic and pessimistic writers do, by referring to the various fates suffered by people whom I've happened to run across in my lifetime. Furthermore, I don't want to make madness out to be a specifically Austrian or Upper Austrian phenomenon. We shouldn't exaggerate our importance. Also, I don't want to suggest – here, more than anywhere else in what I've said so far – that this tendency to madness is to be interpreted according to the formula of "madness equals genius" and thereby prove our genius, even supposing that it's really a more pronounced tendency among our fellow countrymen than among other people. It's actually nothing more than the normal sort of anxiety – here, there and everywhere, just it's always been for thousands of years.

If, however, I refrain, as I should in view of these facts, from any kind of sentimentality, I am nevertheless compelled to say a few words about precisely those people who, inhabiting spiritual houses, suffer breakdowns in their spiritual and emotional health. It's quite obvious that especially in this kind of community many people suffer mental breakdowns. Even in your own House the rate of mental collapse and incapacitation is very high. And if you don't notice it and nobody else does in your Abbey, nevertheless the foundation for attracting such notice elsewhere later on was laid here. This is what I call homemade madness. Clinical medicine refers to it as ecclesiogenic psychosis.

Of course I'm aware that a religious person – that is, a person who has to ask questions and stubbornly demand answers – is by his very nature more at risk than someone who isn't involved or is merely indifferent. But it's also possible to devote one's whole life to some spiritual issue without being touched or affected by it in the least; in other words, basically without understanding anything about it at all. One can't help getting the impression especially with priests who are unusually healthy, active and full of life, that they probably don't take theological or ecclesiastical matters very seriously. It's unlikely that any God-fearing person would be quite so boisterous and cheerful. Isn't it true that anybody charged with the salvation of souls has to be forever troubled, for otherwise why should it be referred to as *caring* for souls? And why, otherwise, are there so many souls in a condition that demands our care? Even so, wherever faith is, there doubt is not far distant. But the doubt of true questioners often plunges doubters into despair. Their questioning and disbelief eventually culiminate in bouts of despair, or, as those learned in Latin would say, *primum dubitatio, deinde desperatio.* When doubt is neighbor to the heart, then will the soul soon drift into melancholy, as Wolfram von Eschenbach says. Actually, as you may remember from your Middle High German class, my dear Abbot, he says: *Ist zwivel herzen nachgebur, daz muoz der sele werden sur,* or "When doubt over the heart has power, Then the soul must soon turn sour."

What I actually want to say is that many of the children who come to you in Freimünster are grave beyond their years, grave even beyond their spiritual condition. Viewed in this light, they are at risk. Either they will end up doing something important or else they will end in disaster, like our prize pupil Isidor Seitenstettner; or they will end in both, if the disaster is in no hurry to happen. I would like to defend and exonerate you against attacks from enemies of your system of training and education – in the final analysis, against enemies of the Church as such – by asking people to consider what difficult raw materials you have to start with. You, along with your religious and lay teachers in the Abbey Preparatory School, the Boarding School and the Seminary, assume a great responsibility, much greater than that of teachers in the public schools, because you hold the whole essence of these young people in your educational hands. And, given this responsibility, the critical observer can't help but put in a critical word regarding your educational habits and your punitive expeditions, as well as the whole educational complex under your jurisdiction.

In former times, it was said that life was good under the shepherd's crook. Or, to put it differently, the Church, with its material and spiritual privileges, was the goal many young people strove for, especially if they were the sons and daughters of poor parents. But many well-off parents, too, dropped off their children at the gate. According to Benedict's *Rule* – that is, specifically according to Chapter LIX, *De filiis nobilium aut pauperum qui offeruntur*, The Offering of Sons by the Nobility and the Poor – it was only the parents and the Abbot who negotiated their admission and even set up a contract, a regular contract for delivery and receipt. *If a member of the nobility offers his son up to God in the monastery, and the boy is still a minor, then his parents are to provide him with a legal document. They then offer up the boy by wrapping that document and his hand up in the altar cloth together with a sacrificial gift. But if the parents are utterly without means, they simply write out a document and offer up their son along with sacrificial gifts in the presence of witnesses.* We don't need to discuss the motives behind these offerings. Of course, in some cases it was actually a substitute for exposure, that is for putting children away. Or else it was a way of reducing the number of one's heirs; or family planning medieval style; or family politics; or a cabal without love; or the result of plots and intrigue. (We even know of cases when relatives, brothers or fathers, got rid of some unwelcome rival in this way, but then that person, supposedly safely buried away deep in the monastery, worked himself up the ladder to become Abbot, Bishop, or perhaps even Pope, and then paid them back in kind if not kindness.) That's how it was, and it's clear that there was a great deal of crowding at the gate. Benedict's *Rule* gives an account of this in Chapter 58, where he discusses and regulates not only the admission of children but also, and above all, the admission of adults as *fratres* or monks. One should let the newcomer wait at the gate, so the saint writes, in order to see if he won't change his mind after all: *If someone comes and persists in knocking at the door, and if he nevertheless uncomplainingly endures being treated badly and denied entry for four or five days, persisting all the while in his plea for entry, then he should be granted admission.*

In short, abbots were able to select. The supply was greater than the demand, which is why the abbots established a numerical limit on admissions. They were certainly entitled to do so, but what they were not entitled to do was to arbitrarily send home or dismiss problematic or difficult candidates. Even the criteria used in selecting people for admission were questionable, since certain categories were excluded, among them children of single parents; people practicing certain trades, from butcher to hangman, along with the children of such tradesmen; people who were diseased or disturbed; and so on and so forth. But even more than merely questionable were the criteria used for exclusion and excommunication. Benedict would not have been a saint if he had not foreseen this danger and warned his abbots especially to avoid the arbitary exercise of power in expelling and removing the sickly and the sinful. *Secundum Benedictum, Regulam capitiis XXVII: Qualiter debeat abbas sollicitus esse circa excommunicatos, How the Abbot Should Care for Those Who Have Been Excluded. The abbot should take the greatest pains and should be zealously circumspect and unrelenting in his efforts not to lose a single one of the sheep that have been entrusted to him. He must be conscious of the fact that he has assumed the care of sick souls rather than a tyranny over healthy ones. And let him fear the threatening words spoken by God through his prophet: Ye eat the fat, and ye clothe you with the wool, ye kill them that are fed: but ye feed not the flock.* What you considered fat, you took for yourselves; and what was weak, you discarded, my dear Abbot. Benedict is quoting Ezekiel here, from whose book these lovely and at the same time terrible words are taken, and which in Latin read as follows: *Quod crassum videbatis adsumebatis, et quod debile erat proiciebatis.*

I've always had an uneasy feeling that the Church takes no real joy in complicated and difficult people, nor in so-called intellectuals either, although I don't like the word "intellectual" and even less those who apply the word to themselves. Their presumption is in fact self-contradictory. Whoever claims to be an intellectual is *eo ipso* a pseudo-intellectual. But it's clear that in former times the Church must have treated its intellectual minority better. For example, the sorts of things Saint Augustine describes can't be compared unqualifiedly with contemporary pastoral or social-conscience theology. My dear Abbot, you should promulgate material, not spiritual, humility. For heaven's sake, does one really have to sink to the level of a sheep if one wants to be included in your pastoral theology? When Christ says that you have to become like unto a child if you want to enter the kingdom of heaven, then, of course, you shouldn't interpret this idea of "becoming childlike" as a species of spiritual infantilization. The Lord is here alluding to purity and simplicity of heart. Even Saint Francis Bernadone of Assisi had studied long enough – indeed, had not only read books but even written them – when he came to the conclusion that everything written, with the exception of the Holy Scriptures, was worthless. Studying books and throwing them away – there's a method for you. But you can't reach this stage by taking short-cuts. You've got to read the books first before you throw them away.

Only after people have finally fallen into complete dotage or succumbed to utter madness can they count on receiving assistance from State and Church. Only then is society prepared to take official cognizance of their existence again. And society does take account of their existence; they can count on that. They will be lodged and cared for. Society protects such people from themselves, and itself from them, by confining them in prison-like institutions. Now they have become objects of pity and compassion, of welfare. *Quod debile erat proiciebatis*. The Church, my dear Abbot, should do a great deal more in the way of caring for souls, so that its pity won't be needed anymore; I want to make a plea for more pre-institutional and less post-institutional care. The Church should invest a part of the money that it raises in its Charitable Fund for the preventative care of souls. Incidentally, here's a concrete piece of advice, since we're on the subject of charity. You should act according to the motto, *plus amoris, minus caritatis*, or more love and less charity. The Church and society should work to achieve more spontaneity and less tension in the area of sexual relations, then we might be able to get rid of a great deal of whatever it is that makes nursing care and charity so necessary. Never fear, my dear Abbot, I'm not one of those people who expects to solve every problem in the world by adopting this measure. Not every problem but some problems anyway.

Yes, my dear Abbot, religious people, even religious people,

make mistakes; and one of the mistakes they make while caring
for the souls that are entrusted to them is – and here I'm back
where I started from – that they don't comport themselves as one
has a right to expect them to; and that they don't preach in the
way they should. Even during Holy Mass they don't look like
priests and certainly not like celebrants. They no longer belong
to the Order of Melchisedec. If for once one of your young *patres*
happens to climb up into the pulpit, one gets the impression that
he's actually a workman up there fixing something. Or could it
be the sacristan who's gone up there to dust and see if everything
is all right? Please, my dear Abbot, it's not Father Adalbert's fault
that he isn't as tall as Saint Boniface was, nor does it matter that
he isn't. After all he doesn't have to found Fulda or chop down
a forest or rid it of wild boars – that's a job the Benedictines
managed to accomplish a long time ago. But the fact that he not
only isn't a great preacher but, insofar as his sermons are concerned, is a mere dwarf and a churchmouse, that's something that
catches the eye – though unfortunately it doesn't catch the ear.
Most of the time little people are at least able to talk big. That
he's afflicted with a weak, thin and squeeking voice is regrettable
and of course it's not his fault; but that he preaches badly is
outrageous because, after all, preaching is his profession.

Admittedly, the new loudspeaker system is a nuisance. It
hasn't improved the acoustic situation but actually made it a lot
worse. I'm already considering whether I shouldn't start going to
Church equipped with some *Earpax* or earplugs, because one's
ears can be damaged – badly damaged – not only by these lax and
feeble sermons or by the droning asides (often, alas, electronically
amplified), but also by the melancholy music and, in general, by
the "humble" rhetoric employed during these so-called spoken
masses. Protected by *Earpax*, I would at least be able to devote
myself undisturbed to the sublime, the profoundly and spiritually
exalting pleasures of Fischer von Erlach's divine architecture.
When I hear the celebrant – that is, insofar as one can call the
cult-worker who is fumbling around up there a celebrant, since
there's no question of any celebration or festivity going on –

when I hear the priest up there saying *Pax vobiscum*, then I think to myself that he really ought to wish us *Earpax* instead. Only my piety and my readiness to sacrifice myself have prevented me thus far from resorting to these extreme remedies. The new liturgy has actually succeeded in turning the Mass into a genuine sacrifice.

Nowadays preachers hardly bother to prepare their sermons anymore. They simply rely on inspiration; and inspiration is unreliable. Inspiration fails them, that's one of the things about inspiration. "Something will occur to me," your young *patres* say to themselves, but regrettably I often discover that not only does nothing occur to them, nothing occurs at all, a lot of nothing. The spirit wanders where it listeth, alas.

Of course, my dear Abbot, the fundamental reason why the Mass and the sermon so often go wrong is faith, namely lack of faith. Whoever isn't really convinced of something can't speak convincingly about it. If a travelling salesman loses his nerve and shows up depressed and demoralized at some apartment door, then he certainly isn't going to sell a vacuum cleaner, not even a hairpin. That's the be-all and end-all of traveling salesmanship. The salesman simply has to believe in himself and in his vacuum cleaner. And the priest has to believe in God or else he's sold down the river. There are similarities and differences between priests and salesmen, but with the former it's not an easier but, in fact, a lot trickier and more difficult job. When in the old days, during my years at the Abbey Preparatory School, Father Lambert – God rest his soul – mounted the pulpit (or God's exalted crow's-nest), then a murmur would run through the audience, and we got ready for a powerful and overwhelming experience. You could feel that Pater Lambert's sermon and Fischer von Erlach's archictecture fitted together and worked together, because, as you know, Fischer von Erlach didn't just build churches but was also a military architect, a great connoisseur of military matters. You could feel how the two suited each other. A sermon like that was an attack, the pulpit was a Field Marshall's vantage point. And a sermon like that didn't just demand something from the audience but also from the preacher. Pastor Lambert exerted himself not only acoustically, but also spiritually and pastorally. And when at the end we had said our "May God reward you," after a rhetorically overpowering crescendo lasting for several minutes, followed by a cadenza and the *cursus velox*, as well as our concluding "Amen," then we verily knew what we were thanking the exhausted, almost collapsing priest for. We thanked God that the preacher had delivered a mighty sermon to us in His name. Nowadays it often seems to me as if we're thankful that the preacher hasn't bothered to say much of anything and has finished up, thanks be to God, in five minutes. Nowadays, it's almost a vast relief when we say, "May God reward you." Sometimes I get annoyed and I think of the "May God reward you" as a curse or a cry for revenge. May God punish you for this sermon, Father Adalbert.

While your young *patres* don't quite know what to say, 160,000 books, not counting manuscripts and incunabula, gather dust in your Abbey Library, all books from which we could learn a great deal that our contemporaries ought to be informed about, or from which we should simply start reading out loud. I'm often of the opinion that it would be better simply to read out loud some part of the Scripture or some text drawn from the Church Fathers. I know of a number of passages in Augustine that would interest me a great deal more than anything modern or pseudo-modern or seemingly up-to-date. And with this, my dear Abbot, we have now entered the Library; we've joined the Librarians and the Archivists; and we're drawing ever closer to the Vault from which the Chalice disappeared.

When I told the gentlemen from the Vienna Police Department about the Library, they grew extremely nervous and restless. "We're not interested in your books," they said. "What, for Heaven's sake, do the Abbey books have to do with the disappearance of the Arnulf Chalice? My dear Dr. Einberger," they asked irritably, "did the thieves steal books or did they steal a chalice? Or might it be that the thieves paused to investigate the collection before they stole the Chalice?" At this point, my dear

Abbot, as I began to tell them about the books and, in passing, mentioned that there were 160,000 of them *in toto*, not counting the manuscripts and the incunabula; and when I made it look as if I was about to have to begin going into greater detail regarding several of these 160,000 books, as well as needing to discuss more generally the problems of cataloguing them according to subject matter and the Dewey decimal system, then they suddenly wanted to forget all about me and said: "Enough! Enough already," they said. "We're not going to make any headway if we go on like this. You keep telling us an immensely longwinded story about the Library and the Abbey's collection of books. Unfortunately, however, you're not telling us a detective story," the Viennese continued testily. "We're dealing here with a criminal case," they said. "A serious offence, a grave offence against property; and you're telling us a story that is not a detective story but something about the *Confessions* of Mr. Augustine." My dear Abbot, at this point the gentlemen from Vienna were ready to dispense with my collaboration altogether. There was too little action in my report for them, they said. My stories had too little action in them. One of the gentlemen from the Federal Police said that I was a poet, but a poet incapable of action. I listened patiently to everything they said. I kept quiet and let them finish talking. And then I said: "So, now you've finished talking." And then, my dear Abbot, I put a new bee in their bonnet.

"Gentlemen," I said, "let us assume that in order to reach the Vault the thief had to pass through the Library, or at least pass through the last room in the library, provided of course that he entered the North Wing not through the first but through the second door. But no matter, even if he entered through the first door – because, as Father Ambrosius claims, the second door is usually kept locked, even though he can't remember whether that was so in this particular instance – but even if, as I said, he entered through Door Number One and crossed into the North Wing by way of the Liutbert Room, that is to say, even then according to the first hypothesis, the Library must have been accessible to him; in fact he already stood within the boundaries of the Library, namely in that part of the Library that is named after the noted scholar of Humanism and Reformation studies, Liutbert Armbruster. He was a Benedictine monk from Fürth in Bavaria who subsequently held an appointment at the Benedictine University in Salzburg, became Dean and later even Rector there, and was furthermore a Corresponding Member of the Academy of Sciences of the Upper Rhine in Strasbourg – in other words, a man of very considerable accomplishments. This is where the Unknown Person, or the Unknown Persons, stood," I said. "And now," I said, "set your investigative brains to work. What is Said Person doing in the Liutbert Room? What could he be doing? What would you do? Don't get excited, Gentlemen, I'm only speculating. If I didn't possess any moral scruples," I said. "If I hadn't been raised a Christian; if I hadn't received a Christian education from my parents in Andach and from the monks in the Abbey Preparatory School of Our Dear Lady in Freimünster, and if I had managed, like the thief of the Arnulf Chalice, to work my way all the way up to the Liutbert Room of the Library of Our Dear Lady in Freimünster, then, as someone who knew about the treasures that I now had within my grasp, I certainly would not have relieved the Abbey of Our Dear Lady of Freimünster of the Arnulf Chalice. I would have known of something better to take, gentlemen." My dear Abbot, you should have seen the faces of these people from Vienna. "If I'm standing in the Liutbert Room and know about everything that's within my reach and if I stop to think about which way I should go, then I certainly would not bother to steal the Arnulf Chalice, not I."

"To begin with, I assume that there is no practical way of selling an object that's unique. Everybody knows the Chalice. It's depicted in hundreds and thousands of historical and art-historical treatises and books. Its actual value as a piece of metal, moreover, is relatively small. When some mid-level manager or high-level bureaucrat helps his wife off with her jewelry after the Opera Ball in Vienna, then he's holding more actual gold and silver in his hands. You could have a gold tooth and an earring made out of the gold that's contained in the Arnulf Chalice, but not much more. For that matter, people often vastly overestimate the value of objects used in the Mass. The value of the Arnulf Chalice, Gentlemen," so I said to the Viennese, "is essentially an ideal and spiritual value; but it also possesses a legal value, as far as its rightful owner, the Freimünster Abbey, is concerned. The Chalice, as a gift from the Duke, entailed a legal title; a legal claim and a privilege were attached to it. So far, while carrying out our investigations, we've sorely neglected to consider the aesthetic and ethical value of the Chalice. We've got to establish for ourselves a historically accurate mental picture of how the original recipients, along with their heirs up to the present day, conceived of the Chalice and its significance. And then, on the basis of this contextual knowledge, we've got to imagine what the thief must be like. Given the lack of tangible facts, we've simply got to piece the thief together imaginatively. We've got to ask ourselves the question, and try to answer it, as to whether the thief had any idea of what it was he was stealing, and if he did, then how much did he know. We can and simply must make our deductions from the starting-point of the Chalice, *a corpore delicti ad delinquentem*, working from the object taken to the person who took it. At the present stage of our investigation we have nothing more than the Chalice to go on; that is, we don't have the Chalice anymore, we have a Chalice that's lost and various pieces of information relating to it, that's all that we have to go on, or that's all that we don't have to go on. And now we've got to start, *ad personam*, to deduce the thief from the Chalice."

"Whenever groceries are stolen, the police knows immediately what kind of people constitute the logical group of suspects. You've got to look for a grocery thief among people who are hungry. Of course, even there you have to take other factors into consideration. What sort of groceries were stolen? If somewhere a kilo of caviar is reported stolen, I'm naturally not going to go off looking for the thief among poor, starving people, since ordinary people don't think of caviar as food and hardly recognize it as such. Mere mortals simply have no idea what caviar is. They probably think that, as far as this black substance is concerned, it's not waiting to be eaten and digested but already has undergone the process of digestion. In other words, speaking respectfully or disrespectfully, it's a pile of crap. Or when whole truck-loads of wheat disappear or are sold through a fence, then I don't look for potential thieves among people who are anti-social or suffering from malnutrition. Somebody who is anti-social doesn't do things like that. Instead, I would snoop around the big flour mills. The only person who cheats on his taxes is someone who either pays taxes already or ought to pay taxes. Or," I told them, "let's consider a case that actually happened here in Freimünster. Two tires of the same size were stolen from a big truck. That's a crime that certainly wasn't committed by someone who rides a bicycle. Of course you've also got to take re-sale into consideration, namely somebody speculating on getting rich by selling stolen goods to somebody else. These are all basic *Rule*s of criminal investigation, so simple and straight-forward that one really shouldn't have to waste one's breath on them."

"Let's see what the Chalice has to say for itself," I said. "Let the Chalice speak. The Chalice is a) unique, and b) of real value only to its rightful owner. So the question arises: Was the thief less interested in stealing the Chalice – actually, it's not really question of theft anyway, since, taken literally, the facts of the matter indicate that there was no attempt to bypass any measures to protect against theft. Witness the lax, credulous and bene-volent manner displayed by the Abbot of the Abbey of Our Dear Lady of Freimünster, as manifested in the irresponsible failure to lock any door whatever, including the door at the main gate. In short, the thief was not so much interested in stealing or abduc-ting the Chalice, in order to delight in its possession or gain material advantage for himself by selling it, as he was motivated more than anything else (perhaps exclusively motivated) by the hope of injuring its rightful owner, the only entity for whom the object has any real (spiritual and practical) use. But to whom might such a motive be attributed, Gentlemen? Do you now see why I have placed so much emphasis on the enumeration of potential enemies of the Abbey and the Church, as well as focusing on that group of people whom I have designated and described – far too broadly and indiscriminately, I admit – as unbelievers? That's also why I have combed meticulously through the lists of names of everyone who was employed during the last ten years in the Abbey or in the dairy farms connected with it, including people who were previously employed and subsequently left or were fired, especially those who left in bad odor. I asked myself who might have acted out of revenge and who out of pure malice, that is pathologically and without motive. I even took care to unearth the slightest hints of vandalism, destructiveness and violence among the students staying in the Abbey dormitory. I looked at the desks in the classrooms. I even examined what the boys had gouged or carved into the wooden tops using their pocket knives or the points of their drafting compasses. "A thorough detective," I said to the Viennese, "must never leave the least, the tiniest stone unturned; he has to explore the outermost limits. And I really did go to the limit: I even analyzed the drawings on the walls of the washrooms. I really left no stone unturned, Gentlemen. I left nothing of this sort – of the toilet sort – out of consideration but also nothing of the spiritual-religious sort, of the intellectual-historical sort that you, Gentlemen, evidently have such difficulty in understanding and coming to terms with."

"*Calix loquitur*, the Chalice speaks: '*Unicum sum.*' The Chalice, Gentlemen, is a unique thing, an absolutely singular object, if I except for the moment the copy that is displayed in the Abbey Museum, whose existence of course we also have to take into account. Attached to the Chalice," I said, "there is a legal title, a right transferred to the Abbey by Arnulf the Founder in the fulness of his might, though of course we must also take note of the fact that a foundation is to be distinguished from a gift or from an endowment. The Founder remains the *instans primum*, so that the landed property of the Abbey of Freimünster continued to be part of his territory even after the Foundation had been established. The Abbey lands did not constitute, within the federation of the Duchy and the March of Bavaria, an extraterritorial entity." That's what I told the Viennese, in order to elucidate the difference for them and make clear what sort of Imperial titles were linked to the symbol of the Chalice. I also attempted to explain to the gentlemen from Vienna what the status of the farmers was on the territory of the Abbey, a status by no means to be equated with that of serfs or people without rights, as has been claimed by critics specializing in patchwork history and propaganda.

Now my audience was growing restless again because they were of the opinion that in saying all this I was once more digressing and going too far and becoming irrelevant. But I replied that all this was very relevant indeed. "You simply can't know, unless you know the whole context, what actually was stolen. Because the Abbey of Our Dear Lady of Freimünster wasn't robbed of one kilo and twenty grams of iron, or one kilo and twenty grams of some metal alloy, but of a Chalice that is over a thousand years old, in other words, of an object made of precious metals that have been shaped and crafted. That is to say, the Abbey wasn't robbed merely of some gilded vessel that, according to the documentary evidence of the *Inventarium instrumentorum*, has a capacity of two heminas. That kind of loss wouldn't matter much; in fact, it wouldn't be worth wasting one's breath over. However, in order to be able to grasp the full implications of the crime and in order to be able to reach meaningful conclusions about the thief, as well as about his motives and his origins, one needs to pay attention to these facts and to these circumstances."

"The Chalice," I said, "has value only for its rightful owner. Nowadays to be sure, it only has souvenir value because, of course, the Dukes of Bavaria are long gone and the political context has changed completely. That means that we also have to take into account the variable factor of time. If, for example, somebody had stolen the Imperial scepter and globe during the terrible period when there was no Emperor, then of course the thief would not automatically have become Emperor himself, and he also would not have been able simply to cut a slice out of the globe either. Still, his action would have had a completely different contextual meaning and it would also have been condemned, punished and penalized differently from the way we would punish it today. On the basis of this example," so I told the Viennese, "the need for a diachronic *and* synchronic mode of investigation should by now have become both plausible and self-evident to you, along with the need for a structuralist interpretation of the phenomenon of crime in general and of this crime in particular." Thereupon I distributed among these gentlemen various materials relating to the history of your Abbey and to the history of the Chalice that I had brought along in my rucksack. I then asked them to read through these materials and study them carefully before our next meeting.

"Not only is the stolen object able to bear witness," I said to my colleagues from Vienna, "but so can – and even more tellingly – those items that were not stolen. I ask myself: why did he leave this or that thing behind and limit himself to stealing only the Chalice? Just because he wasn't strong enough to carry anything heavier? Was he built small and slight like Father Adalbert? Why did he neglect the manuscripts and the books? There are similar problems with the manuscripts and the codices as there are with the Chalice. They too are unique, often registered, catalogued and described, and they therefore hardly constitute merchandise that's easily disposed of. Besides, it's primarily state-supported collections, national libraries, literary archives and, generally speaking, public institutions that have an interest in this kind of document. But public institutions usually don't buy things on the black market because, once they've concluded the purchase, they have to declare it and make it public. As a rule, public institutions don't publicly make fools of themselves by dealing in illegal merchandise. Though, of course, that's been known to happen too. If it's true what I read in the last issue of the magazine INTERPOL, then it's fairly common for Central American countries to turn to the black market to buy the gold they need for minting their medals and collector's coins. The most impudent way to transact this kind of business is to personally (or impersonally) steal something from the State and then sell it back to the State. In order to make a transaction like this work, you only need a State that's in an advanced state of disorganization and decay. Such places do exist. But that sort of thing is, no doubt, only possible in Central America. Taking everything into consideration, therefore, I would say that the unknown thief acted wisely in not bothering with the Manuscript Archive. Still, there are parchments stored in there which, strictly in terms of their cool cash value, would put a chill on the Chalice, as for example the so-called *Codex Perennius*. I have my doubts, nevertheless, about the unknown thief's ability to find his way around in the Archive. Pater Ambrosius administers a vast disorder in there."

"What do you mean by 'disorder,'" says Father Ambrosius. "I know my way around. What you see here may strike you as being disorderly, but it only strikes you as being disorderly because you're unable to find your way around. A disorder in which you *can* find your way around is an order. Looked at from the structuralist point of view, one could argue that you yourself are part of a disorder; you lack the celebrated so-called competence, you lack the keys and the code to be able to decode and decipher what you consider to be disorder. You find it impossible to deal with a system that's unknown and strange to you. What you see in my Archive is no disorder but a system that's unknown and strange to you. Everything in my Archive has its meaningful place in a system. I administer, you might say, a systematic disorder. In cybernetics this kind of *systematic* disorder is called an order. My order is an orderly disorder. In special cases, namely when the process of distribution follows certain rules, when the intervals and frequencies of the individual elements are aesthetically governed, that is, when they are set in rhythmic or parallel sequence but are nevertheless continually and necessarily interrupted and infused by so-called digressions and interferences, then, my dear Inspector, what you term disorderly and messy is not only orderly but actually constitutes an artefactual order and ornament." Thus spake Father Ambrosius.

"I would not go so far as to describe my Archive as a work of art, though I would have no difficulty at all in finding equivalencies among the papers and objects and furniture that are lying or standing about there. These objects or elements are connected with each other by means of structural relations; they are *controlled*. There is an unlimited number of positional links among them, without even mentioning the internal links. All of this may strike you as chaotic and full of rigamarole, because you're not one of the initiated. For me it's a cosmos. There are no cosmic orders as such, my dear Inspector; there are only various cosmoses viewed from the varying perspectives of intelligent observers." "I want to thank you most sincerely for this introductory course in Information Theory," I said. "It's impossible to deal with the question of order and disorder without taking the observer into account," said Father Ambrosius. "Order and disorder in whose eyes? Everybody terms his own disorder an order, and they're right and entitled to do so. I think of your order as a disorder, just as you think of my order as a disorder."

That's the philosophy of anarchy and order, of cosmos and chaos, as espoused by Father Ambrosius Hirschbach *Ordinis Sancti Benedictii*. You know all about it already, you don't need me to describe it more fully for you. Rumor has it, my dear Abbot – and that's something you probably don't know about because, as his Superior, you're not supposed to know about it – Father Ambrosius has often used (or rather abused) various old sheets of paper or parchment as kindling to start a fire in his barrel stove in the Archive. I don't want to believe it, but I do believe it, honorable Father. *Credo quia absurdum est*; I believe it *because* it's absurd to believe it. Once, late at night in the Tavern, I sidled up to him and discreetly grilled him about it. He only smiled slyly and said: "The things people poke their noses into." "Well," I said, "the Abbey has so many manuscripts that are of no use to anybody except to be catalogued and edited by linguistic and literary scholars. You're in a splendid position, Ambrosius, you live in the land of plenty. Only I don't know, my dear Ambrosius, if you're really carrying out your duties when, as the Archivist in charge of old palimpsests and all those parchments which our thrifty ancestors produced in their monastic offices and scriptoria – well, of course they were not actually our ancestors, if we go along with the assumption that the Brothers and Fathers practiced celibacy. Be that as it may, they were always busy scraping pieces of parchment clean and recycling them, even if only to present posterity in the end with some prescription about brewing snake-oil to cure horses ailing from the colic or from worms. Even so, you're not really fulfilling your Archival duties when you make use of these artifacts to engender a little fleeting energy in the form of warmth, and specifically during the *status nascendi* or initial stages of this process."

This is pure anarchy, in practice if not in theory. It may be of course that Father Ambrosius's primary intention here is to simplify the administration of his Archive and so manage to achieve a kind of order in the place. Quite frequently problems – political problems, too – have been resolved by procedures resembling this one. On the other hand, it's always been my impression that an archive was a reservation where conservation was supposed to be the order of the day. "Yes, yes," sighed Father Ambrosius, "I know, there are different opinions about administering archives. Even among specialists in the field there are different views about the nature, function and operation of archives and manuscript collections. Life in this world is an eternal struggle," Ambrosius said, "an eternal struggle. Conflict is the father of all things. Cheers, my dear Doctor," he said. "Cheers," I said.

Ambrosius, the Enlightenment man. Ambrosius the Josephinian. For, my dear Abbot, that is how, or more or less how – much like Father Ambrosius – the Imperial state officials under Joseph II managed to haul away our monastic treasures when the majority of Austrian monasteries were suspended or dissolved. Whole wagonloads of books and manuscripts were carted off to Vienna, or should have been, but as we know, a lot of them never made it. When they got stuck in the mud on the way, the Imperial officials and their wagoneers threw precious folios – from the Abbeys of Pupping, Engelzell, Suben, Reichersberg, Spital, Ranshofen, Lambach and God knows where else – under the wheels of their covered transport wagons to provide traction. How many wonderful books from the Upper Austrian monasteries perished at that time in the bottomless roads of Lower Austria. That too was the time when the treasures of our noble Upper Austrian culture were trodden down underfoot by horses and put to the wheel in Lower Austria and Vienna. It was barbaric, more than barbaric; it was brutal, bestial. From Upper Austria to Lower Austria to Vienna, that, my dear Abbot, is a direction that leads one way only, namely down and downward and down underground. I then proceeded to give the gentlemen from the Federal Police in Vienna an account of this episode too. "Gentlemen," I said, "go into your Viennese libraries and examine and read the books and manuscripts from Upper Austria that the Emperor had his minions confiscate and expropriate, or as we would say nowadays, steal from us. Read those books and get an idea of what the country north of the Enns River is like, and when you've finished reading you can come – but only then – and start investigating the theft of the Chalice. This is also, Gentlemen, good medicine against attacks of metropolitan arrogance. When your bureaucratic predecessors from the time of the Emperor Joseph or the Empress Maria Theresa threw or placed those precious Upper Austrian codices and folios under the wagon wheels in Lower Austria, they were making the only use of those precious Upper Austrian books that they knew how."

None of the Emperors, my dear Abbot, and not merely Joseph II, never treated us with proper respect. They hauled everything away – the books from our monasteries and the salt from the Imperial mines. God save, oh God protect our gracious Upper Austrian culture. Our game too was shot dead by the Viennese hunters. Even today the fauna in the area around Bad Ischl haven't recovered from their depredations. The game still hasn't been won back from the Monarchy. Everything was hauled off and shipped to Vienna. The only thing the Imperial retinue left behind was illegitimate children. Whenever the Court swarmed out towards Upper Austria, there wasn't a single woman between the summit of Mt. Dachstein and the Bohemian granite plateau that was safe. There were numerous gentlemen swelling his Majesty's hunting parties who were wont to continue their activities after the actual hunt had ended. This they did by pursuing women into their lairs. Even today, my dear Abbot, I'm still surprised when I go to visit my sister who lives near Salzburg and see peculiar and quite un-Upper Austrian-looking people sporting pronounced lower lips. Originally there was no such lower-lip face around here. This pouting species isn't autochthonous. This rare phenotype with the hanging dewlap is an import; it's a secondary type, my dear Abbot. It's on such occasions that I know that I'm hard on the track of the Habsburgs. It practically stinks of Emperors.

People from the big city have always misunderstood the countryside as a place where they could spend a summer vacation. The Imperial big city folks were looking for either summer recreation or winter cold but they weren't looking for Upper Austria nor did they find it. Just like big city people still do today, they think that country people have nothing better to do than wait for them and then, when they appear, wait on them. And then wait to see if they'll come again. That's why the Emperors too were dumbfounded when another type of news made its way back to Vienna from the rural areas located near the banks of the Enns River. As, for example, the time when the farmers got up a rebellion in Upper Austria. Mr. Emperor got himself a real surprise then. He was astonished that there were such violent hotheads among the resolute yeomen who banded together and rose up in open rebellion, not only against holy religion, but against Our Apostolic Majesty himself. But who gave them permission to do so? That was a question asked not only by the open-mouthed Ferdinands in Austria. And in this respect nothing has changed.

At that time one of these yeoman might have delivered a sermon to his fellow farmers that would have gone more or less like this: *Just keep in mind, all ye farmers, what you've been made to suffer and endure, how you were considered not to be humans but mere asses and oxen who have to eat any old thing that's tossed in their direction, who have to do everything that they're told to do, everything that the masters drive them to do with their boots and whips. Remember all that, ye farmers. And now after we overcome the masters, don't be stupid like the asses they think you are. A reckoning has to be made. Therefore, ye farmers, burn and scorch, ye farmers, and beat everything down that refuses to join you. Take whatever you find, it's yours by right because it was stolen and plundered from you in the first place. Rage like the devil; wreak havoc by day and by night.* And indeed, my dear Abbot, that's what the farmers set out to do. For example, in a contemporaneous biographical account from Wels, it says: *And in the end the loose rogues in Wels grew so insatiable that they wouldn't even eat good beef anymore, but only chicken and capon, venison and fish. God only knows where the already impoverished burgher was supposed to get it from. They wantonly spilled the beer onto the ground, along with those wines that weren't good enough for them. They were only prepared to drink the very best wines.* That was the news, my dear Abbot, from the shopping center known as the City of Wels which, as you can see, might have chosen 1976 as the occasion to celebrate not only the three hundred and fiftieth anniversary of the Peasants' War, but also the founding of its famous folk festival. And in another report to the Emperor about the farmers' mood at the time – a report that I also read to the gentlemen from the Federal Police – it says: *They behave like maddened tyrants when they get their hands on some Imperial or Bavarian soldier. A few days ago they captured three Viennese soldiers. Of these, they flayed the first alive; and in the case of the second they burned both his eyes using his own firing fuse and then hanged him from a tree by his feet. As for the third, they cut three strips of skin out of his body, hacked off his nose and ears, and ordered him to return to the Viennese camp and report what he had seen and what had happened to his companions.* My dear Abbot, I am deeply pained by what it says in this authentic report. Even the Viennese detectives made big eyes when they heard it. "Now you've got action," I said, "since a while back you were complaining about a lack of action in my reports. Here you not only have action, you even have a crime and an atrocity. Gentlemen, that's how the supporters of centralized government and the supporters of provincial rights used to behave towards each other."

On the very same spot, my dear Abbot, where the unknown thief stood, the thief who stole the Arnulf Chalice from you, namely in the Liutbert Room (which at that time was not yet called the Liutbert Room), on that very spot there also stood in 1626 the leader of the Peasant Rebellion, Stefan Fadinger. But he, along with his followers (among them several small leaseholders from the Abbey), behaved in a quite civilized manner and, as we know, neither stole nor plundered anything. He also left the Chalice undisturbed, for otherwise we wouldn't have had any trouble with it now. Perhaps the proximity of Luther's writings about the Reformation and the other Humanistic books put him in a gentler frame of mind; we just don't know. Perhaps it was due to your predecessor in matters of the Mitre, Abbot Patricius Stebner, who may have read him a little something out of Luther's 1525 treatise, *Against the Thieving and Murderous Gangs of Peasants: Therefore, let whoever may, smash, strangle or stab them, openly or furtively, bearing in mind that there is nothing more pernicious, injurious or diabolical than a mutinous man. Just as when you have to beat a rabid dog to death: if you don't beat him, he will bite you, and a whole country along with you.* And perhaps Abbot Patricius Stebner may have explained to good Stefan Fadinger that Luther was referring here to farmers; and that, to be precise, the farmers here occupy the position of object in the sentence, not subject. The subject is the princes. Translated into German grammar, so Patricius Stebner might have instructed the farmer Stefan Fadinger from St. Agatha, this means that the princes are the active principle in the sentence; their authority is in the nominative case, whereas the farmer is part of the predicate. He is in the objective case. The farmer's role is cast in the so-called dehumanizing accusative. Everybody, however, is supposed to be subject to authority. This lesson in religion may have had something of a sobering and disillusioning effect on the Lutheran. It also may be that the Abbot went a step further and provided the leader of the rebellion with some food for thought by referring to the case of Thomas Münzer, whom they had tortured and hanged exactly one hundred years earlier in Mühlhausen (that's in Thuringia).

I am merely speculating about all this, my dear Abbot. The fact of the matter is, however, that the farmers only ate an opulent dinner in the Abbey, which they forced Katherina Schindler's predecessor to cook for them, threatening her in somewhat rude and unpolished language and making nasty remarks about the possible consequences in case she failed to cooperate. Then they left and went elsewhere. This event or, rather, non-event – that is, the habitual looting practiced by the farmers elsewhere and omitted in Freimünster – is interpreted favorably by the Abbey Historian, Father Dr. Anselm Brenner, as a sign that the farmers were demonstrating in this way their gratitude for the good treatment that they had received as Abbey leaseholders, as well as, generally speaking, for the Abbey's many acts of benevolence during the period of settlement. But it strikes me as unlikely that at this turbulent period they would have bothered to make a detour to Freimünster merely to give thanks. It was not a favorable time for offering up thanks to God. At that time the farmers simply took unceremoniously what they needed; etiquette was not one of their priorities then. Basically, Anselm Brenner doesn't know a lot more about the role of the Freimünster Abbey during the Peasant Wars than we do about the thief of the Arnulf Chalice.

It's clear, however, that the farmers weren't quite so timid and pious in the Premonstratensian Abbey of Schlägl in the Mühl district; there the peasant warriors really behaved like peasant warriors. In these differing circumstances, a good historian like Anselm Brenner resorts to anthropology and explains the peasants' behavior by referring to the characteristic psychology of the inhabitants of the Mühl district. Having been oppressed and intimidated more brutally than the average Upper Austrian to begin with, they supposedly became fiercer and angrier after the uprising than did their countrymen from the other Inn districts, that is, Hausruck and Traun. It was in the Mühl district too that the Bavarians seem to have been on their absolutely worst behavior. It seems that the soldiers under the command of Count Adam von Herbersdorff (who acted as representative for the interim Bavarian government in this part of the country north of the Enns River) instituted regular expeditions into the Mühl district for the purpose of procuring song, drink, women, and rape. There is really no other way of interpreting the report about the origins of the revolt in Lembach: *It really started in Lembach in the Mühl district when, after a procession attended by the farmers, they rose up because the soldiers kept pricking and teasing them with needles, likewise because they raped their women in their homes, and because they tried especially to steal their horses, which they needed for hauling their wagons away when they proposed to leave the district. These soldiers had for some time been occupied with doing absolutely nothing but gorging themselves on sweet wine and brandy, cider, beer and vast quantities of food and drink both night and day, blaspheming against God, committing immoral acts, bullying the children of respectable people and tripping them up, and, in general, arranging for a large part of the law-abiding population's larders to pass through their stomachs.*

Three hundred and fifty years have passed since the Bavarians pricked and teased the farmers in Lembach with needles, raped their wives and stole their horses; three hundred and fifty years, since Count Adam von Herbersdorff instituted his dicing competition in the field at Haushammer near Frankenburg, and let the farmers roll the dice for their lives. That's a long time. But not long enough nor so long ago that I can't imagine or conjure up a vision of what happened then. Whatever it was, it certainly wasn't a rustic idyll. And even today, after three hundred and fifty years, there's no reason to celebrate or to spout crocodile-tear oratory. My dear Abbot, I can't find the memory of 1626 funny. At best I can make fun of the celebrations of the three-hundred and fiftieth anniversary of the Peasants War. Just what was it that was being celebrated, my dear Abbot? I don't understand. Did they celebrate the fact that three hundred and fifty years had elapsed since the farmers were pricked and teased with needles and then finally massacred by the thousands?

If, my dear Abbot, I had anything to say about it, then I would have allowed only requiems to be sung in commemoration of the Upper Austrian Peasants War, along with instituting country-wide special training sessions dealing with our inability to grieve. I wouldn't have commissioned an opera, my dear Abbot. Instead I would have set up competitions and awarded research grants with the specific aim of presenting and describing similar, if more subtle, acts of compulsion, constraint and repression occurring in our own day. Then we might have been able to say truthfully that we've learned something from history. I'm afraid, however, that we've learned nothing from history. People always claim that history teaches. Always, that history teaches. Of course history teaches, my dear Abbot, but first humanity has to enroll in history class; otherwise history can't teach anything. Above all, one has to arrive at the right and not the wrong conclusions, and make the right and not the wrong deductions from studying history. Mankind has to be ready to accept instruction. Further-more, one can't just approach history aesthetically or numerically and algebraically. It's not enough to memorize dates, nor is it enough to think of the past as something beautiful; no, above all history has to be approached morally. To omit morality is to commit a malicious act of inhumanity.

In this connection, my dear Abbot, and by way of conclud-ing this melancholy chapter about the Peasants War – that is, before I return to the Chalice and to our criminal case and its investigation – I want to remind you of the Army Commander Count Gottfried Heinrich zu Pappenheim, who thought war was a very beautiful thing. In his report to the Commander in Chief, the Bavarian Elector, about the Battle of Emling Wood near Eferding, he writes that he can't find words that are enthusiastic or lovely enough to describe this decisive battle: *Your Electoral Highness should have witnessed the most marvellous exhibition of sword-play to take place for many a long year!* He praises the farm-ers to the skies for fighting so beautifully and dying so beauti-

fully. There was no lack of corpses, either. There was a great
surplus of corpses. Close to two thousand dead farmers lay
strewn about in the woods and on the ground as far as Eferding.
And Hans Jakob von Starzhausen, too, one of Pappenheim's bat-
talion officers, reports enthusiastically about the impressive *resolve* shown by the farmers, so that, although virtually unarmed,
they let themselves be *hacked, stabbed and beaten, worse than
buffaloes.* Pappenheim and Starzhausen, my dear Abbot, describe
how they hunted these men down as if they were animals, blowing their hunting horns over long stretches of territory. Another
source provides a further report on how these defenseless farmers, having forfeited in previous battles their pitchforks and clubs,
their scythes, flails, sickles, and whips, now climbed up into the
trees, from which they were then shot down like jackdaws by the
forces of Pappenheim and the Emperor. What a charming scene!
    This, my dear Abbot, has been a footnote to the subject of
aesthetic historiography. It's a subject that enjoys greater popularity among historians than among eyewitnesses. History is too
serious a matter, my dear Abbot, to be left to historians. Pappenheim went on eventually to meet his own death in battle. I'm
afraid he didn't quite realize where he was looking. He was so en-
chanted by the spectacle of the splendid Battle of Lützen during
the war between Denmark and Lower Saxony. Nowadays, however, historical aesthetes no longer die in battle; they occupy professorial chairs and hold on to them for dear life. I know what
these stage-struck Pappenheimers are like, my dear Abbot. In me,
my dear Abbot, you may behold someone who holds no brief for
aesthetics, but who does hold a brief for synesthesia. I'm issuing
a plea for a synesthetic approach to the teaching of history. I'm
demanding that history be taught in a way that satisfies all the
senses. One ought to be able to produce gunsmoke in university
auditoriums. A lecture about war should entail a certain amount
of risk to life and limb. Professors and students should be
required to hold classes on military strategy while carrying out
forced marches at night, in rain, fog and snow. Entries in
university course catalogues should read like this: "The class

meeting on NAPOLEON AND RUSSIA will take place halfway between Zwettl and Klosterneuburg on the night of the 9th of January. STAFF." Above all, however, and as a prerequisite for admission into any History Program, I would not only demand a couple of good grades on a high school transcript, but I would also require sympathy. Sympathy and compassion for downtrodden humanity, my dear Abbot, sensitivity and a capacity for suffering, is what I would demand. And I would demand that utterly rare gift and virtue of being able to bring the past into the living present, together with all its implications for a suffering humanity. Sensitivity and consciousness, not just nosiness and sensationalism. For example, I would make candidates for admission to history departments listen to an historical account of the Battle of Emling Wood, and whoever didn't break down in tears at a certain point during the reading wouldn't be admitted. Unfortunately, I would tell them, the candidate didn't manage to pass the entrance examination. He evidently lacks the required basic human equipment to undertake the study of history.

If I had succeeded in working my way into the Liutbert Room, as once Stefan Fadinger did, or more recently the unknown thief, then I would not have entered Ambrosius' messy Archive with its manuscripts, nor would I have entered the vault containing the Arnulf Chalice. I would have headed straight for the shelf with the incunabula and helped myself. "These early imprints," I told the Viennese, "are neither unique nor plentiful. They are, in terms of the market for antiquities and second-hand books, by far the most reliable and profitable merchandise. They can be sold or auctioned off after a suitable interval with virtually no risk. I wouldn't like to know where the incunabula and early imprints come from that are offered for sale at book fairs by the great auction houses. Sometimes I take a look at the second-hand book catalogues of famous bookstores and I'm convinced that lists of the Most Wanted, or of wrongdoers for whom warrants have been issued, couldn't be any more full of crime than the catalogues of these famous second-hand booksellers. At the same time I'm aware that the bibliophilic merchandise that puts in an appearance in these catalogues some time after its unconventional acquisition is only the tip of the iceberg. Most of it is disposed of secretly or sold under the table."

Habent sua fata libelli, my dear Abbot; but the fate that some books suffer is absurdly curious. Above all I have in mind here the aforementioned books that were exported from Upper Austria to Vienna during the Josephine period of monastic secularization, and which were subsequently offered to us for repurchase, presumably because people in Vienna were unfortunately unable to read them, my dear Abbot. I'm reminded here of the business strategy of one of my classmates, who had a knack for training pigeons. Knowing all the while that the pigeon would fly back to him, he would sometimes sell the very same pigeon twice on successive Saturdays in the cattle market at Wels. But at least he didn't turn around and sell it back to the same customer, my dear Abbot. It's sheer impudence to offer stolen goods for sale to the very person from whom they've been stolen.

My Viennese colleagues kept on asking me how it was possible for the unknown thief to be able to enter the vault without making any audible noise. "Even if you don't take the doors into account," they said, "what about the long hallways and the big, echoing rooms? They inevitably amplify every sound, so that even a cough can't go unheard." "When it's quiet," I told the Viennese, "yes, then in fact you'll be able to hear our oldest monk, Father Einfried, quietly clearing his throat three corners away, down by the south wing near the Refectory. But for that to happen it has to be quiet," I told the Viennese, "absolutely quiet, just the way any noise can only be heard when it's quiet, and this solitary noise in turn breaks the quiet and the stillness. Noise is by definition an interruption of silence," I said, "if you know what I mean. Noise, sound, disturbs silence, but silence does not disturb sound or noise but actually makes their existence possible. That should be selfevident. But we must proceed further and note that noise not only disturbs silence but also disturbs another, different noise. That's an elementary principle of acoustics and music. Tones and sounds resound together, but they also compete with each other; they outdo, obscure and annihilate each other. And presumably that is precisely what happened in this instance," I said. "I'm convinced that the theft of the Arnulf Chalice was executed and carried out to the accompaniment of organ music, and that the music of the Silbermann organ, booming loudly over from the main Church down in the East Wing, covered up every other sound. I suspect that our Abbey musical specialist, Father Reginald, was busy pushing the pedals down powerfully with his feet at the very moment when the thief was gliding softly up the stairs and through the corridors. It may even be that the thief moved in time with the music. It's more likely, however, that Father Reginald had laid down so thick a carpet of sound that even a lumberjack wearing hobnailed boots could have trampled through without being heard. It's clear that Father Reginald, tireless as ever, provided the thief with soundproofing. In the shadow of Reginald's sonorities, the thief could make his way undisturbed. Of course, Gentlemen," I told the gentlemen from the Federal Police, "the organist Reginald bears no direct responsibility for all this. Presumably Reginald was playing organ, not stooge, for the unknown thief, but Reginald is no hypocrite; his assistance was certainly not conscious or deliberate. His assistance was unconscious; he helped the unknown thief, if he helped him (which I must assume he did), *nolens*, not *volens*; nilly, that is, not willy. No doubt at the time he was playing *The Heavens sound His everlasting glory, And echo propagates His name.* And while Father Reginald was playing *The Heavens sound His everlasting glory, And echo propagates His name. The earth, the seas, all spread His fame. Hear now, mankind, their godly story. Who counts the multitude of heavenly stars? Who leads the sun from out the dark? Look, it shines, it laughs. And hark! Lordly it runs its course like Mars* – while, that is, he was intoning, ornamenting, and varying this divine melody according to all the rules of the art of organ playing, while he was busy doing that, the anti-hero of our story, of whose name we were then ignorant, was running off in the direction of the Liutbert Room in order to pick up the Arnulf Chalice. Or did Reginald play *Whoever yields to God's dear sway* instead? Or did he play a prelude? A prelude with a post-lude, or, more simply, a sequel. I made an exact check of the times when the organ was being played during the interval in question. That was not quite so simple as it sounds because unfortunately organs don't as yet come equipped with timers of the sort that are installed in new trucks, to measure usage. Even so I was able to confirm my suspicions. During the interval in question, the organ was in use virtually all the time. Father Reginald played from 6:30 to 8:10 p.m. I also inquired about what music was played and received specific answers. Reginald began by improvising freely on a theme by Bruckner; he then played in succession organ motets by Schein, Schütz and Scheidemann, concluding with organ transcriptions of Beethoven symphonies. Around 7:30 one of his pupils took over and Father Reginald practiced with him the second étude from Gustav Sendrath's organ manual, ORGANUM. In this piece it's primarily a matter of testing the facility of the left hand, something that, according to Father Reginald, caused no difficulty for this particular student because he's left-handed. For that reason he soon switched him to other kinds of organ exercises. At precisely 8:10 p.m. he placed, as he always does, his foot diagonally over the pedals and let it rest there for a moment so as to extract the remaining air out of the pumps, turned off the motor, pulled the keyboard cover shut, and left the choir with his student."

"Bah," said the Viennese. "Nothing but dead ends. What's the point?" "The Porter, the Archivist, the Historian, the Sacristan, the Organist, the Abbot," I said, "they all play a role. The whole Monastery, all of the staff, everybody is implicated. Your method has to be holistic," I said. "It's holistic, or it's no method." The Viennese, on the other hand, claimed that it was only possible to talk about a method when there was some kind of limitation, some principle of selection. According to their view, the investigator needs first and foremost to be bold in bridging gaps; it's a matter of simplifying complexity, of abstracting, of isolating the significant detail, of narrowing and focussing one's point of view. You shouldn't look at everything but at something, at a selection of things, but then you should examine this selection carefully and minutely. My method errs by spreading everything too wide and too thin, insofar as my procedure can be called a method at all. My imagination runs away with itself, they said. I, however, maintained against them that one had to begin by spreading one's net wide. Whoever starts by limiting himself *a priori* isn't really making a selection. For abstraction is contingent on concrete detail. Before I can step back and generalize, I have to step forward and look at the unlimited totality of phenomena. Only then can I start selecting from among what there is. "Give me a solid place to stand on and I'll move the earth," said Archimedes. But first you have to find that place to stand on. Maybe someday we'll also be able to say with Archimedes: "Eureka, I found it."

One of the questions that at first struck the Viennese as being completely beside the point was the question of the rucksack. By referring to the rucksack I actually meant them to consider the whole complex of problems relating to the thief's means of transport. At the beginning the Viennese were much too enamored with the hat box that bore the inscription *Ziller Always Suits*. The gardener had found it the day after the robbery in the grass near the gate. This box really fascinated the Viennese. As far as they were concerned, everything depended on this box. I never treated the hat box with contempt, my dear Abbot. Nobody can accuse me of underestimating the hat box and its testimony. I was very grateful for the box, but for me a box is no dogma. That's why I said that the important thing was to put some sense into this box; by itself this hat box has no meaning. The very first time I inspected it, I said right away that we absolutely needed to look at the hat box dialectically. The Viennese, however, danced around the hat box as if it was the Golden Calf. For them the box was the solution to the mystery. "Hold on," I said, "there's no doubt that the box is a clue," I said, "but it may have been planted there deliberately to mislead us. I don't mean to diminish the reputation of the store," I said, "but *Ziller does not always suit.* We really do need to ask ourselves, whom does Ziller always suit? Or, rather, whom does Ziller suit in this instance? More than anything else, next to the matter of the hat box, we need to consider the matter of the rucksack." "What do we need a rucksack for," inquired the gentlemen from the Federal Police, "if we've got a hat box?" Soon they started calling me Detective Rucksack, using the term ironically, much as one would refer to a Rucksack Stockholder or a Rucksack German. These Big City folks were always using expressions like rucksack, milkmaid, bicycle, bicycle clips, belt buckle, ear muffs, hot water bottle, province, garden allotment, kitsch, doghouse. At the beginning provoative words like these played an important part in the vocabulary that the Viennese used in conversation with me and my staff. Presumably they wanted to provoke us into acting impulsively, perhaps in order later on to be able to exclude us altogether from the investigation.

The fact of the matter is that on the evening of August 18th, Father Robert was standing by a window in the physics lab located in the Mathematics Tower. Happening to look pensively down into the Provost's Garden, he noticed a man with a rucksack who was making his way towards the passage connecting the Provost's Garden with the Forum. Father Robert later officially placed in evidence that it had been a peaceful autumn evening, just about the time when twilight was falling, and that his (Father Robert's) mood had been very much in harmony with the evening. He had heard the organ in the distance. Then the bell for Vespers had rung. A flock of birds had flown serenely homeward across the darkening sky. A gentle evening breeze had touched and caressed the willow tree standing near the Laurenz Fountain. Father Robert was also able to provide me with precise information regarding the feelings which the man with the rucksack had evoked in him. This was the case because those feelings had arisen in the context of a state of psychic exhaustion characteristic of the hour of nightfall and, given the nature of such feelings, they were absorbed by his mind at a moment when it was not at the peak of concentration. His mind was therefore largely unprotected and vulnerable to external impressions. These feelings wcre, so he said, extraordinarily intense and enduring, but also joyous, even if not altogether pleasurable. At the same time they were actually a little melancholy and painful. Father Robert groped for just the right words to express the emotion he had felt at that particular moment and he tried out the following words one after the other: *wanderlust; regret for lost youth; itchy feet; high school skiing class; the St. George Boy Scout Troop.* He also tried out other words, testing each one, but in the end he was unable to find one that satisfied him, no matter how right they seemed at first. Finally he described the state of his feelings by reciting two proper names – those of the German author Thomas Mann and of his protagonist Gustav von Aschenbach. Subsequently I asked my Viennese colleagues to read Thomas Mann's story "Death in Venice" in order to help clarify matters, but this suggestion irritated them beyond measure. Their highest ranking officer had once seen a film of the same name. He made very disparaging, contemptuous and, above all, ironic remarks about the person who had written the screenplay. My dear Abbot, I have never heard anybody speaking so ironically about Thomas Mann. "We're not looking for some perfumed corpse in the Lido," he said, "but for the thief of the Arnulf Chalice and for the Chalice itself." I replied that despite the fact that my own critical opinion of this particular literary work was not so very different from his own, I nevertheless had recommended reading it precisely because it pertained to the case and to its speedy resolution. They should read it because only in this way could we come to understand our witness, the Abbey Physicist, Father Robert, and evaluate his testimony objectively.

"You just can't trust a man with those kinds of feelings," remarked the leader of the delegation from the Federal Police. "A man who goes off into trances and mental lapses, as Father Robert apparently does, must undoubtedly be liable, during these states of psychic absence and ecstasy, to mistake a rucksack for a suitcase or a rucksack for a hat box. People like him," he said, "have been known to see apparitions and visions! The kind of psychic state revealed in Father Robert's testimony – soaked and impregnated as it is with nightfall, autumn and twilight, brimming over as it is with decadent nostalgia, *weltschmerz*, nobility, intuition and decay – that kind of emotional and psychic state provides a fertile soil for visionary and hallucinatory experience, for wild imaginings and ideas, but not for truthful testimony. These lyrical types," he said, "are simply useless as witnesses. These dreamers and occi/accidentals (as he said he would like to call them) orient themselves according to the occident, but it would better for them to orient themselves according to the orient. They should once and for all change direction and look towards the East; they should be sober, awake, rested, full of energy." He said that he did not want his words to be interpreted politically. "Just put an end to serenades and soirees! Let's have a matinee at last!" So he said.

After hearing his testimony, he said he couldn't help but take Father Robert for one of those absentminded professors who are never of any use in accident cases, or at best only as victims. "It's not a rare occurrence for one of these moonstruck characters to be run over," he said. "Somehow or other in every accident, whether it's in traffic or at work, poetry plays a part. Poetry plays a great role in catastrophes. That's the function of poetry," he said. Whenever, for example, his officers were called in to assist with an accident that had occurred in some work place, then, he said, they knew from the outset that the victim was going to be some kind of poet, or that he actually *was* some kind of poet in those cases where the accident had turned out to be fatal. "A poet, that is," he said, "in the broadest sense of the word – a dreamer – but not seldom also a poet in the more restricted, even in the literal sense. Let's say the police is called in regarding an accident in a carpentry shop. A young man working the bandsaw or the milling machine has pulled his hand back too late and gotten his finger caught in the works. And it turns out that this young person spends his free time turning out poems by the cartload! And while he's working in the shop he keeps thinking about the poems he's working on during his free time, instead of thinking about his work while he's working, or rather instead of not thinking at all but just working. While it may seem strange to the general public, it's not at all strange," he said, "for somebody who spends his free time writing poems on his own, to stick a finger into a planing machine or some other dangerous machine. 'I just put my fingers down and bid my hand goodbye. Now the finger or the hand is gone.' That's sad," he said. "Poets are all mutilated," he said. He said that he thought poetry was a disease like anemia or epilepsy. In his opinion, nobody suffering from poetry should be allowed to have a driver's license, or to go out into the streets or crowded places alone. "Such a person ought not to be able to get married either or enter into any other sort of contract, and he should not be able to give testimony or act as a witness. The testimony of such people is by definition useless," he said. "Such people can't tell men and women apart, as in the case of Aschenbach. Yuck," he said. "Such people," he said, "simply make a mess of everything you manage to get out of them. Their testimony is a work of art, full of contradictions and loose ends, utterly useless for the purposes of an official inquiry. It's the same with Father Robert's rucksack," he said. He was unable to put any faith therein, he said. This Rucksackman who is supposed to have walked from the Provost's Garden to the Forum on the evening of August 18th, was in his view, so he said, a phantom, a kind of fata morgana, maybe even Morgan le Fay herself.

The Viennese detectives were deeply disturbed by the rucksack. Probably this rucksack, which Father Robert Inder had seen hanging on the back of the man from Regensburg, offended their aesthetic sensibilities. The idea that a thief should carry his loot out by the main gate in a rucksack struck them as simply too ridiculous. It's not easy to think simply; it's much easier to think complicatedly. Ideas of genius are always simple ideas. A rucksack! If only it had been a duffel bag. It's true that duffel bags figure more frequently in detective stories. Naturally, the Viennese denied that their evaluation of the evidence – the testimony and the leads provided to them by the local population – had been in any way affected by aesthetic considerations.

But it wasn't the first time that a paradigm shift had taken place. I notice it again and again, my dear Abbot, how the ethical, the aesthetic and the noëtic are either mistakenly thought to be identical or else confused with one another.

A person thinks he's reaching a judgment on ethical grounds, but allows himself to be blinded and deceived by looks and appearances, and so he can't arrive at a judgment on truly ethical or moral grounds. Another person claims to be examining some issue from an artistic and aesthetic perspective, but nevertheless is influenced and governed by his moral prejudices, and so is misled into aesthetic *and* moral confusion. Nevertheless, my dear Abbot, everybody claims that they're only interested in getting at the facts and at the truth, but if you look more closely then it's not hard to discover that a great many other interests, besides noëtic ones, play a part in their philosophical game, to wit, advantages and considerations of an external – purely external – nature. It is the task of investigative science to clarify the real motives and mainsprings of human judgment and action.

"Of course," I told the Viennese detectives, "one also has to bear in mind the so-called qualitative leap. I'm referring to the qualitative leap, in distinct contrast to the quantitative leap of dialectical materialism. There are human objects, products, and particularly artefacts that are aesthetically so perfect that we can unhesitatingly speak of them as morally good too. On the other hand, however," I observed, "it is by no means necessary for an excess of aestheticity to trigger a qualititative leap. There are works of art – or at least works that are meant or intended by their creators and authors to be works of art – that have already exceeded that furthest limit. Many books and pictures are simply too beautiful to be true. The loveliest books and pictures, the so-called loveliest books and pictures, consist without exception of lies and falsehoods. These lovely books and pictures," I said to the Viennese, "suffer from a redundancy, from an abundancy, from an excess of artifice and aestheticity and literaturicity and poeticity. They're kitsch," I said. The Viennese replied that what I was saying was very abstract and led nowhere. They didn't seem to notice that so far as this particular digression was concerned, I was only interested in gaining time and catching my breath. I needed more time in order to rehabilitate my chief witness, Father Robert Inder, whom they were intent on making look bad – not, by the way, a particularly difficult task. My aim was to restore people's faith in Father Robert.

"I have the feeling," I said to the Viennese, "that you would only be satisfied if you were provided with some incredibly attractive, super-intelligent, and eminently respectable witness. A witness who merely tells the truth isn't good enough for you."

That reminds me of how in the old days, when the annual general spring cleaning of the Freimünster Abbey Church was scheduled for the eve of the Feast of the Name of Mary, only virgins were allowed to enter the church. According to tradition only virgins were permitted to participate in the great purification of the Sanctuary of Our Dear Lady of Freimünster. But at the same time the inns were packed with young fellows who, while looking out of the windows at this virginal cleaning crew, would make suggestive remarks as they proceeded towards the Abbey. Nor was it unusual for there to be among these Vestal virgins one about whom some young man or other, or some young men and others, could well have taken an oath regarding the imperfect state of her intactness. "Well, lookey here," they said. "Erna is there too." In the meantime, however, this custom has also died out; in fact, virginity itself is not customary anymore. Nowadays we have to resort to books to find out how chastity and restraint used to be practiced. We have to consult the old writers, such as the works of Adalbert Stifter, the greatest of Upper Austrian writers – his "Indian Summer," for example – in order to get some idea of how chastity used to be conceived, because nowadays it strikes us as an utterly exotic condition. Unfortunately, it's impossible to observe these phenomena *in vivo* anymore; it's something that can no longer be studied in a living state.

Stifter and purity, my dear Abbot! How often did they criticize him and his books for being sterile and antiseptic, for not being realistic enough. His characters, even the workers –

insofar as one can use the term "worker" for the picturesque woodcutters who pop up now and again in his stories – all spoke a refined and genteel language (classic, in a word), using complete sentences, just the kind of language an Upper Austrian school inspector would have expected and demanded from children during his inspections and visits to schools. But, my dear Abbot, what's the point of all this petty, small-minded, altogether absurd criticism and faultfinding when you consider the immensity of Stifter's linguistic skill and craftsmanship. It's a case, my dear Abbot, of hounds baying at the moon – no, at the sun. The Abbey of the World's Redeemer in Kremsmünster has good reason to be proud of its pupil, Adalbert Stifter. Freimünster, unfortunately, possesses no pupil of comparable stature. In his story, "The Woodsman," dating from the year 1847, Stifter speaks of Kremsmünster simply as *the Abbey*. He writes: *There, as noon approaches, in the remote distance where the gray and violet of the flatlands thrusts a ribbon into the ethereal blue of the great mountain range, there, if it had been visible, one might have seen the glittering white point of the Abbey. It is there that the observer of these events spent so many years of his childhood, and there too that his heart and budding soul first found delight in so many joys* ...And later:.. *off to the Abbey, whose towers must surely now be gleaming in the sunlight...* In his writings Adalbert Stifter has built a truly beautiful monument of affection and devotion to the Abbey of Kremsmünster which had raised and educated him.

Even today, my dear Abbot, it is not unusual for there to be artists who are graduates of Abbey schools, but they are scarcely proud of their Humanistic education; on the contrary, they boast of having been expelled from the Abbey boarding school because of some act of delinquency or disobedience. And in their short stories or long novels they triumphantly describe their adolescent insubordination and rebelliousness. They are proud of their faults but they scourge the real or imagined faults of their teachers, especially of their religious teachers and supervisors. Some prefect who once upon a time presumed to slap one of these scions of the Abbey is unhesitatingly denounced as a vicious sadist. If, however, the prefect placed his hand on his pupil's shoulder, then there can hardly be any doubt that he must have been a died-in-the-wool homosexual who was wallowing in the most loathsome pederastic sewer or had lured minors into some lewd web of vice. My dear Abbot, it is well known that a teacher must not expect gratitude. On the contrary, he has to expect every imaginable kind of ingratitude. His profession is much less a matter of education and teaching, and much more a matter of serving as a target for aggression. In a word, my dear Abbot, a teacher is nothing more than a masochist who has security of employment, someone whom everyone – pupils, parents, bureaucrats – are entitled to beat up on. He gets paid for swallowing everything. "What else do you expect?" the public asks its teachers. "After all you get all those long vacations..." Being a teacher requires a great receptive capacity. It's best of all when the teacher is really a masochist; that way at least he manages to get a little fun out of all the nastiness and humiliation. It's even possible for a masochist to find fulfillment in this profession. That, my dear Abbot, has been proven conclusively and is a fact. But the sort of memorials that graduates of renowned abbey schools have been writing recently, pickling their former teachers in vats of satire and derision, makes a mockery out of any sort of real recollection and exceeds all endurance. The immense amount of immoral selfrighteousness, complacency and arrogance that's contained in the outbursts of these moralists! Adalbert Stifter, on the other hand, my dear Abbot, was cut from very different moral cloth. And it's not as if he was unfailingly praised and spoiled during the years he spent in the Abbey, from the moment that his grandfather dropped him off at the Kremsmünster gate in 1818 until he graduated in 1827. But that didn't prevent him from writing as follows: *Since those unforgettable days of my earliest youth that I spent in Kremsmünster and that I can unhesitatingly call my most beautiful days, because they were the purest...* And he writes that he would like to paint a picture of Kremsmünster in order to hang it up in his bedroom – as in fact he subsequently did.

My favorable opinion of Freimünster isn't the result of my having grown older, nor is it the product of nostalgia or of sugar-coating the past; it is rather a feeling I've always had. That is why the members of the so-called Association of Freimünster Alumni in Vienna once thought of making me their President. When I started studying in Vienna, I was known for my pro-Freimünster views and proclivities, and that's why many of the members considered me the logical candidate to preside over the so-called Association of Freimünster Alumni in Vienna. But, my dear Abbot, those who thought me the most logical candidate for the Presidency of the Association of Freimünster Alumni in Vienna were sorely mistaken. Those who intended to propose me for this office had found in me the absolutely wrong man; they underestimated me completely! For the kind of memories that these people foster and cultivate in the Association, along with all the other associations and clubs of this sort – such as, let's say, the Seitenstett Alumni or the Saint Paul Alumni or the Heiligenkreuz Alumni, etcetera, etcetera – didn't suit my idea at all of how to recall the past. In this respect I hold very different views.

I attended the meetings of the Freimünster Alumni in Vienna a few times but I was never able to find anything to my liking. For my taste, the members drank too much and talked too much nonsense. Most of them behaved in ways that were diametrically opposed to everything they had learned in Freimünster. They behaved in ways, in other words, that would never have been permitted here. Aside from bottled spirits, they shared no kind of spirituality. Naive as I was, I thought at first that things might be changed for the better. But all my suggestions for elevating the tone of the meetings were met with incomprehension and utter disregard. The veterans observed that they didn't need any elevated tone, they just wanted to keep hoisting their beers. Although there was no lack of so-called establishment people among the Freimünster alumni – they included quite a few doctors, business people, lawyers and professors – all these gentlemen had no use for anything but socializing, alcohol and idle gossip. Some of them would even quite spontaneously promise to help you with this or that difficulty, perhaps arranging to get you a loan or a new job or something along those lines. However, aside from the fact that many of these promises were made under the influence of alcohol and were forgotten the next day in the wake of a massive hang-over, and aside from the further fact that, plunged as they were in a state of intoxication, many an old goat overestimated the help he could give, and many a young fox the help he would receive, aside, that is, from these facts, I personally didn't want to get anything for free but was determined to make my own way. That is why my interest in the Association of Freimünster Alumni waned very quickly, as did their interest in me. Both of us realized we weren't meant for each other and wouldn't grow old together.

So there I was, not feeling particularly sorry for myself, alone, unable to establish a connection either with those who suppressed or diabolized the years they had spent in the Abbey, nor with those who abused the Association to commemorate their pasts in quite different ways. Nowadays, whenever I think back on this period of my life, it strikes me like a chapter out of a *Bildungsroman*, a novel of inititiation. Besides, I'm convinced that – without suggesting that it was really comparable – my experience in Vienna was like the early experiences of Adalbert Stifter or of Anton Bruckner who, to be sure, was a lot older when he came to Vienna. It's just that there is a shared Upper Austrian element in the lives of Upper Austrians in Vienna. Upper Austrians have similar experiences in Vienna, chiefly, of course, similar experiences of disillusionment. In my case, I spent much of the time that I wasn't studying law in reading – mostly reading the writings of Adalbert Stifter. Feeling as I did about my old school, it was only natural that Stifter should have been an example and ideal that I hoped to emulate, after having been disillusioned by the would-be iconoclasts as well as by the Association of Freimünster Alumni in Vienna. All his life long Adalbert Stifter venerated the memory of the Kremsmünster *Abbey*, just as I will keep alive until I die my fond memories of the Freimünster Abbey and its venerable school. I told the Viennese investigators that it was a high honor and a grave duty for me to be able to assist the Abbey at this critical juncture with all my professional expertise and with my long years of investigative experience. "For you," I said, "it's just another criminal case like so many others; but for me the recovery of the Arnulf Chalice is very close to my heart." And, my dear Abbot, without wanting in hindsight to make myself seem important or interesting, I really do think it was due to my personal commitment that I finally managed to get the upper hand of those unfeeling old boys from Vienna. Of course, I was also helped by my familiarity with the local circumstances and my acquaintance with the Fathers.

As for the testimony of Father Robert, that's a separate chapter unto itself. A physics teacher with so much imagination and intuition isn't just a little suspect as a witness. It was precisely in this particular witness's biography that the Viennese got very busy nosing around, and they really did uncover some surprising things, as I was forced to admit. For example, that he had once been a leading researcher in the field of perpetual-motion studies; that he had repeatedly foretold the coming of a decisive new development in perpetual-motion research; but that in the end he had been forced to rework his perpetual-motion machine into an early-warning detection device for earthquakes. Of course, I was aware of all this from having observed it myself. I had talked many times in the Abbey Tavern with Father Robert about his machine and his kinetic optimism, and I often smiled to myself about his machine, his kinetic optimism and his peculiar ideas. But at the same time I saw nothing in all of this to compel me to dismiss his testimony in the case of the Arnulf Chalice. And in the end it was in fact a tip from him that led me to my conclusive triumph...

I've always been puzzled why a Benedictine monk – that is, a man who adheres to the *stabilitas loci* prescribed by the holy Regulator – should, of all things, have picked on a subject like perpetual motion. Benedict once contemptuously dismissed the Gyrovagian monks as *numquam stabiles, semper vagi*. For his part, Father Robert Inder characterized stability of place, along with the capacity for persistence and monastic *constantia*, as the basic prerequisites for dealing successfully with all important problems in the physical and natural sciences. "A person," Father Robert said, "who is always on the go or on the move is completely incapable of understanding anything about the nature of motion and kinetic energy. One needs to possess within oneself an infinite store of potential energy in order to understand what kinetic energy is. According to my way of thinking, a person has to act with absolute and complete calm, and, while being at the same time relaxed – that is concentrated but not tense – must be able to contemplate motion-in-the-world in such a way as to fathom its inmost secrets. A person, on the other hand, who merely hurries and stumbles hectically through the world and through life, presents too high a degree of frictional resistance, generates much too much friction, and in fact gets all hot and bothered whether travelling by road, train or air – that is, by any means whatever. A person like that fragments into little bits and pieces. Once that happens," he said, "you can be sure that he'll never get around to achieving anything of real significance. Neither in physics nor in any other scientific or humanistic subject of study can you expect anything but jokes from a jack of all trades; that is, you can't expect anything constructive, innovative or pathbreaking. A great researcher, however, whether in the natural or in the humane sciences, is in some sense always a monk, regardless of whether he actually is a monk or not. Anyone working on some great idea has to take care, above all, not to waste time on trivial matters. His relationships with other people have to be kept limited but they should be amicable and rest on solid foundations. In the lives of most of the great researchers in the natural or humane sciences – in their private lives too – one can see," he said, "an above-average degree of loyalty and faithfulness to their fellow human beings – also to their wives if they're men; or to their husbands if they're women. Often, however," he said, "it's not a single individual who matters most to the great artist or researcher in the natural or humane sciences, but Nature, or Intelligence, or Art itself. This substitution of one's work for a person is by no means a rare phenomenon. After all, in the final analysis, all great artists and scientists are married to their arts and to their sciences. That's true and the case," he said, "even if some people who occupy meaningless positions in their marriages *and* in their work use the latter as an excuse with their dissatisfied spouses and so try to make themselves look important. In the end," so he said, "it's simply a quantitative problem, a question of setting priorities, of time, of attention – of divided or undivided attention."

But from the Paulistic point of view it is of course, as far as the man is concerned *better to take a wife, than to burn*, and, as far as the woman is concerned, *better to take a husband, than to burn*. Paul himself, my dear Abbot, views this whole matter entirely from the man's perspective. Actually, I've been attributing to and foisting off on the Apostle Paul rather more progressive views on emancipation – and on Father Robert Inder too, because during our conversations in the Abbey Tavern, Father Robert always cited St. Paul more literally, that is, quite literally. With Paul it's the man who takes and chooses the wife, and the woman who is taken and chosen.

"Not everybody is able," so Father Robert said, "to accommodate and sublimate his erotic energy so completely through Art as was the case with Ludwig van Beethoven. His *distant beloved* really was as *distant* and as unknown to Beethoven himself as she still is to the Beethoven scholars of our day. Beethoven simply wanted to create an impression. In fact, the distant beloved is merely a pure mystification, fabricated entirely as a way of keeping himself going in social suuroundings that were utterly uncomprehending of the self-restraint he exercised for the sake of his music. It was a society, moreover, given to nasty innuendos and false suspicions. In short, Beethoven did it so as not to be denounced and persecuted by the petty bourgeoisie as a madman or a pervert; he did it in order to be left in peace and to be allowed to do his work." So Father Inder said. In addition, he said that it was perfectly correct for white candles to have been lit on Beethoven's coffin – the white candles that in former times were a symbol of the deceased's chaste and unmarried life. "For Beethoven," Inder said, "there really had been nothing but music. But, as I mentioned before, all great artists and scientists possess large quantities of potential energy, or more to the point, rich inner lives, imaginations – also inner tensions, to be sure – but withal an extraordinary calm, a lucidity and sense of superiority; and, finally, a capacity for extroversion, for transforming potential energy into motion. Motion arises out of calm. Whoever wants to prove himself in the arts or the sciences," he said, "first and foremost has to *preserve* himself. More than anything else, he has to protect himself from sources of irritation and distraction."

As his true model for a scientist, Father Inder repeatedly referred to Johann Gregor Mendel, the great naturalist and Abbot of the Royal Abbey of Brünn, a person whom I too admire immensely. It's simply impossible to dig up anything disparaging about Johann Mendel. "If you, my dear Viennese colleagues [I said to my quite undear Viennese colleagues], if you are always finding fault with anything and everything, then in the cases of Mendel and Father Robert's admiration for the great scientist and provost Mendel, it's simply not possible to make valid objections or criticisms. There is a great deal that speaks for Mendel," I said. "Everything speaks for Mendel." Of course, I found it necessary to explain to the Viennese that Johann Gregor Mendel was also to be reckoned among Vienna's victims. The *also* was intended by me to refer to my own difficult position *vis à vis* the headquarters of the Federal Police. I took the liberty to remind them that it was above all arrogant professors from the University of Vienna – great scientists and researchers whom, to be sure, nobody today has ever heard of, unless, that is, they're somehow connected with the life of the world-renowned and unforgotten Johann Gregor Mendel. In that case it may of course happen that people will run across their names as marginal figures. I took the liberty, I say, to remind them that it was some Viennese scientific popes (self-appointed popes) who had failed to take proper notice of the provost from Old Brünn. They snubbed and ridiculed him at a meeting of the Association for Scientific Research in Brünn, where this man of unassuming countenance first presented the systematic results of his work in the field of genetics. "What's the significance of this little farmer's son from Heinzendorf? What does this immigrant parson from the boondocks of remote Silesia think he's discovered? Nothing that we in the Imperial Capital haven't thought of ages ago! If there had been anything in it at all, then no doubt we would already have known about it in Vienna." They didn't even bother to discuss Mendel's results. The slender, unassuming Provost from Old Brünn simply couldn't make a dent in the armor of the pontifical bigwigs from Vienna. The popes had decided against the Provost.

The Viennese simply couldn't get it through their swelled heads that Father Gregor had made his experiments with peas. They called Mendel's genetic theory a peabrain theory. In the opinion of the Viennese these experiments should have been carried out using animals, big animals, preferably elephants or lions. They considered Mendel's association with peas an expression of his picaninnity. In the meantime the Viennese scientists too have come to the conclusion that it isn't the size of the research object that makes for the significance of the actual research. Nowadays you can even see Viennese behavioral scientists waddling tamely and modestly behind flocks of unassuming grey geese. But it was different then. What also displeased the Viennese about the methods of the little prelate with the nickel-frame eyeglasses was that he didn't proceed mentalistically and in terms of wholes, but classified the appearance of his plants according to their individual characteristics. Quite obviously they thought it was a scientific weakness for a researcher not to be able to make a survey of a whole phenotype in one single brilliant stroke. Mendel was too petty and picayune for them; they had a completely different conception of what a great and grandly conceived scientific discipline should be like.

Mendel's way of doing science was to some degree democratic, but the Viennese scientists followed the Imperial model. Scientifically speaking, too, they were Monarchists, even monarchs themselves. Johann Gregor Mendel, on the other hand, had already instituted team work at the experimental stage; he had trained several Lay Brothers for this purpose and they provided him with a great deal of help. The Viennese gentlemen, on the other hand, were individualists. To be sure, each one of them was surrounded by assistants, but these scientific helpers were basically trained only to make coffee for their masters or to run down to the restaurant when the great man had forgotten his umbrella. These assistants were stooges, flunkeys, gofers. But above all they were a claque. They continually had to tell their bosses how great they, the bosses, were. For their services, and as a reward for their endless running back and forth, lugging books, opening and closing windows, applauding and making coffee, they would be mentioned in a footnote in one of their boss's articles. Over long periods of time these references were, in the case of the average assistant, the only trace of the scientific existence of these obedient and serviceable minions. Such was the fate of the academic footsoldier.

Even during my own time as a student, my dear Abbot, remnants of this feudal professorial heritage still survived. You could immediately recognize an assistant from the way he carried himself. There was something unmistakably servile about him. The assistants acted as if they were always waiting and listening intently for some command that might possibly be issuing forth from somewhere in the higher regions. They only spoke of their professor in whispers and in a way that suggested they were uttering the Name of the Most High. No matter what or whom they met with in their surroundings, they would invariably evaluate it from the point of view of their lord and master. They had learned to look at the world through the eyes of their professors. The assistants always told their students only what their professor might or would say regarding this or that issue, but they never said what they thought of it themselves. The professors for their part kept their assistants in line by applying the ancient Roman strategy of *divide et impera*; that is, they played their assistants – they always had more than one; some even had whole hordes of acolytes – off against each another. So, for example, they might say, "Lately your colleague, Dr. Wuderl, has been making progress a lot faster than you." And immediately the panicked Doctoral Assistant would begin to step on the academic gas.

Every assistant wanted to be closest to the heart of his lord; every one, my dear Abbot, would have liked to have been St. John. The further, however, the services rendered by the assistant were removed from his actual academic discipline, the more private and, as it were, intimate they were, the more beloved he would be entitled to consider himself. The ultimate honor was to be allowed to help the professor's wife with her shopping. It was also a matter of course that the assistant would share his professor's general outlook on everything. Just like the professors, the assistants were also mostly freethinkers and freemasons. But that was just about the only thing that was free about them. In actual fact they lacked any sort of freedom despite calling themselves freethinkers. Basically they were serfs, retainers, domestics, servants without livery. You could tell who the professors were because of their gowns, and who the assistants were because of their shabby clothes and cute leather heart-shaped patches – hearty symbols of their loyalty – sown on the elbows of their shapeless jackets, or else because they were wearing sleeve protectors. Every one of them, my dear Abbot, every single last one of them would have dearly liked, as I said, to have been the professorial equivalent of Christ's Favorite Apostle John, but in the end, alas, it often turned out that they were nothing more than an absurd crew of jackanapes.

And of course accidents would often happen. Suddenly one of them would explode and out would pop a Judas. The human messiness of this inhuman business would suddenly emerge unmistakably in various spectacular and notorious cases involving the law and the police. I'm thinking, for example, of the case where an assistant of the Dean of the Faculty of Philosophy insulted his boss, that is shot him, while the latter was standing opposite, declaiming a funeral oration on the other side of a grave wherein they had just deposited another professor. At any rate, in this particular instance the facts were easier to grasp and to ascertain than in the case of the theft of the Arnulf Chalice, which remained unsolved for so long. The motive too, as it turned out, was pretty straightforward.

As a consequence of their way of looking at things – that is, the way I've just described – the Viennese professors found a man like Mendel very peculiar and rather repulsive, since he habitually worked on friendly terms with his Monks and Lay Brothers. All his co-workers were kept fully informed about what they were checking up on, observing, keeping track of, noting down, comparing and evaluating. And then there was Mendel himself, not wearing a professorial gown but only a plain gardener's apron over his habit. He almost looked like a servant. "That's exactly," so said the Viennese, "what the janitor looks like in our old Alma Mater, the University of Vienna..."

What the Viennese rejected in Mendel wasn't primarily, however, his appearance. What they rejected most of all was his astonishingly modern methodology, a methodology that had virtually anticipated structuralism. In 1865 Mendel's analysis of the nature of characters and factors, his conception of the *type* as a combination of structural characteristics resulting from a process of controlled genetic selection, was of course utterly unheard-of and actually shocking. In the context of the final official report I'm making at this moment, it is surely unnecessary to delve into all the historical or theoretical implications of Mendel's innovative scientific methods. The few points I've made so far regarding the Mendelian links with cybernetics, information theory and structuralism are sufficient, but nonetheless I needed to raise them briefly for the following two reasons. The first reason is that in subsequent years Mendelism was badly misused as a pretext for the murkiest kinds of speculations about race and eugenics. For this misuse, of course, Mendel is in no way responsible. He never had anything to do with such things, my dear Abbot, nothing at all. He would have despised all those people who claimed to be his followers from the bottom of his agrarian and monkish soul, despised all those who thought they could get some ideological mileage out of his scientifically rigorous and experimentally verifiable results. He had no sense whatever for such nonsense.

Another group of people understood him a lot better and more correctly, that is, those who made use of his work outside the borders of the so-called Thousand Year Reich – exiles, in other words – in order to develop and extend structuralism into every other field of knowledge. It was not the ignorant National Socialist specialists in heredity who were Mendel's heirs, but those men and women who were chased out of the country by the representatives of the mad doctrine that now prevailed in the German universities. Mendel would have given these narrow-minded nationalists and racists, with their blood-and-earth theories and idealized peasants, a piece of his mind. Just like the down-to-earth peasant, my dear Abbot, just like the true man of God that he was. He would have shown them whose evil progeny they were.

It is revealing in this context that, even after the whole ghastly business had ended, Austrian and German scientists only managed very gradually to re-establish a connection with international developments in the scientific world, or as one might say (putting it metonymically) before they re-established a connection with Johann Gregor Mendel. If it's true what my brother-in-law told me – the husband of my sister in Ebensee and the father of your pupil, Werner – then as late as the mid-fifties when he was studying literature in Vienna, he ran across unreconstructed biologists who were adamantly opposed to a structuralism that was, in their eyes, a decadent, nihilistic, destructive method that had been invented by Jews. But in Vienna it was still the rule that writers were rooted in the brown soil like trees. In Vienna all the old-fashioned theories involving genealogical trees were still in the process of growing fashionable. It was no different in the Law School where I studied after the War. We learned a great deal about Germanic Justice, but we were told very little by our professors about Germanic injustice.

And secondly, my dear Abbot, great ideas like Mendelism always run the risk of being trivialized, turned upside down or misunderstood. Something similar happened to me during the time I was working alongside the gentlemen from the head office of the Federal Police in Vienna, though of course I don't mean to imply any comparison with Mendel because of that. But, as it turned out in the end, the Viennese disregard for my suggestions often had dire consequences for the investigation. Quite often they even acted in direct opposition to me, as in the case of Father Inder's testimony. Because of my continual warnings and my persistent complaints they even started calling me Jeremiah. They claimed I was a hater and despiser of Vienna, something I am not and never have been. They simply didn't understand me. Once the Chiefmost Inspector said to me: "My dear Dr. Einberger, wasn't there somebody from Upper Austria not too long ago who was a big Vienna hater? Didn't he live in the Men's Association Hostel in Stumper Street?" That's when, my dear Abbot, I really lost my temper and really blew my stack, because I saw what he was driving at. "Are you perhaps referring, Sir," I asked him, "to that false prophet from Braunau whom back then you and your fellow Viennese compatriots overwhelmed with cries of joy in the Heldenplatz?" And then I added: "I will *not* be compared with that man. I have as little to do with hatred for Vienna as Johann Gregor Mendel had to do with the 'Nordicizing' of the Germanic race. In reality my attitude toward this city is one of critical sympathy, or, in the final analysis, of love." "Well, that's something Vienna can be grateful for," one of them sneered.

As for Mendel, the Augustinian Chapter of the so-called Royal Monastery in Brünn really did him no favor when they elected him Prelate. Of course he was a good and conscientious Abbot, but it wasn't long before his many administrative responsibilities kept him from his beloved scientific work. And then, after the Government in Vienna instituted the notorious tax on religious foundations in 1875, Mendel never had a moment's peace again. When he died on January 6th, 1884, he was a broken, lonely and embittered man. After the severe bouts of depression he suffered in old age, death came as a relief to the Abbot.

I have given a great deal of thought to Johann Gregor Mendel, not just to the researcher in heredity and the pioneer in genetics, but also to the man of God and the Abbot. Is it right to burden a great scientist by putting a mitre on him? Ought cardinals and bishops to be great theologians as well? Sometimes, in any case, it seems as if Rome doesn't think so... Is it still possible to rely on God to give brains to somebody whom he is also endowing with high office in the Church? Recently I heard somebody say the opposite – that when God gives somebody a job in the church, he first takes his brains away. And when a cardinal whom I know and who in my opinion is intelligent was asked if he was interested in becoming Pope, he replied that he was not since he wasn't crazy. But this is not the place or occasion to retail jokes about the clergy. Here we are rather faced with the serious question of the role of the abbot, my dear Abbot. What is the best way for the abbot to carry out his difficult task? In reflecting on this subject I take as my starting point the name which this monastic office bears. Benedict too, for that matter, does likewise in his *Rule*: *An abbot who is worthy of heading a monastery must always bear in mind the title with which he is addressed; and he must justify the designation of "maior" with his deeds. For the pious and the faithful flock see in him the representative of Christ in the monastery. After all, he is called by His name, in the words of the Apostle: Ye have received the Spirit of adoption, whereby we cry, Abba, Father.* It really gives me pause that so many positions in the Church are designated by the name of "father." Almost all the words for clerics with priestly functions are derived from the name of father, starting with the Pope – the Holy Father – down to the Parson and the Father and the Abbot. Oddly enough, the Bishop of all people, however, has nothing fatherly in his name. If it's true that the word for "bishop" derives from the Greek "*episcopos*" and that *episcopos* means "supervisor," then an Archbishop must literally be a "Supersupervisor." As for the Pope, according to the rules of historical grammar, he is a *pater* who didn't undergo the Old High German sound shift. Presumably he didn't participate in the sound shift because he was too dignified.

My dear Abbot, I really do hope that you don't think I'm being frivolous merely in order to get satirical mileage out of the fact that priests, while unmarried by definition, are so fond of providing themselves with, and getting themselves called by, names having to do with father. That's not how I do things nor is it the way I am. Even though I must admit that in some cases my experience of actual, physical fatherhood was not only no obstacle but in fact fostered in me a kind of spiritual fatherhood. I'm thinking especially of St. Augustine. In the ninth book of his *Confessions* Augustine writes about his son. My dear Abbot, whoever reads this passage without being moved to the depths of his being was never a child, a son or a daughter, was never a father or a mother.

The story begins with Augustine telling how he went on a pilgrimage with two companions, Alypius and Adeodatus, right across Italy in the direction of Milan, where he was to be instructed and baptised by Ambrosius. Of Alypius Augustine writes that he had already advanced to the stage *of walking barefoot over the wintry soil of Italy, an act of unusual hardiness.* That's an observation which, given the fact that Augustine came from North Africa, must not surprise us. With people from the North, on the other hand, it was almost *de rigeur*, once they had crossed the Alps into Lombardy, for them to take off their shoes and toss them into the Po, continuing onwards to Rome and not just to Canossa. But I digress. Augustine (a name which means the Exalted, the Augmenter, the Addressed-to-God-Our-Lord) writes of his son: *We also took the boy Adeodatus along, my son in the flesh, the fruit of my sin. You had made him so well! (Tu bene feceras eum.) He was about fifteen years old; and he was more talented than many men of rank and education.* And later on he says: *There is a book written by me called "The Teacher." The person who carries on the dialogue with me there, that's him. You know that all the words put in the mouth of my interlocutor there are his thoughts, the thoughts of a sixteen-year old. And there were a great many more things, even more astonishing, that I witnessed in him. His talent was so immense as to terrify me. (Horrori mihi erat illud ingenium.)*

My God, my dear Abbot, who *was* this precocious Adeodatus who died young? If Augustine said that he, Augustine, was overcome by *horror* in the face of his youthful intelligence? Only those who have never read a line of Augustine could dismiss Augustine's remarks about his son's intelligence as the product of partiality. With Augustine it was certainly not a case of his having gone ape over his son. To be sure, nowadays parents only say of their children either that they are particularly intelligent or if their grades – which these days are referred to only as *School Reports* – seem to prove the contrary, they say that their children, although *intelligent, very intelligent,* and very gifted, are nevertheless *lazy.* The parents say that fundamentally my son or my daughter is very *intelligent* but he/she is also *rotten lazy*; my son is a lazy loafer, the father says. There are only *intelligent* children nowadays, very many of whom, however, are *lazy, rotten lazy.* That little bum is just so awfully lazy, they say; that lazy, little, naughty twirp just won't budge for anything. Nowadays laziness is held in high esteem. It's almost a crime not to be *lazy.* Whoever works hard, so they say, needs to. Whoever works hard seems to possess no talent. Best of all, however, now and forever, my dear Abbot, is a talent for working hard. In my opinion, a talent for hard work is a *conditio sine qua non.* Whoever doesn't possess a talent for hard work can, in the final analysis, only boast that he has squandered, wasted and dissipated his talent. Incidentally, my dear Abbot, since just a moment ago I used the expression *gone ape* to refer to the phenomenon of uncritical approval and permissiveness of parents *vis à vis* their children, I would like to point out that monkeys have a healthy, nurturing, and vital relationship to their progeny. It's safe to say that monkeys don't feel any *human* affection for their offspring. Thus, to use the expression *going ape* to describe such infatuation is an insult to the so-called lower primates; *going ape* in the absence of natural instinct should be called *going human.* No orangutan would ever say of its offspring that he is an intelligent and highly gifted brat but also lazy, rotten lazy. It would not occur to a gorilla to say such a thing.

As is well known, when it comes to one's own children the critical faculty often breaks down, but what then takes the place of the critical faculty is unfortunately only rarely a sensible kind of love. Usually it happens that parents simply go ape. But that sort of infatuation makes parents go blind as well. That is why nowadays schools can hardly get anywhere with their pupils, because the Parents' Association would never allow their children to be encumbered and bothered by having to learn something. If it can be done with a smile and without any effort, then they don't mind; but there must never be any suggestion of compulsion. No question whatever of compulsion. If you look at the way our schools are run, you can't help but feel that discipline must be a dangerous thing. Soon they will compel the parents – those few who might be inclined to raise their children in a disciplined way and with some respect for discipline – to sign a release form assuming all risk for their actions, much as people are required to do in hospitals before serious operations. Benedict's *Rule*, my dear Abbot, recognizes the role of parents in the education of their children; it takes a favorable view of parents' cooperation in the formal education of their children. Nowadays it is always said that the parents should work very closely with their children in the home. And they really need to do so because they don't allow the school to do its proper work anymore but only hinder it from doing its work. But how are the parents supposed to teach their children about subjects which they prevent the schools from teaching, when they don't know or understand those subjects themselves? Schools nowadays have their hands full in trying to get rid of and making the children forget all the nonsense – the incorrect ways of doing arithmetic along with a variety of other benighted views – that the parents have inflicted on them. The truth is that the school and the parents don't work together, they work against each other, they neutralize each other; the school negates the family and vice versa. The biggest contribution that families could make to the formal education of their children would be to make no contribution at all, that is, to refrain from doing anything whatever. And that is precisely the role that Benedict ascribes in Chapter 58 to the parents of pupils in the abbey schools. After they reach the gate, the parents turn around. The parents bring their children to the abbey school and then they turn around and go quietly home. If they happen to be well-to-do, they first leave some money to pay for their children's school expenses.

We need real fathers in this fatherless society. We need fathers, my dear Abbot, not superfathers; but as it is we only have subfathers. Whenever I take a look around I never see any fathers; I only see dads and granpas, and likewise on the maternal side, nothing but moms and grannies.

A father should not be authoritarian, but he should be an authority. To be authoritarian is, in fact, nothing more than the unjustified assumption of authority; an authoritarian father is no authority, he is a posteriority. There can be no authority without competence, responsibility and legitimacy. A good father – and a good abbot – has the advantage of experience over his children and charges, and he *loves* his children and his charges. That is, he makes use of his experience in the right way to help them. By dipping into the depth of his experience, he comes to realize what the right way is. He knows what will, in the final analysis, help his charges on the road to salvation. In a word, he knows what salvation is and he knows how to transform his knowledge into reality. And because of this knowledge, he also knows what detours he can allow his charges to take as they make their way toward the ideal; he knows when to give them their freedom but he also knows how to restrain that freedom. He knows when he has to draw the line and insist on having his own way in the interest of his children, on having it even, if necessary, against the will of his children. If he fails to act in this way, then he makes himself guilty. Later on he can't simply excuse himself by saying he did it because he loved his children. He did *not* love his children; he was in fact careless, inattentive, sloppy and lazy. I realize, my dear Abbot, that my image of the father is a little idealistic and conservative, but I happen to think that Nature is also very old-fashioned and conservative. Fatherhood itself is a conservative matter; biology is conservative and traditional. It's very traditional for children to be created, conceived and born; it's traditional that they can't manufacture themselves, that they have to begin in a small way.

And what a joy it is, my dear Abbot, to obey a good father, a real father. In such cases obedience comes easily and spontaneously. That's true of an abbot as well. Then too, it is not merely a matter of obeying the whims of some arbitrary and autocratic figure, but the authority of a sovereign human being who is himself subject to governance. Specifically *in casu monasterii* it is the authority of the *Rule* that prevails over the abbot, but in all cases – the Pope, the bishops and the abbots – it is the authority of the Bible. In this way the giving and taking of orders is fitted into a coherent hierarchy and is derived from a precedent set by the gospel. We yield to the authority of those who themselves must yield.

My father, my dear Abbot, was still a father. Perhaps that is why I have a tendency to be paternalistic. If I had had a worse experience of fathers, if I had not been the son of a father and a mother but merely the child of a dad and a mom, I would probably talk differently. But wouldn't I then actually have to talk all the more the way I do? Doesn't somebody whose education went wrong know a lot better what the difference between a good and a bad education is? Unless, of course, his progenitors and educators went so far wrong that he can't even figure out what's right.

I remember – it's my first conscious memory of my father and it dates back to my fourth year – how during a terrible storm my father went out of the house into the raging elements. The rest of us, that is my mother and we seven children, were standing in the front hall trembling with fear, while my father, readying himself for his task, put on waterproof clothing and huge leather boots in a room which, because of its function, was called the "Sow Kitchen." When he went outside he passed us as we were all drawn up in two rows in the front hall. It's a picture I'll never forget. While it was thundering and lightning and the storm was whipping rain and hail in through the door, my father appeared, keeping his head down low so as not to hit the frame of the Sow Kitchen door that my mother was holding open for him. The only light came from continual flashes of lightning, and we watched as he rushed – the personification of FEARLESS-NESS – out the main door and down the steps, vanishing into the storm. Mother shut the door and we returned to the living room, where we resumed the prayer that had been only briefly inter-rupted. What Father was actually going to do out there, I didn't altogether understand (I was only a child) but I had no doubt that he was going to attempt some heroic deed in order to make the storm abate. Later on I learned that he was only rushing out to protect the waterwheel but he didn't succeed in doing so. All he could do was watch how the huge advancing masses of water swept away the wooden contraption that had already been ram-shackle for some time. As far as I was concerned, however, my father was performing immensely heroic deeds out there in that hell of thunder and high water, in that howling darkness of raging elements that made one's teeth chatter. Probably he was battling monsters, giants or dragons, just as St. Michael had done, and all for our sake, for the sake of his family. He was risking his life out there because he loved us.

When, my dear Abbot, I reflect on the significance of the abbots who were your mitred predecessors in Freimünster, then I always imagine them in the following setting: I envision the individual abbots who are depicted sequentially in the Great Hall and whose deeds are recounted in the Abbey Chronicle in vari-ous historical contexts. In other words, I transport them in my imagination into other centuries and, knowing their capacities and personalities, try them out to see how they would have acted in various historical circumstances, especially critical ones. A father has to prove himself by conforming to my image of what a father should be; and an abbot has to prove himself to me above all by conforming to my abbot-image in critical or even disastrous situations. So, for example, I try them out one after the other in the context of 1626 and the Peasants' War. Or perhaps I look backward to the time of the Turkish invasions or the Hungarian onslaught and try out individual abbots like Florian Hölzel, Carolus a Mari, Rupert Breitfarth, Gerhoch Raffetseder, and so on, and so on. Or I take a look at the years from 1934 to 1938 – a very tricky thing to do, since those years presented a challenge that many of these highly-placed religious gents might not have passed with flying colors... Because already more then 500 years ago there were authoritarians among the top-ranking clerics who displayed certain proto-fascistic tendencies by trying to lord it all over everybody else. I am well aware that you are in the habit of looking back at the 1200 year-old history of Frei-münster from an escatological and teleological point of view, abetted and fostered therein by the Abbey Historian, Father Dr. Anselm Brenner. That's why you've become convinced that God always put the right man in the right place in the Abbey at the right time. But I say that you should also make provision for error when dealing with Providence. For I believe it holds true in only a few cases or only in a negative sense. That is to say, given this or that situation, I am convinced that this or that abbot would have ruined the Abbey.

It's not difficult to divide the abbots up into hawks and doves; but the Lord did not always send the right bird at the right time. For example, there can be no doubt that the dove of peace named Breitfarth arrived at the wrong time. At that particular moment a man with political savvy like Konrad Sachser would have been more useful, a man who was more given to the *vita activa* and less to the *vita contemplativa*. In retrospect, however, it's hard to escape the impression that the more active personalities, the more energetic doers and shakers, actually in the end managed to accomplish less good, while undoubtedly causing more harm, than the more gentle and pious ones. Unquestionably at many moments of crisis the smartest thing to do was to retreat into the *vita contemplativa* of the Oratory, hole oneself up and hibernate safely behind the walls of the Abbey. You don't always have to explain things by referring to the power of prayer or the ways in which prayers were answered, although of course in my Christian opinion that plays a role too. But you can also see it in purely natural and secular terms – no action may be the most appropriate kind of action. So, for example, during a hard and snowy winter I can either go outside with shovel and scraper and wage a hopeless war against piles of snow, or I can stay inside my apartment, turn up the heat, drink tea and wait for spring to come. A great deal of harm has been caused in the course of history by acting impetuously; in 90 out of a 100 cases the rush to action means a brush with disaster. "To move is to prove;" yes, that's true, but only if you're moving through fields or woods, or in your study at home, and not on the battlefield or on the so-called field of so-called honor.

I am not contradicting here what I said earlier about the necessity of not avoiding confrontations. The operative word here is "necessity." Which, of course, is again not to say that one should seek out a confrontation for the sake of a confrontation, as Abbot Sebastian Preiner – the most choleric of our abbots – did. He had too much surplus energy; sometimes he could hardly walk for excess energy. Translating all this into pathological terms, I draw the moral that only sick people lead really healthy lives. As a rule healthy people lead very unhealthy lives, they live their lives to the full – or rather to the fool. You have to fall sick first before you can become healthy. Healthy people have no idea what health is. An Austrian writer once remarked that sick people get more out of life than healthy people do; that's just how it is, my dear Abbot, sick people get more out of health. As for the abbots, those who were bursting with excess vitality and activity often used their energies unconsciously to precipitate a crisis. If things got worse, they felt better. Great men, so it is said, only flourish in times of crisis; the eminent statesman is less effective in peace and in keeping the peace than in war and in declaring war and in waging war. But war isn't enough; if at all possible, it has to be world war. Many politicians won't budge for anything less. But let's not delve into that, my dear Abbot. I also like trying out the abbots of Freimünster – your predecessors, among them several striking personalities – to see how they would have performed in our current situation. How would these various individuals have behaved if the Arnulf Chalice had been stolen during their administration? How would they have reacted against the Viennese team of detectives? I used to get so deeply involved in speculating about these probabilities and possibilities that sometimes, while I was working with the Viennese Federal Police, I would suddenly say: *That's something that Abbot Hölzel would never allow you to do!* Or I said: *This is the kind of thing that his Honor Carolus a Mari won't approve of.* Or I said: *Crossexamining a witness in this way is something that Abbot Raffetseder would never permit you to do with someone whom he is in charge of.* Or, as I unfortunately have to confess, I even said: *That's something that you can maybe get away with in the case of the present Abbot, but in the case of August Preiner, he would have seen you in hell first.*

When I argued in this way, the Viennese used the term *the investigative subjunctive* for it. They meant it as an insult. "Thanks, Gentlemen," I said," I'm highly honored. You acknowledge thereby that I have imagination; that's a great honor. For I certainly count myself among those people who are able to go beyond the indicative and reach a level of investigative thinking and working in the subjunctive mood as well – no, not only in the subjunctive but also in the hypothetical case and the optative mood, even in the condition contrary to fact. That is something I owe – among other things – to my solid humanistic training in the Preparatory School of the Abbey of Our Dear Lady in Freimünster. Gentlemen, I said, I'll go even further and call forth for the purpose of my investigation and research the whole range of Indo-Germanic potentialities, also with respect to number. You're always wondering if there was only *one* or if there were *several* people involved. You're only familiar with singular and plural forms, but I distinguish among singular, dual and plural forms. I also take cognizance of the twofold number – the venerable dual – as a distinct form. Two thieves are not simply a plurality of thieves. Acting in pairs, in fact, requires from each individual a quite distinct and specific mode of behavior. Just think of the duo of stooge and thief, or think of the teamwork required between a thief and his look-out man. Lots of crimes are also committed by combinations of big and a small persons, old and young men, or men and women. We simply have to learn how to use the dual as a distinct mode of investigation in police work. It's the same way in our field as it is in music. A duet doesn't simply consist of several musicians; if a duo or a duet is supposed to harmonize, then the harmony must be founded on a certain substantive and formal recognition of duality and dualism. Perhaps," I said to the Viennese, "we will even have to take a step beyond the dual and advance to trinity – yes, perhaps even quaternity – as distinct reference points within police work. And then, Gentlemen," I said, "we will have to return to the verb, to the part of speech that describes action."

"You accuse me of practicing the so-called *investigative subjunctive*; you tell me that I think too much in the optative mood and drift off into wishful thinking. But I consider all this to be a compliment; I express my thanks and also my conviction that we will in future also have to pay more careful and precise attention to the *genus verbi*, that is to the gender of the verb. You are only aware of the active and passive voice. You say either that *some unknown person has stolen the Arnulf Chalice*; or you say that *the Arnulf Chalice was stolen by some unknown person*. But that's not enough; that's much too crude, as far as I am concerned. For I am also familiar with the so-called medial voice, a form falling between the active and the passive. Every beginning student of Greek learns the form which appears, for example, in the verb *paidomai*, meaning neither *I educate* nor *I am being educated*, but something like *I to me educate*. It's a form that's hardly possible to translate into German. German, Gentlemen, has no distinct medial form. But who is to say that the thief was a German-speaker? Might not the person who stole the Chalice have been a Greek, perhaps even a Greek who was using the medial voice? In any case, we also have to take into account other possibilities provided by other languages. Imagine, Gentlemen, how complicated the case would become if the Chalice had been stolen by someone who belonged to a non-Indoeuropean language group! Or think of the aspect form which exists in the Slavic languages." I told the Viennese that the diplomatic and political advantage which the Russians possess over the West was probably due to their more sophisticated verb system. How pathetic by comparison is a highly analytic language like English! Simple and primitive, clumsy, just like American politics.

A language like Russian, with its wealth of forms, of course trains its speakers how to think, whereas thought is impoverished by the simplification and radical reduction of grammatical forms characteristic of a language like English. I also explained to the Viennese how the decline of the Roman Empire was directly linked to the diminishing number of grammatical forms and to the morphological levelling in the areas of flexion, declination and conjugation, a phenomenon which is especially evident in jurisprudence. This vulgar decline is classic. Hence the Romans – the ancient Romans, namely those of the golden Latin period – used the word *barbarism* as one of their worst insults. When they used the word *barbarism*, however, Cicero, Horace and Quintilian did not mean to refer to the lack of culture of the neighboring Germans, Asians or Africans; they were referring instead to a grammatical phenomenon, an error, a question of faulty linguistics. For example, the Romans would call barbaric any offence against congruity, such as the failure of noun and adjective to agree in gender, number and case, or of subject to agree with predicate in person and number, and so forth. *You be Roman. He come from Brindisi. You called Angelica.* Or as a Viennese detective said: "We're missing the *corpus delictus.*" My dear Abbot, *hic est enim calix Arnulfi.* It's *here* that the Arnulf Chalice is to be found. The great Roman grammarians were convinced that *barbarism* would soon end in the universal *barbarity* of the human race. "Congruity," I told the Viennese. "Congruity, Gentlemen! This is a linguistic concept that evoked or must have evoked a corresponding conception in administering the law and implementing punishment. Isn't it true that in precisely this area too – that is, the area of defining and sifting evidence – we are always dealing with questions of agreement, of fitting together elements and larger groups of elements, so-called complexes? Isn't it true too that we keep asking ourselves what fits together: Chalice and hat box, or Chalice and rucksack? What is the link between playing the organ and stealing the Chalice, and so on? And don't we also have to consider the question of who stood to gain from the point of view of congruity? What is it that leads this or that witness to testify in this or that way? Is he lying? And if he is, isn't he acting in incongruity with religious principles – that is, if he happens to be a monk or a member of the monastic community in general?"

Once, before noting down his answer, one of the Viennese asked a perplexed monk if he was related by blood or marriage to the thief? It's not that the detective meant to entrap the monk with this question; it was just that he got his investigative contexts mixed up. He asked a question about congruity of the sort that is asked of witnesses in the presence of the accused, but it was a question based on an error of congruity. *Cui bono*, the Romans used to ask, who benefits, who gets something out of it? And so forth, my dear Abbot. In this way I expounded the principles of judicial and social order just as Wilhelm von Humboldt would have done, deriving them step by step from the structure of the language and moving forward from the classical period to the present time, cutting across various cultures, but without neglecting for a moment the relevance of all these speculations to the present case. And the further I got, the greater was the incomprehension of the Viennese. It's possible that I may even have gone a little too far. They were just about getting ready to throw me out. In any case, the Chief of the Investigative Unit from the Federal Police remarked that he didn't expect any real help from me in solving the case, only rhetorical *tours de force*.

On the first Sunday after the disappearance of the Arnulf Chalice – oddly enough it happened to be the Laetare or Mothering Sunday – you held a sermon during the ten-o'clock mass that was very typical of you and that, in my opinion, no abbot preceding you could have held. It bore witness to your great goodness, as well as to your profound simplicity, if not to your naiveté. You appealed strongly and earnestly to the conscience of the thief. But how do you appeal to someone's conscience when he has no conscience? You preached your sermon as if the thief was among the congregation, presumably under the impression that a thief will often return to the scene of his crime. There was a lot of talk about introspection and change of heart and penance. You said – and it's something that made me think highly of you because it showed you had a sense of humor – that the thief of the Chalice had apparently taken the phrase *place of grace* somewhat too literally. Among your predecessors, at best Heinrich von Gellersburg, the jester among our abbots, would have been capable of cracking a joke like that. One to nothing in your favor. "Go into thyself, my son," you said, "and repent." I, however, was already sure long before coming up with the clue about Regensburg that the thief would not go into himself but would go abroad, because that's where he would be able to get rid of his loot if he was going to get rid of it anywhere. But I admit, my dear Abbot, that it was touching how you spoke out of the depths of your paternal heart and made use of the language of the parable of the prodigal son and then even alluded specifically to it. It's a testimony to your ability to make things seem up-to-date that the parable of the prodigal son (Luke, 15, 11 and following) seemed almost made to order for the case which we were dealing with, barring a few minor alterations and pertinent additions.

In this respect you were following the best traditions of preaching, for behind this kind of modernizing there lies the venerable doctrine of the fourfold scriptural meaning, one of whose fathers is undoubtedly Augustine. You must surely know the sixth section of Book 4.6 of the *Confessions*, where he writes that because of his philosophical background he had difficulty understanding the writings of the Saints, and that it was the sermons of Ambrose, Bishop of Milan, that helped resolve this difficulty for him: *I was delighted that I now no longer needed to read the old writings of the Law and of the Prophets with the same eye as before, when I had reproached the Saints for writing nonsense because I thought they had meant what they had written literally; but of course they did not mean it literally. And with immense joy I often heard Ambrose cite the phrase – doing so as if he meant to impress it upon his people with the utmost emphasis – that the letter kills, but the spirit – yes, the spirit – gives life.* What Augustine is implying here, and what he discusses at greater length elsewhere, certainly has nothing whatever to do with the way certain preachers – such as your Father Adalbert, for example – succeed in accomplishing a feat not provided for in the *ars praedicandi* or "Art of Preaching," namely of always ending up with their habitual subject, no matter what text they started off with. Just as there are people outside the Church who, no matter what the subject is, always come round again to talking about their chronically habitual subject, whether it's some disease or military service or their children. They are singleminded monomaniacs, always reminded almost immediately by everything they come across of their illness, their military service or their children. Leaving aside illnesses, military service and so forth, that's of course true especially for the Number One Subject: sex. That's one of the principal current manifestations of foulmouthedness.

I myself have given much thought to the proximity and distance of various phenomena in the visible and invisible worlds. And I am often shocked, my dear Abbot, how close the most contrary and contradictory elements lie to each other. There are oaths that consist of precisely the same words as prayers. It is said that Spaniards and Poles have the most horrible curses and oaths. That's not the result of chance. Or I'm struck by the following thought: an atheist who indulges in blasphemy is an absurd atheist. The atheistic sentence *God is dead* can almost be read as part of a prayer. Whoever says something like that seriously is asking to be baptized. He is seeking the community of the faithful. My dear Abbot, when somebody fails to keep order in his head he will soon lose track of where anything is. For, in fact, everything is as close to everything else as the words are in a dictionary. In a normal dictionary the greatest distance between words is at most 30 centimeters; that's the distance between the first word on the first page and the last word on the last. Only 30 centimeters separate *aardvark* from *zymurgy*. Things that are otherwise difficult to reconcile and radically different from each other are, when seen from this perspective, not only close to each other but actually provoke and evoke each other. Love turns easily into hate, freedom into tyranny. Incidentally, my dear Abbot, the neighbor who's before *abbot* in the dictionary is *abacadabra*, and the neighbor who follows him is *abdicate*... However, during the great anniversary year the Abbey was not just commemorated, it was also looted. And of course it is no mere coincidence that the Arnulf Chalice – the show-piece of the 1200 year old Abbey of Freimünster – disappeared precisely during this anniversary year and not long after (and as a result of) the great commemorative ceremonies. It was simply because of all the tremendous publicity that the attention of the general public was attracted to the Chalice. And not just to the Chalice itself, but also to its preservation, to the circumstances of its safe-keeping, its *inadequate* safe-keeping.

My dear Abbot, I have always considered announcements of great exhibitions – and, in fact, all sorts of announcements of great events, such as state visits etc. – as a form of notification and information to thieves, saboteurs, terrorists and every kind of miscreant. I have even found and read bulletins that were deliberately put before the public eye – that is, with the active cooperation of the Federal Police – in which things were said explicitly, fully and in great detail which the Police does not want the public to know. The Police said things they don't want to say. The Police, so it was said, does not want to betray things it is betraying here. And even if you take into consideration that now and then the Police uses this kind of bulletin to set a trap, by way of providing misleading information, still the genuinely informative value of these bulletins is very great. The criminals know anyway if they are supposed to take the whole thing in a positive or negative light, if they ought to believe what's being announced or the opposite. Soon matters will have been brought to such a pass – that is, if the current neuroticizing and criminalizing trend continues – that great events will either have to be cancelled altogether or else take place in secret. But of course it won't be possible to keep a great event secret anymore. We've already reached the stage, my dear Abbot, where the announcement that the State, or some corporation or private individual owns or has acquired a valuable object has to be viewed as an inexcusable and irresponsible act of stupidity. It serves only to invite or even encourage and instigate assault, robbery, manslaughter and homicide. I also know of fully a dozen unimpeachable political truths whose public utterance would entail the immediate liquidation of the speaker. You only have to go into some radio station and say this or that, and your life isn't worth a plug nickel. Oddly enough, in the middle ages this condition was called *cowardly*. To be a coward, so I've been told on good authority, used to mean that you were a *cow herd*. Nowadays, only those who are in the medieval sense not *cowardly* are in the modern sense *cowardly*.

And among those events which soon won't be possible anymore is the event of celebrating a great anniversary, along with great commemorative events such as exhibitions, receptions, prize award ceremonies and so forth. My dear Abbot, as a conscientious police officer, I take no joy in the fact that buildings such as famous museums and vaults nowadays have to be viewed exclusively as possible targets, as objects, that is, which provoke and stimulate the unceasing and often quite imaginative efforts of criminals. It's become so that museums and banks can only, on the one hand, be regarded from the point of view of their vulnerability to attack and theft, and, on the other, in terms of how they can be protected, shielded and defended. While, as I say, I take no joy in such developments, nevertheless I do not regret various nasty things which have failed to happen because of the increased danger, higher risk and concomitant hysteria resulting from the possibility of terrorist acts. In some cases I'm even sincerely grateful. And in other respects too people's consciousness has been raised. It's a melancholy fact that it was once impossible to rid government officials of their criminal feeblemindedness except by terrifying and horrifying them. Even now, though enough terrible things are still happening, multitudes of peaceful and reasonable citizens' campaigns are failing to persuade the powers-that-be to change their policies. It's a sad fact that many of the horrifying things proposed by the VIP's for reasons of alleged constraint and necessity, can presumably only be prevented by correspondingly horrifying actions. Rational argument, for example, won't gain any concessions from them. And as we've learned from history, but not only from history I'm afraid, it is simply and plainly necessary now and then to eliminate somebody in order to stop him from eliminating a great many others.

I'm surprised, my dear Abbot, that there is so little interest these days in the philosophy and theology of tyrannicide, a species of social hygiene that enjoyed great popularity during the Middle Ages and the early Modern period. It would be a good idea for powerful scientific organizations and foundations to establish and lavishly endow courses on this subject in, let's say, the philosophical and theological faculties of South American universities. How would it be with a course in theological ethics: "*Tyrannicide, a lecture course with practical exercises?*" Also subjects like outlawry and the venerable tradition of safe-conduct ought to be researched. And so forth, my dear Abbot.

In other words, as I was just about to point out a moment ago, in the future different possibilities and ways of celebrating anniversaries and commemorations will have to be found. That's been made quite evident by the 1200 year anniversary celebration of the Abbey of Our Dear Lady of Freimünster and everything that took place in connection with it. And as for memorializing deceased artists and politicians, I don't want to keep you in the dark about a proposal of mine that should particularly appeal to you as Abbot of a Benedictine monastery. As an appropriate form of commemoration, we should revive a venerable form of religious devotion: that is, we should pray for the dead, and not just on anniversary days or in anniversary years. Prayer is in my view the most beautiful way of commemorating the dead. After all, the dead are rarely honored in memorial speeches or services; mostly it's the speakers who honor and celebrate themselves with their display of skilfull and brilliant turns of phrase. The dead are mis-used and merely made into an occasion for the speaker's own self-glorification and gratification. The dead can't defend them-selves. Often I get an uneasy feeling that the dead are being de-secrated. If, for example, the classic German writers were able to hear the things the living say about them, they'd be spinning in their graves. But, my dear Abbot, on the rare occasions when this kind of memorial speech happens to be successful, it's always because it contains some religious element. On these rare occa-sions one always becomes aware of some deep connection between the speaker and the person invoked or spoken about that can only be described as mystical – a friendship and a love that extend beyond the grave.

Such speech is really invocation. Whoever can't speak in this way should keep silent. Mere clever chatter is, in view of the seriousness of the occasion, scandalous and sinful. Speakers of this sort should be made to learn Chapter 6 of Benedict's *Rule* by heart: *De Taciturnitate, Of Keeping Silent: We propose to do what the Prophet says: I said, I will take heed of my ways, that I sin not with my tongue. I will keep my mouth with a bridle, I was dumb with silence, I held my peace, even from good. Here the Prophet indicates that at times one should refrain even from good speech for the sake of taciturnity.* And later Benedict quotes from the Book of Proverbs: In *the multitude of words there wanteth not sin. Death and life are in the power of the tongue.* Oh, my dear Abbot, the quantity of pointless speeches I had to listen to, while I was study-ing law, and afterwards! *Si tacuisses, philosophus mansisses*, as the Romans said. *If you had kept silent, you would have remained a philosopher.* This Roman proverb proceeds from the amiable assumption that the person who is now talking hooey was once upon a time a lot smarter. Somebody who wasn't a philosopher before has nothing to lose. That's probably the assumption most people make. "What can I possibly lose?" they no doubt say to themselves. If you don't have a good reputation as a speaker, you can't risk losing that reputation. But better than the best speech about the departed is a prayer for his soul. This is not only the most worthy but also the most necessary and useful thing to do; and this is not only the Christian point of view but also the point of view and conviction of all other universal religions.

You don't have to be an ardent advocate of purgatory in order to believe this. The Church – particularly the Catholic Church – has gone a little too far in speculating about the nature of purgatory, following here the lead of Pope Gregory the Great, whom scholars sometimes refer to as the creator of "vulgar" Catholicism. But that makes no difference in terms of the rightness and usefulness of praying for the dead. And though you shouldn't misinterpret my words as arising from arrogance or pride, I would like to affirm that, judging from the lives of several eminent artists and politicians, prayer hasn't been pointless or ineffectual. Think of the vast numbers of people who speak or write about Goethe! But who prays for him? Isn't prayer something that students and professors of German actually owe him? Every year medical students hold a memorial service for the souls of the dead whom they've dissected in their anatomy classes. There ought to be a similar custom among literary scholars and critics. For what they owe their victims, or what they have done to them, isn't negligible. In many instances probably saying a single Our Father would have been better and more appropriate than a couple of dozen articles and books. If you've read a lot about dead poets, then you're moved to supplicate God in fervent prayer that he should spare his departed servants from further maltreatment at the hands of so-called scholarship. Preserve, O Lord, his soul from the Powers of Hell, and his work from literary criticism and scholarship. Lord, do not permit his work to fall prey to critical hacks. Lord, grant him eternal peace. In the case of another group of poets, however, one would like simply to plead with God not to take their own work into account because it's no more than one continuous sin committed against ethics and aesthetics. O God, we beseech Thee not to heed or regard his work. Turn Thy eye away from his work.

When I was still a boy in Preparatory School I imagined that in Heaven the list of books prohibited by the Church was always open for inspection and that whenever some writer came asking for admission, the heavenly gatekeeper, St. Peter, would consult the *Index librorum prohibitorum* to see if his name was included. And woe unto him if it was! I even speculated about whether the books were read and the censorship handled separately in Heaven, or whether the latest reports of prohibitions from Rome were simply adopted and appropriate entries made. In other words, I wondered if the heavenly and the earthly lists were in congruity. That's how I used to speculate about the Approbation of the Church. Nowadays, of course, I don't think about it in those simple, childish terms anymore, but even so I'm still absolutely convinced that there is a connection between books and morality, and that someone will eventually have to assume responsibility for the books.

It would be easy to apply to books the doctrine of venial and mortal sins. According to this doctrine, in the case of mortal sins one needs to take into account the following three factors: the degree of severity; free will; and knowledge. It's in connection with the last of these factors that the most logical and efficient defense of writers might be undertaken. Lord, forgive them, for they know not what they write. Nowadays there are books and dramas from which the devil himself could learn a great deal. There are provocative books and pictures which have served to "stimulate" generations of adolescents, including adolescents no longer in the state of puberty. If what they do or manipulate while or after reading these books is a sin, and if this sin is also credited to the account of the authors of these provocative and seductive books, then it looks bleak – very bleak – for these authorial gents. After all, it is written that it would be better for anyone who offends one of these little ones – that is, leads them into sin – that a millstone be hanged about their necks and they were drowned in the depth of the sea. If, my dear Abbot, the incitement to sin is also a sin, then unquestionably the authors of these books continue to influence their readers from beyond the grave. They continue undiminished in their sinfulness even after they're dead. They possess, as it were, an earthly sin-factory that keeps on operating and producing sins after they're gone... That's the curse of the wicked literary deed, that it must go on breeding further wickedness.

Some writers have tried to exculpate themselves by publishing such books anonymously or pseudonymously. But I'm very skeptical about whether they don't know up there about who wrote what books. And it may be that they even have access to a Dictionary of Pseudonyms. There's no doubt but what they're aware up there who the authors of these texts are. We can be assured that there will be no divine miscarriage of justice, such as falsely accusing somebody or holding him responsible for something he didn't write or commit. But, my dear Abbot, there simply aren't sufficient millstones left to meet our needs if we're going to take the scriptural injunction literally. Not only our morals but also our milling methods have changed over time. That's something that I, as the son of a miller, am fully aware of. That's something you can take my word for. But even that makes no real difference to the issue at hand. Updated and translated into the technical terminology of modern milling processes and mill construction, the injunction would run something like this: "It would be better for anyone who offends one of these little ones that a pressure drum or an automatic aspirator, spiral separator or scourer, or a Pelton wheel or a Kaplan turbine be hung around his neck and he be dropped into the depth of the sea." If this change were actually carried out we'd be equipped with a really splendid spare parts facility on the ocean floor. We could then put a whole range of automatic literary mills into operation down there.

My dear Abbot, nowadays all writers – not just those who produce unmitigatedly obscene, vulgar or pornographic stuff – generally strike me as resembling big manufacturers or owners of great aesthetic automatic milling operations. They go at it like Swabian industrialists. Their very prolixity is a sin. Even if it isn't a mortal sin or one that cries to high heaven for punishment, still it is a sin. Our scribes have simply set up their production facilities to conform with those of modern manufacturers, and now they push their raw materials day-in and day-out through the automatic milling machinery. They grind everything up extremely fine; they produce nothing but double-0 grade flour. Whereas others produce only grist, or else groats or bran. In contrast to earlier periods, writers nowadays are very conscious of market forces. In earlier times, writers didn't give a miller's damn about the market. Writers these days, however, are even proud of how capitalistically corrupt they've become. They consider themselves realists, no matter how surrealistic or way-out their actual productions may be.

Millers, as practitioners of an honorable craft, don't deserve to be compared with writers. Nevertheless I would like to suggest one further slight comparison between milling and writing. My father didn't own an automatic mill because, as he would often say, "When it's automatic, you don't need skill to mill." My father used traditional methods when he transformed his grain into flour. He still used so-called windbags. These consisted of a whole row of bags placed under the roof and filled to the bursting point with air, a procedure that was supposed to introduce a kind of aerodynamic balance into the milling process. A mill like my father's had, as it were, certain quite natural vegetative and visceral needs. In fact, the mill often and quite visibly suffered from excessively high pressure, but my father knew how to keep it healthy.

I'm reminded of my father's so-called windbags when I think of the present state of literature. Windbag after windbag. Every year writers fill their bags with air and bring them to the Frankfurt Book Fair. They don't even use hot air, but only old, stagnant and unventilated air. And the more these fellows jump up and down and insist that their work is absolutely natural – the spontaneous overflow of vital impulses or some necessary and direct expression of life – the more I'm convinced, always bearing in mind my father's windbags, that their writing does indeed exemplify a natural process, but only the natural pathological condition of flatulence and metiorism, an illness characterized by the presence of excessive stomach gas. An ironic writer once remarked that he couldn't keep his ink dry anymore; but these guys can't keep their air dry anymore. Their intestines are lazy and their sphincters defective; that's their problem. That's how they produce wind.

Given my views on how books get produced, I know I'm in agreement with St. Francis of Assisi. He too didn't think much of books, with some very few exceptions. But those exceptions were written a long, long time ago. In this respect I don't think there's much hope for present-day writers. I don't really believe that we can count on getting a book during the next hundred years. I mean a book of significance, a real book deserving the name. I believe we've written ourselves out. Besides, the public wouldn't know what to make of such a book, a real book. It wouldn't be able to take cognizance of it. The way the public gazes blankly, rather like a chicken, at the annual analities of a few literary folks suggests that it is incapable of taking notice of anything really new or significant. The literary public stares fixedly, as if hypnotized, at the latest productions of a dozen or so scribblers. The newspapers and the critics feverishly await the publication of the new X and the new Y. My dear Abbot, just as the individual's capacity to absorb new phenomena is psychologically limited, so too with the literary public. The cultural pages of the newspapers are finite in number. Their interest and receptive capacity are, for practical purposes, permanently occupied. Not only human beings but the public too have, as it were, only two eyes. And both eyes are already being sat on by a relatively few authors and publishers with their big, fat arses. The public's capacity for digesting books is hogged by cliques and clucks. Well, my dear Abbot, I could care less. I read Virgil, Augustine and Erasmus.

My dear Abbot, let us pray for the departed. Let us not talk a great deal about them but simply number them in our prayers. Let us take a cue from your Abbey architect, Karl Friedrich. Year after year he drives over to St. Florian on October 11th, the anniversary of Anton Bruckner's death, and there he deposits a bouquet of lilies on the master's sarcophagus in the crypt. Afterwards he attends mass and returns home to work. That's the act of a real man, an act very much after the heart and spirit of Anton Bruckner himself. It's an act of pure piety, my dear Abbot. I've often had to take Friedrich under my protective wing because there are plenty of people whose enmity, envy and ill-will he has provoked. They've done their best (or worst) to depict his piety – of which the annual Bruckner commemoration is only a single instance – as a pretext for drumming up architectural business. And even though I am fully aware of temptations of this kind, I have always continued to defend Friedrich against such allegations. Friedrich is no pharisee. That there is such a thing as pharisaism and that there are more pseudo-saints than saints is, of course, also true. In his Filser Letters, Ludwig Thoma – the great Ludwig Thoma – writes that candlestick-makers tend to be extremely devout Catholics, seeing as how the clergy constitutes their principal clientele.

I learned the meaning of pharisaism after the Second World War. In the period of famine following the war, lots of people used to come to my father's mill in Andach and beg for flour. Now, my father was known far and wide, just like Friedrich and Anton Bruckner, as a pious and religious man. But he was no pious hypocrite – no sanctimonious prig; and he wasn't a bigot either, my dear Abbot. He was a plain Christian. Now, in front of my father's mill there was a bridge spanning the stream, and in the middle of the railing at one side there was a meter-high cross sunk into a concrete pillar. We children were encouraged to follow our parents' example by making the sign of the cross when we walked past it. It was a custom that in those days right after the war the so-called hoarders had also adopted and taken advantage of...Some of them even went so far as to decorate the cross with flowers that they had picked on the way from Wels to Andach and then stuck into a tin can attached with a wire at the base of the crucifix. For some of these people, however, it wasn't enough to simply make the sign of the cross, but they had to fall down on their knees as well. Several, moreover, performed these pious gestures so conspicuously and so demonstratively – not only for the crucified Redeemer, but also with an eye to the windows of my father's mill – that their latent significance became obvious. In fact, they genuflected less to Christ than to my father.

And now, my dear Abbot, you'll see that my father was not just a man of piety but above all a man of good sense. To begin with, he gave everybody something. Even today I'm still shamed by the gratitude people feel for him and that they transfer to me when they happen to meet me. Secondly – and that's why I said he wasn't just pious but also had good sense – he always took these ostentatious gestures of piety or pseudo-piety at face value. "What hunger and despair these poor city folks must be suffering," he would say, "that they're willing to go against their deepest convictions and humiliate themselves by genuflecting and making the sign of the cross." As far as he was concerned, that was sufficient proof of their dire necessity. "Necessity teaches people to pray," he would often say. But for him it was in their prayer that he saw the evident proof of their necessity... Often he would look out of his milling-room window and watch the awkwardly pious contortions performed in front of the cross by these suddenly converted Catholic pilgrims from the city. Then my father would say: "If things get bad enough, even the devil will take to eating flies." That's what he said. It may be that many people who were given something by my father at the mill-gate thought that what they got was due to their gifts of guile; and it may be that these people later made fun of the "sainted" miller. But in fact my father had penetrated into the very depths of their souls, saying: "If things get bad enough, even the devil himself will take to eating flies." He knew full well that these people were conforming to necessity rather than desire.

Theology describes humanity as essentially flawed and defective. And unfortunately theology is right. That human beings are forced to live in deficiency, even while passing their days in excess – in outward excess – that fact makes them deficient too as individuals. I'm reminded in this connection of our German class in the Freimünster Preparatory School. Our German teacher,

Father Rudolf, had a weakness for so-called Christian essays, a weakness that various of my schoolmates habitually exploited with essays that were thickly coated with Christian sugar. In Father Rudolf's view, an *excellent* essay had to mention God at least five times, otherwise it couldn't be an *excellent* essay. God and the German classical writers were Rudolf's weakness, although the latter were actually Protestants when they weren't downright atheists (or pantheists). In his grading he would gladly overlook errors of orthography and defects of style if these inadequacies were substantively compensated for by chunks of humanity, morality and religiosity. God had to be mentioned, no matter if God was misspelled. So long as God had been referred to, you could count on a good grade. Naturally this led to the most deficient choristers in Rudolf's orthographic choir singing about the Lord God strictly according to the notes, hoping in this way, as it were, to make the grade. That's how our German class was transformed into a training ground for hypocrites. *In speech alone resides the speaker's bliss*, says Wagner in the "Night" scene in the first part of Goethe's *Faust*; and the schoolboy says in the "Schoolroom" scene: *You may take home safely whatever's set down in black and white.* Oddballs like this, my dear Abbot, also have a right to exist. *A good man knows deep down where the right way lies*, said Father Rudolf. But if I had been the German teacher I would have quoted Goethe as follows at these pharisaical essay-ists: *This business makes me laugh. Oh, I'm weary of all this gadding about. You're not man enough to catch the devil by the tail. You take big words into your little mouth. What clever man wouldn't find his master in the Vatican? If you want to know how to act properly, then just go and ask the noble ladies. You're like the spirit whom you're trying to grasp. If it's not from the heart, if you don't feel it, you'll never catch it. And now that the whole world has turned cultivated, the devil follows their lead.* And so on, my dear Abbot, with Goethe as companion through the entire year. And at the end I would have written *not satisfactory* or *unsatisfactory* (as it used to be phrased). Not *satisfactory*, not *excellent*, but *not* satisfactory.

As you know, several months ago, when we were at the lowest ebb of our investigation, I asked one of your current lay teachers of German, Werner Reich, to assign "The Theft of the Arnulf Chalice" as an essay topic for his 5th year German class. He agreed, and I then took the trouble – partly for professional reasons, partly for pedagogic and didactic ones – to look through the resulting 25 essays. Although th⁄ Viennese thought nothing of the idea, the effect, my dear Abbot, was nonetheless startling. I was astonished to find that the same "Christians" and "Moralists" were still at work, even though I know that Werner Reich feels no particular susceptibility to these kinds of moral/ethical stratagems and in any case doesn't reward such compositions with specially good grades. One of these goody-goodies wrote the following essay:

Some unknown guy took the famous Arnulf Chalice from the spot in the Abbey of Freimünster where it always was. Now it's no longer there in that spot where it used to be, but you can be sure God knows where it is now because God knows everything. Maybe the thief will try to defile the Chalice by filling it with beer, because he thinks nobody can see him, but God sees him with His all-seeing eyes. The Police, I'm sorry to say, aren't omniscient, because they're made up entirely of fallible human beings. "Errare humanum est," as it says in Latin, or translated into German: "to err is human." Unfortunately, we pupils of the Abbey Preparatory School can't do nothing more than pray to God to enlighten the Police Department and give their dogs good noses to help them locate the track leading to the place where, maybe, the thief is at this very moment defiling the Chalice by drinking beer out of it. We also pray fervently to the Mother of God, the Patroness of Freimünster, to help solve this crime. The Honorable Abbot has said that when we've reached the end of our tethers, when everything looks hopeless, then we've got to call on St. Jude – who helps in hopeless cases – to help us. That's his special job, and though his name is really the same as Judas, he's got nothing whatever to do with the evil Judas, whose last name was Iscariot, because St. Jude's last name is Thaddeus. Judas is a beautiful name; it's only that one Judas made it bad for the others. Judas Iscariot was a traitor or what we would nowadays call a criminal. The Police, whom in those days they called bailiffs and catchpoles, didn't have no trouble with him because he hung himself. That's a really terrible way to go. But Father George says we shouldn't judge even such folks because nobody knows how it was at the very end, and judgment is reserved unto God alone. But it sure don't look good for Judas. It is well said that whoever judges himself has already been judged. But perhaps Judas had second thoughts at the very end. Father George says that we shouldn't condemn the thief of the Arnulf Chalice either. He may still change his mind. My father always says that it's unfortunate that there ain't no death penalty nomore. If it was up to him, he says, we would reinstitute the death penalty. My father says that he would use the stolen Arnulf Chalice like a cookie cutter to cut a round piece out of the thief's stomach. And then he would hang him up for a while on the nearest tree, so as to give his feet some rest. My father served in the Army for quite a long time, that's why he's a little hardened, since the Russians didn't treat them with velvet gloves either. Father George says that his attitude is understandable but not quite right. Father George says it's better to pray for the enemies of the Church than curse them. And that's what we want to do too; that's the right thing for us pupils of the Preparatory School of the Abbey of Our Dear Lady of Freimünster. It's really out of the question for anybody start to cursing here.

Freimünster, so it is said, is a *Place of Grace*. But what does that mean, a Place of Grace? Without delving any further into the opinions of ordinary people or into folk piety – not that I look down on these things in any way; on the contrary I find them right and good – I am compelled to confess that for me a Place of Grace is a place where people work and pray who are in a state of Grace, who are blessed and gifted with Grace. The most visible expression of such a Place of Grace and graciousness is to be found in its architecture.

It is sometimes said that Christian art was not and is not necessarily or even primarily produced by Christians, but often, on the contrary, by non-Christians. I don't believe it, my dear Abbot. For true art is already halfway to religion. The great Church architects of the past were not just Christians, they were theologians. In any case, they belonged to a spiritual elite. It is often said of splendid buildings that they represent ideas translated into stone. That may be a metaphor but it is not a bad one. And it works the other way around too. Sometimes I see buildings, mostly modern buildings, and I know immediately that the architect had no idea of how to build, not the slightest shadow of an idea. You have to think of the art of building as something wholly spiritual and religious. We should also take the concept of an *architectural sin* very seriously and interpret it in a theological sense. A badly designed building, like a bad book, has a soulless effect on people long after its creator's demise. But a good building continues to live on as a good deed performed for the sake of humanity. In such buildings, the architect's intelligence and his love are always and forever being expressed.

When I think of buildings like this, I am reminded of the Passau Cathedral. This Cathedral, designed by C. Laurago during the High Baroque period, is a true Place of Grace. My dear Abbot, the Passau Cathedral isn't just a Place of Grace and an idea translated into stone; the Passau Cathedral is a proof of the existence of God, an irrefutable proof of the existence of God. It wasn't just once that I made the journey on foot together with my father from our house in Upper Austria to Passau. Every year we made the trip to Passau at least once, and then another trip in addition to Altötting. And when we finally entered the Passau Cathedral after walking for a long time, it was like arriving in Jerusalem the Golden. I can't find words powerful enough to describe that feeling of coming home, of being enveloped in safety, that I felt when I entered – when I immersed myself in – the Passau Cathedral; it was like being absorbed and bathed in light and warmth. At first I was simply stunned to the point of forgetting who and where I was. My father actually had to rouse me out of a trance when we got up to leave after a service or mass or simply after visiting the Cathedral. C. Laurago's architecture liberated and enlarged the little youngster I then was.

I simply have to resort to the words *rapture* and *ecstasy* if I want to convey some part of the joy I felt in this work of art.

Also the word *sweet*, which nowadays, alas, has lost most of its semantic value. It's probably because of the Nazarenes, or rather because of the vulgar manifestations of aesthetic Nazarenism, that it's become impossible to make any meaningful use of the word *sweet* anymore. Perhaps there is a connection here too with all the sugar substitutes, with saccharine, and maybe even with diabetes. It's unfortunate too that we associate *sweet* with cuteness and prettiness, as when we say of decorative church angels or putti that they're "sweet." But when I use the word *sweet* in connection with Laurago's architecture, then I expect it to be understood in the sense of the Latin words *suavis* and *dulcis*, both attributes and epithets of Christ. *Sweet* Lord Jesus. That's the *suavitas Dei*, the sweetness of the Lord! In the *Song of Roland*, the Franks call their homeland *sweet*; they long for *douce France*, for *sweet* France. It's in this sense that the Passauer Cathedral is *sweet*, sweet like the homeland of the Franks, the great and mighty, the glorious land of France. As you know, Roland's men were ambushed near Roncesvalles in the Pyrenees; they died in a place far from their *sweet* homeland. And it's from the intense memory that these doomed men have of France that we know what the word *sweet* means.

The encounter with a magnificent work of architecture can shape a whole life, and can alter it too. I'm convinced that most vocations to the priesthood are somehow connected with architecture, and with the spatial experience of churches, monasteries and priories. We tend to overemphasize the importance of the word in this process. In my opinion the word actually plays a lesser role than architecture or music. Poetry and scholarship must accomodate God in words; but the plastic arts can reveal Him, can make His presence visible, sensible, tangible. A church, an altar – a monstrance!

And there's more, my dear Abbot. Architecture – the very fact of being housed – actually constitutes the greater part of such happiness as still remains to us after being expelled from Paradise. We are cast out and banished, but at least we can manage to crawl in under cover. That is why architecture, good architecture, always has an animalistic component. Good architects habitually build in places where animals tend to make their lairs, and they build in such a way that the resulting edifice is also a burrow and a cave. The mightiest cathedral must in some sense always remain a dog house. That's what is so incomprehensible about the art of great architects: that they are able to treat large spaces intimately; that they use stones to produce the effect of weightlessness; that they are able to extract monumentality out of miniatures; and intimacy out of monumentality. How do they do it?

A mighty fortress is our God, my dear Abbot. "Fortress" comes from "fortify," meaning to make strong. A good building – I include Churches here too – is always something of a place of protection, a hospice, a sanatorium. Nowadays public buildings are finally being designed to be accessible to the handicapped. That's a good thing, but still no attention is being paid to the aesthetic aspects of construction. My dissatisfaction in this respect has nothing whatever to do with the feelings of a few esoterics, aesthetes and hyper-sensitive eccentrics. It goes deeper. The inhospitability of modern buildings – of many modern buildings – oppresses and offends the great majority of people; it makes them ill and even homeless. Architects nowadays are building depressive structures; they are creating spaces that produce agoraphobia even among normal people – collapsible houses, in a word. It takes a really strong and "healthy" person not to suffer a collapse when entering some of these rooms. Entering many buildings these days means, purely from an architectural perspective, putting life and limb at risk. Too few architects have any idea what psychology and psychiatry are about. Technologists are as a rule removed from life; they are in fact against life. They build elevators that are absolute nightmares, to name only a single instance. They talk about transparency and then they build elevators without windows or light, triply enclosed by automatic doors. People are then imprisoned in cells utterly devoid of any view or hope, or buried in coffins that would put fear and trembling into any half-way normal human being. Whoever gets stuck in one of these things during a power failure is as much as buried alive.

There's no simple provision, like a crank to move the elevator up or down, no little window to look out from, nothing to offer you some slight glimpse of hope.

But to return to the subject of architecture. I find it highly significant that textbooks refer to the chief architectural movement of this century as *Brutalism*. According to the textbooks, exposed reinforced-concrete is the greatest architectural discovery of the century; and exposed reinforced-concrete is also the preferred medium of Brutalism. *Brutalism*, my dear Abbot, comes from *béton brut* or what we call exposed reinforced-concrete. *Brut* is derived from the Latin *brutus*. And here I would like to ask for a moment's indulgence, to give me time to read out the entry for *brutus* in my copy of Karl Ernst Georges' *Comprehensive Latin-German Dictionary: brutus, a, um (cf. Oldind. gurüh; Gr. barys; Got. karus, heavy), I) heavy, cumbersome, ponderous, solid weight, Lucr. 6, 105: tellus, Hor, carm. 1, 34, 9: corpora, Apul de deo Socr. 9, II) metaph., blunt, unfeeling, 1) physical (animate) Eccl. (vide Bünem. Lact. 2, 5, 40), 2) spiritual dull, unfeeling, unreasonable, blockheaded, a) about living beings and their states etc. (rational), b) about inanimate objects, fulmina, meaningless, Plin. 2,113 Superlative: brutissimus.*

And under the entry for *brutalis*, I find in Georges the following definition: *bestially irrational.* Thus Georges. So, taking my cue from the word itself and from the dictionaries, it's clear that even with the best will in the world, there are not a lot of positive overtones here. I recall in this connection what I was telling you earlier about *Barbarism*. For *Brutalism* is a variety of *Barbarism*. As far as I'm concerned, I'm unable to discover anything revolutionary in exposed reinforced-concrete. And as for the placement – the deliberate placement – of the plumbing and the drainage systems out in the open where they can be seen, all I can say is: "Hey, suit yourselves."

My father always told us the story of how our grandmother, his mother, when she grew old and bedridden, often spoke about how she wished to see the Passau Cathedral just once more before she died and hear once more the great Cathedral organ.

Then she would willingly die. "Just to see the Cathedral in Passau once more!" she said. Can you imagine, my dear Abbot, anybody these days saying, as they're lying on their deathbeds: "Just to see the exposed reinforced-concrete once more, then I would willingly die?" You can't imagine that either, I'm sure. At best one could kill somebody by providing them with a final view of some exposed reinforced-concrete buildings.

My dear Abbot, the Passau Cathedral has accompanied me throughout my whole life. Of course I see and experience the Cathedral differently now than I did when I was a boy, just as I now feel quite differently about Baroque art generally. But my sense of its worth has not diminished; on the contrary, if anything it has grown greater. It's only that my spectrum has expanded; I've developed a taste for other styles, such as for the Romanesque and the Gothic. It gives me great pleasure to pass from the Abbey Church in Freimünster to the Gethsemane Chapel, from the Early Baroque period back into the Romanesque-Gothic, and then, moving at once backward and forward, from the Romanesque-Gothic into the Baroque. A walk through the centuries. Or a walk around the fountain in the cloister, if the drunken porter doesn't interrupt me by stumbling into view... I often reflect, whenever I take this kind of visual bath in the old architectural monuments, that I probably wouldn't be able to survive in a country that didn't have an old culture. Living in America, for example, is unimaginable to me; it would mean my death. For what do these poor Americans have? Nothing, my dear Abbot, nothing at all, except for every conceivable variety of Brutalism.

By the way, at a very early stage in the investigation I pointed out to the Chief Federal Investigator from Vienna that we should keep in mind the possibility that the Chalice might have been spirited away to America. It wouldn't be the first time that venerable European cultural treasures had been hauled off to America. After all, as you very well know, so I said to the Chiefmost Investigator, what the Americans can't get ahold of legally or what they can't photocopy, they steal. We can take it for granted that ever since Columbus discovered America several centuries ago, many people have emigrated to America for whom staying in Europe was simply too hot of an option. Speaking euphemistically and avoiding the vocabulary of the police station, modern Americans are nothing more than the descendants of adventurers. Americans are capable of just about anything. Their conceit and arrogance *vis à vis* Europeans has always struck me as ridiculous. It's often said of the Russians that they claim to have invented everything under the sun but that's simply not true. In principle, no; it's the Americans, the Americans who are the greatest and the best. It annoys them that it wasn't an American who discovered America, but a European. They needed a European to do that for them. Christopher Columbus had to discover America. That was a great deed which, to be sure, nowadays looks more and more like a mistake, a misfortune, and not just for Native Americans.

Just think of all the American tourists, my dear Abbot, who visited us during the Anniversary Year. How they stood in front of the Chalice and said: "*Wonderful, beautiful, very nice.*" And in the Church: "A mighty fine place!" "*Wonderful, indeed, really.*" But nevertheless it always turns out that everything in America is better and more beautiful. Freimünster is an old Abbey; Freimünster is over 1200 years old. But I can tell you, my dear Abbot, if it was standing in America, it would be even older.

The Americans, my dear Abbot, imitate everything, everything without exception. They photocopy whole libraries in Europe and then set them up again over there in America. The New World has practically photocopied the entire Old World and then re-assembled it over there. The bright and eager Americans have shoved us all into the shadow, my dear Abbot. And the day will come when they'll shut off all our lights. Modern American foreign policy towards Europe must be the absolutely vilest political policy carried out in this dark century, superseded only by German Hitlerism. Whenever I think about the relationship between Americans and Europeans, I'm reminded of the Lombard *Song of Hildebrand*. Father and son face each other in battle. The father reveals his identity but the son doesn't believe that his opponent is his biological father. "You're an old, crafty Hun," Hadubrand says to Hildebrand. In the version we have it's the father who is then forced to kill his hot-headed and deluded son – or at least that's the outcome we have to conjecture, since of course the last part of the *Song* is missing – but in the Scandinavian tradition there is also a different ending, one in which the father is killed.

And once the Americans almost finished us off – or me, anyway. Back then I was waiting along with many others for the American bombs to drop on us in Wels in the deep Brewery Storage Cellar. The dead were lying by the hundreds out in the streets. For them the ERP, the European Recovery Progam of the Marshall Plan, would unfortunately come too late. Smashed and torn to shreds by the American bombs, they unfortunately had no more use for American powdered milk. Most of the people taking shelter in the Brewery Cellar back then, my dear Abbot, spent the time crying or praying quietly, or both, while the Americans dropped tons of bombs from the air down onto the city. *Welaga nu, waltant got, wewurt skihit.* "Great grief, mighty God, great sorrowful deeds are happening."

Here, my dear Abbot, I can't help but relate an episode out of history, a story in which the Lombards, the Germans and the Americans also play a role. It is one of the saddest stories I know. You probably know it already...

In the year 529 in Latium in the Italian province of Frosinone, on a mountain 519 meters high, an Abbey was founded by Benedict of Nursia. The spot had previously been occupied by a pagan temple. However, this Abbey, which is considered to be the Mother Abbey of the Benedictine Order, was destroyed for the first time by the Lombards sometime between 581 and 589. After its reconstruction in 717, the Abbey fell under the protection of the Carolingians and began to grow in importance. Charles Martell's son Carloman; Rachis, King of the Lombards; Adalhard; and Paulus Diaconus, all entered this monastery. When the Abbey was destroyed by the Saracens in 883, the monks took refuge in Teano, and later on in

Capua. In 950, the Abbot Aligernus, a disciple of Odo of Cluny, returned to the mountain. The Abbey's great period began in the eleventh century with Abbot Richer of Bavaria (1038-55) and was brought to its absolute height by Frederick of Lorraine (1057; later Pope Stephen IX) and especially under Abbot Desiderius (1058-87; later Pope Victor III). Among the 200 monks inhabiting the Abbey at this time were numerous scholars, such as the theologians and historians Alberic, Amatus, and Petrus Diaconus. In 1071 Pope Alexander II consecrated the Basilica (whose decoration had been partly carried out by Byzantine and Arab craftsmen). During the twelfth century the Monastery was the only place in the Western World where Ancient Greek was taught. Decay set in when the Kings of Sicily attempted to interfere with the rights of the Abbey. In 1230 the Emperor Frederick II expelled the monks and garrisoned the Abbey with his own soldiers. For a brief period the Abbey made a recovery under Abbot Bernard I (1263-82). In 1321 the Abbots were elevated to the status of Bishops by Pope John XXII (until 1367). In 1349 the Abbey buildings were destroyed in an earthquake. The Abbey was rebuilt, but it was only in 1504 that a renaissance began with its fusion with the Congrega- tion of Santa Giustina in Padua (thereafter known as the Congre- gatio Casiensis). New buildings were constructed in the 16th and 17th centuries, among them the Early Baroque basilica. After 1799, the treasures of the Abbey were looted successively by the French, the Neapolitans and (after 1860) the Piedmontese. In 1866 the Abbey was declared a National Monument and the monks were put in charge of its preservation. During the Second World War, when in 1943/44 this area was declared a cornerstone of the German line of defense, the Monastery was completely demolished by Allied bombing in February 1944.

This, my dear Abbot, is what you'll discover if you look under the entry for *Monte Cassino* in *Meyer's Encyclopedia.* That's the situation, my dear Abbot. A saint gathers a group of monks around himself, builds a house on a mountain in order to pray and work with them, and then there comes a succession of Lombards, Saracens, Sicilians, French and Germans. And in the end, following the Green Devils, there come the Allies with their bombs and annihilate what's left. Not forgetting Mr. Marshall's subsequent European Recovery Program.

Of course, my dear Abbot, it's not difficult to hit a Benedictine Abbey; you don't need to be a genius to bomb a Benedictine Abbey. There's no strategic advantage anymore in building on elevated sites as the Benedictines used to do, instead of following the example of the Cistercians and building in valleys. If anything, the strategic advantage now favors the latter. Even Americans are capable of destroying a Benedictine Abbey. Let's forget the Americans, my dear Abbot.

In my view, a good specimen of architecture, whether it's a church or a dwelling, always has to be in some sense a place of refuge. It has to be a *tabernaculum*, which means something like a tent or a hut, or even a wooden shack. It's connected with the Latin word *trabs*, *trabis* (f), which means *tree* or *beam*. And taken literally, the word "tabernacle" is the diminutive form of the word "Tabern" or "Tavern." Whether it's "b" or "v" makes no difference; intervocalic "b" has a tendency to become "v" or "w." I once took advantage of the opportunity to point out jokingly the connection between tabernacle and tabern to the keeper of the Abbey Tavern. Your tabernacle, I said to him, is the drawer in which you lock up the cash, for otherwise I can't make out anything that's in any way church-like about you. "What do you expect?" he said. "If you want something else, you have to talk to the Abbot about it. It's for him that I work and collect payment here." And that's why, my dear Abbot, I herewith turn to you and observe that in Chapter 53 of the *Rule*, *De hospitibus suscipiendis*, *Of the Reception of Guests*, Benedict seems to have had a rather different conception of hospitality in mind than the one practiced in your Tavern or, for that matter, in all the other abbey taverns, wine cellars and shops in the country. Benedict makes not the slightest mention of any sort of payment. The staff in the monastic hospices, hospitals and inns were paid in God's currency. It wasn't just the abbots who sought to outdo each other in the degree of Christian hospitality they offered when lodging and accommodating their guests, but the Bishops also made a contribution of their own to the spirit of hospitality. They established so-called Bishop's Courts in the Cathedrals. Nowadays the porters in the so-called Bishop's Courts would be utterly dumbfounded if some poor devil turned up asking for a room or a night's lodging. They would probably refer him to the Railway Mission, that last, pathetic, Christian remnant of past munificence and charity.

Insofar as the monasteries are concerned, my dear Abbot, our faithful predecessors took care to found and build them in just those places where they could count on their being sought out by lots of strangers and travellers in need. The monks did not isolate themselves, or if they did, then only in such regions and places where, because of their very isolation and remoteness, they could count on having to provide assistance to distressed travellers and wayfarers. That is why the monks established themselves on the Great St. Bernhard Pass and on other mountain passes too, as well as at river-crossings, gorges and ravines. Once upon a time, my dear Abbot, the monks used to employ bloodhounds to seek out their impecunious clientele. That's how they wooed the poor. And that's what I call Christian. Nowadays it's more likely that a priest would get himself a huge mastiff in order to keep the rabble at bay.

A dog is a dog, my dear Abbot. There are no sectarian or religious differences among dogs, even though the St. Bernard does look extraordinarily lovable, pious, modest and good-natured. After all he bears a great name, the name of Bernard of Clairvaux, the eminent Cistercian Abbot from France and the founder of the "Bernardines," which, as you know, is no separate order but merely a distinct movement within the Cistercian Order. If, let's say, a St. Bernard and a Boxer were standing next to each other and if one were to ask passers-by which of the two was Christian and which heathen, then surely everybody would at once identify the St. Bernard as Christian and the Boxer as heathen. The St. Bernard simply looks so faithful. In this way we've projected religious sectarianism deep down into the animal world, although of course the Bible already makes provision for a kind of theological zoology, as for example in condemning the snake whose head is to be crushed. And there are other diabolic animals too. The rat, for instance.

From the point of view of food and drink, my dear Abbot, the monasteries form part of a long and honorable tradition that reaches back to ancient Egypt and Mesopotamia. The monastic variety of hostelry represents primarily a continuation of Greek and Roman hostelry. In the Roman Empire a real inn fulfilled several different functions. It was, in the context of Western cultural history, a *mansio*, a lodging, or translated literally, a "shelter"; a *statio*, a resting place; a *mutatio*, a place to change horses; a *popina*, a restaurant; and, finally, a *caupona*, a store, and a *taberna*, a bar. At one time or another the monastic inns have performed all of these functions. But that doesn't exhaust the catalogue of their virtues. In the cultural histories – by the way, I consider the history of hostelry an important, if the not the most important, chapter of cultural history, that is, not just of *cultural* history in general but specifically, I would say, of *intellectual* history. In the cultural histories it is said in this connection that it was due to the good example set by the monasteries that innkeeping was rid of its formerly bad reputation. For, during the late Roman period, inns were not just *mansio, statio, mutatio, popina, caupona* and *taberna*, they were also, *cum grano salis*, bordellos, bawdyhouses and resorts of easy virtue. The innkeepers' wives and their waitresses were not exactly considered pillars of virtue in the community; at best they enjoyed a certain kind of repute. In this respect, the reputation enjoyed nowadays by our Honeys, Duckies, and Cuties is an old and venerable one. *Love a waitress and you'll be cozened./She does, even though she swears she doesn't.* To be sure, the monastic innkeepers haven't succeeded in cleaning up their act altogether. "Thank God," I'm almost tempted to add. I often have occasion to sit in your Tavern and observe the goings-on there. And even though cultural historians assure us that the Abbey innkeepers purified and raised the level of their profession as a whole, even so, my dear Abbot, there still exists a category of customer that is under the impression that the price of beer includes the right to fondle the waitress. Alcohol, as we know, has the effect of loosening one's inhibitions, so that when it gets on towards midnight and a well-endowed waitress leans invitingly over the table as she sets down the beer mugs, or else bends down in front of the table to pick up something or other, and in the process exhibits her *derrière* in all its splendor... well, my dear Abbot, let's not discuss it any further. After all, there's no need to wax puritanical and holier-than-thou.

I once heard a clever professor from Munich lecturing about the Bavarian monasteries. He was particularly concerned with the question of what, on the one hand, is *Bavarian* about the Bavarian monasteries, and, on the other, what is *monastic* about them. That's exactly my question. In my view, the fact that they're Bavarian doesn't prevent them from being monastic or, even more generally speaking, Christian. "Bavarian" and "monastic" are not contradictory concepts. It's only that the Bavarian element modifies the Christian one, and the other way around too: the Christian element modifies and defines the Bavarian one. There is no specifically Bavarian Gospel and there is no specifically Bavarian Sermon on the Mount, but there is a specifically Bavarian interpretation of the Gospel. And the same is true, *mutatis mutandis*, of Austria too – or, at any rate, of Upper Austria.

A good inn, one that really deserves the name, has to have something homey about it; a good tavern really has to be a kind of tabernacle. The Freimünster Tavern is a good example of what a tavern should look like, at least architecturally. A good tavern has to have vaulted ceilings. Its spatial dimensions have to be curved, and the waitress who serves people in this space has to be curved too. And she also has look like something, as they say in my native Upper Austrian dialect. The tavern lay-out should also make provision for niches and the waitress for bulges, if only to help buttress the heavy beer mugs. The need to make sure that the ballast is correct is reason enough to insist on the waitress being a woman of ample proportions. A genuine Bavarian waitress without an armful of beer mugs is simply unimaginable.

Your Abbey architect Karl Friedrich once told me that weakened vaulted ceilings are reinforced by putting extra weight on them. The layman would probably assume the opposite. You have to put weight on the vaulted ceiling in order to make it hold up. That reminds me of a hard-and-fast rule of dentistry. A tooth that doesn't serve because, let's say, the tooth on the other side is missing and so the remaining tooth no longer encounters resistance, such a tooth will soon grow loose and fall out. It's much the same with the Bavarian waitress. She also has to possess the right stature to accomodate the so-called platters or trays on which she carries the pork roast and dumplings and beer mugs, in such a way that all of these elements seem a necessary complement to her figure and shape. The Bavarian waitress has to be weighted down like a vaulted ceiling. A really genuine, old-style Bavarian waitress has to embody that idea of a "whole" which nowadays is once again assuming an important role in architectural design. What a Bavarian waitress looks like, what she wears and what she carries, how she walks and how she talks, how she laughs and how she swears, all of these elements have to add up to and climax in a unity. A Bavarian waitress has to be like the old, medieval parts of Regensburg and Straubing, only younger.

Our Bavarian-Austrian dialect is well suited to provide linguistic expression for the characteristically regional architecture of our people, and specifically for the *mulier bavarica*. For example, there is mention of porches and balconies, of bay-windows and ledges. Most apt, however, my dear Abbot, is to my mind the term "rear quarters." Thanks to the richness of our language, and thanks above all to the countless number of ambiguous words in it, a Bavarian can talk for hours about racy subjects without ever having a single bad word cross his mouth. *The waitress's got a cute lil' zizziwish, / the waitress's got a great big bill, / Jes take a lil' taste from that big dish, / And, buddy, you'll soon be over the hill. / In front she's got feathers. / No feathers behind. / Rip out those feathers, and you'll go blind. / Girls from Bavaria are built solid behind, / With buns that'll make you go right outa your mind. / These gals are round, round, round, / Built great from top right down to the ground.*

Hey, where's my little pussy? / Where's my little hound? / Hey, I ain't fussy. / Come on, gimme a pound. That's what it sounds like in our Bavarian-Austrian dialect, my dear Abbot. That's also pretty much what you'll hear in the Freimünster Abbey Tavern, but of course only when the Abbot isn't around. And if none of the other clerical gentlemen happens to be present either, then you might even be able to hear snatches of the following: *The priest has a cook / The sacristan's got a girl. / Now the altarboys want a look, / Want to give her a whirl.* Or: *The priest likes her bum / The cook likes his too. / Dominus vobiscum: / When night's done / It'll dawn anew.* You probably aren't interested, my dear Abbot, but if you were interested, then you could find rhyming verses like this about every conceivable subject in Walter Schmidkunz's books, but especially about the Number One Subject. There's no point whatever in feeling shocked about it. In Bavaria we say: they don't *devastate* anything. In the parlance of our old dialect, to *devastate* means much the same as to *cause harm.*

Speaking of natural and architectural vaults and curvatures, my dear Abbot, there is, or there used to be, something rounded about Bavarian women (and men too) that wasn't evident elsewhere, or not to the same degree: namely, goitre. The traditional rhyming verses also take goitre into account: *Her goitre's big, / Her face is lean. / So when we hug, / It gets in-between.* Nowadays, the esteem in which goitre is held has diminished, that is, if it was ever held in esteem. Nowadays, in this part of the world, too, goitre is considered to be more of a defect than anything else. But be that as it may, our Bavarian-Austrian region definitely has an affinity for round things. It's not by chance that Baroque is the characteristically defining artistic style in Southern Germany, since the word originally meant "round" or "curved." Austria-Bavaria is a place where everything is rounded up.

Bavaria is to beer, my dear Abbot, as beer is to Bavaria. If you happen to see any of the larger Benedictine abbeys, let's take the Freimünster Abbey for instance, you can't help but think of the great abbey builders and the great abbey brewers in a single mental breath. So let us thank the Bavarian Duke Arnulf of the race of the Agilulfingers not only for the stolen Chalice but also for the brewing patent with which he endowed his Abbey of Freimünster. Truly, the Abbey has put this patent to good use. It must be a heavenly joy for Duke Arnulf and Saint Gambrinus, the legendary patron of beer brewers and beer drinkers, to watch the busy goings-on in the malt-house and the brewery, and to peer down at the vats that have been sending up smoke continuously for the last 1200 years. My dear Abbot, the monasteries have made an immense contribution to the art of brewing. To be sure, it's clear that this pioneering achievement of the monks also has a down-side, once you start to think about it more carefully and deeply. For, after all, as is well-known, beer does contain alcohol. And alcoholism comes from alcohol. If the numbers that are cited in my copy of the Statistical Yearbook of the German Federal Republic are accurate – and they surely are accurate – then in the year 1970, 85,600,000 hectoliters of beer flowed down German gullets and through German kidneys, or to put it into words: eighty-five million six-hundred thousand hectoliters of beer. Many a liver, my dear Abbot, became a casualty in consequence. Similarly in the case of Austria.

I once had the opportunity to point out to your Abbey Brewmaster the possibility of looking at the problem of brewing beer from an ethical perspective (beer is too important a matter to be left simply in the hands of brewers), but I encountered very little understanding on his part. Beer, he said, is *neutral*; beer in and of itself, your Brewmaster said, is a gift from God, *neither good nor bad*. Of course, he said, viewed from the perspective of the brewer, there is such a thing as *good* and *bad* beer, but from the perspective of the moral philosopher, beer is *neutral*. It all depends on what people do with it, your Brewmaster said. Nevertheless, this line of argument strikes me as being rather sophistic and specious. What are people supposed to do with beer if not drink it? Wash their feet in it, perhaps? *Beer that isn't drunk has failed in its mission.* This celebrated phrase was spoken in 1880 by the Prussian journalist and Member of Parliament Alexander Meyer during a debate in the Lower House concerning the taxation of alcoholic drinks. *Alcoholic spirits are produced for a variety of purposes and only to a relatively small extent for human consumption. But beer is only brewed in order to be drunk, and the beer that hasn't been drunk has simply failed in its mission.* That ought to make sense, my dear Abbot, even to a brewmaster in a Benedictine abbey in Austria.

My dear Abbot, I'm no teetotaller. On the contrary, I'm an enthusiastic beer-drinker. I was just having a little fun playing the devil's advocate, while at the same time demonstrating how certain kinds of argumentation lead nowhere. I am of course aware of the theory that everything that God created was good, and that it is only mankind that corrupts everything, abuses it and makes it bad. As is well known, the traditional Catholic theory of sexual instrumentality follows the same line of reasoning, namely that whatever you happen to find hanging around down there in your pants was put there by God with the best of intentions and has simply been misused by mankind. It's all a matter of using your equipment in the right way. Formerly priests interpreted this notion of proper use very narrowly. The interpretation ran more or less as follows: God has provided us with our sexual equipment primarily in order to allow us to keep clean and pass water through it.

Sexual equipment has, however, if I may remind you, a dual function, anthropologically speaking. There's something missing here, my dear Abbot. The Church is being a little too strict when it wants to limit this other way of using of our sexual equipment to exceptional cases, to the rare and lucky occurrence of a good and happy marriage. My way of looking at the subject is in no way licentious. In my view it's a subject that has absolutely nothing frivolous about it. In fact, the Bavarians and the Austrians have never considered the issue particularly important or tragic. That actually may be a function of what is sometimes called their beerility, a word used by way of contrast with virility. Have you ever a seen an excitable or fanatical beer drinker? If a beer drinker gets passionate, he gets passionate exclusively about beer. It's certain that neither Savonarola nor Ignatius of Loyola ever drank beer, or if they did drink anything, then only strong stuff. To be sure, there are enemies of the Bavarians who claim that their sexual problems, as well as their other problems, seem unimportant precisely because of their excessive beer consumption. That is, they are unimportant because they are never aware of them; they never see them. "A confirmed beer drinker," they say, "loses his appetite for everything else, for everything except beer. The Bavarians," so say the enemies of the Bavarians, "drown their virility in beer." And that's a result not only of the number of liters produced by the breweries but also of the number of liters produced by the beer drinkers. "In this way," says an educated North German to the drunken, boorish Bavarian standing next to him in the pissoir, "in this way we're restoring our sexual equipment to its pristine function." "Huh?" says his neighbor.

And a little mug/Can pull out the rug/From under some lug./Then drown him in beer,/Never you fear. And as another rhyming verse has it: *You dim and dirty guys,/ Stick to your beer./ With pens your size/You can't sign off here.* Or like this: *Beat it, you boozer./You're a sozzled loser./My beer's got a huge foam;/Big boozer, go home.* And like this: *There's fight in beer and fire too./But it goes really flat/ When you're feeling blue.* And again: *My old lady says: "Your gun won't fire./Keep drinkin' and I'll get me a gun for hire."* You won't find these last rhyming verses in Schmidkunz, my dear Abbot. I collected them in your Tavern, along with this one: *When you're drinking beer/You're strong as a bull./But when you're back home/You're weak like a fool.* And so on.

That's how they sing, my dear Abbot. That's Bavarian music for you. They don't just sing hymns in Bavaria. Walter Schmidkunz has published more than 1000 rhyming verses. But the composing and singing of rhyming verses is no dead art; it is a productive and living art, spontaneous and unrehearsed. I myself can testify to hearing singers in your Tavern who were able to improvise verses for every member of a travel group of fifty or more people, and do so without a moment's hesitation, *stante pede* or, as the Bavarians say, *stayin'n bed.* Naturally that means they're not all pure rhymes, either in form or content. In this way, an endless song comes into existence which, in terms of its tapeworm-like length, is probably exceeded only by the multi-stanzaic pilgrim and processional songs.

I myself, my dear Abbot, once knew by heart 15 stanzas of the song, "Unto Your Saviour, Unto Your Teacher," and you really had to know them by heart too, if you wanted to keep up with the singing from beginning to end during the Corpus Christi Day procession in Andach. And I mean really keep up with it. Of course, there were quite a few people who found themselves textless after the third stanza, but even so they went on singing the remaining 12 stanzas, using a kind of blurred la-la text. A few simply held back slightly and then repeated their neighbors' words with a certain discernible delay and interference. In this way, we managed to produce a peculiarly syncopated and dis-tanced kind of song, which sometimes almost turned into a canon. I myself competed with my brother in the singing, and so as to remove all possible doubts about my absolute command of the text, I would usually sing a little faster than the others. We sang without using a hymnal – *by heart*, as we would say. It was considered cowardly to use a hymnal. Along with the unmanner-ly habit of diachronic or unsynchronized and time-delayed sing-ing, there was another trick, practiced primarily by the men in the group, of humming along one octave below all the others. That was called "staying under." If, however, the melody itself hit the ground and the bass voices couldn't hold the octave, they would simply stop singing and wait until the melody had once again recovered from its collapse. Then they would resume their singing at the lowest possible point. Of course, all this had nothing whatever to do with Gregorian Chant or with *cantus firmus, tonus rectus* or *a capella* singing. *Firmus* maybe, but not *rectus*.

One special type of singing that is more characteristic of inns than of churches is the so-called sing-along or sing-above. Al-though I've also heard it practiced in church, as for example in the singing of "Star of the Sea, I Greet You." If one singer said to another: "I'll sing along with you. You hold the note and I'll sing above you," then it sounded like a promise of friendly assistance, of a kind of relief. You can count on me; I won't let you down. I'll give you support and keep you going. And woe betide the singer-along or singer-above who didn't keep his promise. "Oh, my," the other one would say. "You're no good. You're a drop-out, a push-over. One can't rely on you." Singing-along or singing-above while using a head or falsetto voice was like performing acrobatics. The singer-above would exert himself to the utmost, expending all his breath in order to hold the high notes. The physical result of all this would be that his face would turn red, the arteries in his neck would fill up with blood and, in fact, his whole neck would swell up immensely. As a precaution therefore the singer-above would first undo his top collar button before starting the singing-above and singing-along. That way his collar wouldn't burst.

My dear Abbot, a person who is singing beautifully is not a pretty sight. In fact, singing – especially so-called belcanto singing – disfigures the singer. I admire the courage of those fat opera divas who get right up there in front of everybody and sing their coloraturas, with their mouths gaping wide and their whole bodies trembling and vibrating from the resonance. Optically speaking, this is quite unappetizing to watch, though often pleasant enough to hear. As a student I went to the opera in Vienna a few times and afterwards I always felt a little ashamed at having watched the tenors and sopranos singing away. I'm overcome by similar feelings when I'm watching television and happen more or less by chance to see a weightlifting competition. In the opera I felt like a voyeur, like someone who had been watching another person performing some intimate act. I almost felt a little irreverent. I had been staring fixedly at the stage while some corpulent lady or potbellied man seemed almost to be oscillating from the effort of singing. This straining and pressing and holding one's breath and squeezing at the upper end of the body reminded me in every detail of an analogous activity at the opposite end of the body which, as a rule, is not performed in public.

Opera originated at a time when people weren't exactly prudish. There are reliable accounts dating from this period which report that no offense was given or taken when some member of the audience, let's say the Emperor in his Box or some important official, broke a little wind. Nothing could be more natural. Suppressing it and holding it back was, however, in their view unnatural. And that's the kind of mentality you have to assume when watching singers. People in those days thought nothing of it. Nothing, absolutely nothing, not even death, was as much of a tabu subject then as it is now. It could be that on the way to the Royal Opera House you might happen upon some public execution. For someone who had just witnessed such an event it could be in no way surprising to watch a person out there on the stage prostituting himself as a singer. Nowadays we consider many things indecent and perverse that our ancestors thought perfectly natural, things that in fact may very well be natural. Our culture is so riddled with repression, my dear Abbot. Art, art itself, is now largely identical with the art of repression, or with the arts of disguise and concealment. You may consult Sigmund Freud if you want to find out what the consequences of all this are, my dear Abbot, but don't expect Detective Inspector Franz Einberger to elucidate for you the harmful effects of suppression and compensation. You'll have to get ahold of that information yourself in some psychoanalytic textbook. Seen in this light, my dear Abbot, there is of course something natural about the denatured and unnatural nature of opera. I'm not really convinced that we should get rid of the opera altogether without providing some sort of substitute first. Of course, there's no question whatever about the expense incurred by opera these days. And after all, what they put on isn't really so great. For that price, my dear Abbot, you could find people who would allow themselves to be watched doing other things besides singing. Above all, I think voyeurs ought to be made to bear more of the cost of their voyeurism. I think it's outrageous – outrageous especially in view of the taxes paid by the Federal Provinces – that a few voyeurs in Vienna have their voyeurism subsidized by the State. The State provides a subsidy of 500 Schillings for every ticket to the opera. But why and wherefore? After all, there aren't any grants awarded to people going into... well, you know where, my dear Abbot.

Back to Bavaria, where you'll find people singing like mad. And not just in the churches. Bavaria is a lively place in other ways too. Once upon a time Bavaria was real monastic territory; it was a Christian, Benedictine bastion, an outpost of the West. It's of course not by chance therefore that the capital of this province is called Munich, which originally meant "where the monks are." Nowadays, to be sure, the name is not quite so apt anymore. No doubt, in the past there were also monks who lived it up, but not quite to the same degree. And if you take a drive out of the city of the monks, along the Isar River towards Freising, and if you're seeking the Land of the Bavarians with your soul, following the tracks of Saints Boniface, Corbinian and the great Bishop Otto, then the reality which you, as a Westerner, will encounter can be rather sobering. Once, years ago, I inquired about the Benedictines, whereupon the Cathedral sacristan told me: "In that case, my dear Sir, you should have come here a little earlier, that is, before 1802. It was at that time," the sacristan said, "that the Abbey of Weihenstephan was dissolved."

Today the Abbey of Weihenstephan is the home of the College of Agriculture and Brewing Technology of the Technical University of Munich. That's actually quite a good way of making use of the Abbey facilities. But since I sympathize even more with the Benedictines than I do with beer drinkers, I feel saddened that in a place where once there was a celebrated School of Divinity people nowadays only discuss beer. In a place where in the second half of the eighth century the oldest extant German book was written – the so-called *Abrogans*, a Latin-German dictionary of synonyms – the only academic discourse today concerns the fine points of brewing. But I suppose one shouldn't waste time crying over spilt beer. Besides, it's always struck me as note-worthy that the first German word that has come down to us in a book is the word *humble* or *dheomodi* in its Old High

German form. *Humble*, my dear Abbot, *humble*, first written down not far from Munich, later to become the City of the National Socialist Movement, the city from which an indescribable and unparalleled Bavarian-Austrian arrogance almost brought the whole of German history to a complete halt. With your permission, my dear Abbot, I would like to make the following critical gloss in connection with the Old High German literary glosses. If in fact another plan – that is, the plan to convert Germany into an agrarian state – had been carried out, then we might logically assume that, instead of Bonn, the suburban town of Weihenstephan with its College of Agriculture and Brewing Technology, would now be the capital of Germany, and not just the secret capital, the way Munich is. The Germans would have been able to manage that. You can count on it. They have a proven track-record for accomplishing other kinds of historical masterpieces.

My father used to say that Germany's misery began with the Reformation. My dear Abbot, what do you think of that? Weihenstephan is not the only Abbey in Bavaria that was dissolved. The secularisation of the monasteries made great strides here too, as it did in other parts of Germany. I once spent a vacation travelling through Germany from abbey to abbey. Wherever I went I found secularized monasteries. And the things they've now installed in these monasteries! One of the most beautiful Swabian Benedictine abbeys, Zwiefalten, so-called because two streams – one flowing from Wimsen in the north and the other from the Dobel Valley in the west – have dug two (*zwie*) folds or *falten* into the landscape: this beautiful monastery now houses a Provincial Mental Hospital. That's how they've managed to transform what was once a cloister into a security ward. Zwiefalten was founded in 1089 by monks from the Hirsau Abbey, led by the famous Abbot William the Holy; it was another in the series of German Benedictine Abbeys conforming to the *Rule* of Cluny. And Hirsau itself, my dear Abbot? We can read in the guidebooks about the fate of what may once have been the most venerable church in Würtemberg, if not in all of Germany, the

Aurelius Church in Hirsau. According to one of the guidebooks, the conditions there after the introduction of the "new doctrine" were as follows: *Two reports written by visitors on 10. 4. 1578 and 19. 7. 1584 provide information about the use and condition of the St. Aurelius Church at the time, namely that the Church was being used by the local forester to store his wood, along with feed for the sheep that were also stabled there. Moreover, the visitors reported that the structure of the Church had deteriorated badly and had even become a casual attraction for patrons of the baths. It was therefore thought advisable to demolish the Church. Accordingly it was pulled down, except for the lower part of the nave, which remains standing to this day. This structural remnant was then covered with a plain roof and consigned, under the designation of "stone barn," to the care of the forester. The building blocks left over from the demolished towers, from the transept with its central cupola and from the Choir with its apses, were all re-used in the construction of the Ducal hunting lodge on the other side of the Nagold River. In 1813 the "stone barn" was sold for 610 guilders to a stonemason named Kopp from Hirsau with the idea of demolishing it. However, he in turn sold it in 1814 for 718 guilders to the leather merchants Zahn & Scholl, who used St. Aurelius as a storehouse for pelts and other raw materials. On 30 September 1892, upon payment of 7000 marks by the Treasury Office, what was left of the Church became State Property. Nevertheless, until 1954 the structure continued to be put to a variety of profane uses, including as a gymnasium and, finally, as a garage.*

A typically German fate for a Church, my dear Abbot: barn, sheepshed, storage house, gymnasium and, by way of culmination, garage. I do, however, want to pay all due respect to the truth by acknowledging that since 1954 the remains of the Aurelius Church have been used in accordance with their original function, even though I can't say that I'm absolutely satisfied with the result.

I had some strange experiences while I was following Benedict's footsteps through Germany. All the places with secularized Benedictine monasteries were still making a living somehow, either directly or indirectly, out their Benedictine past. On the whole, to be sure, there's not much left beyond the old walls and the admiration of posterity for the Benedictines, particularly in terms of their good taste in choosing the most charming bits of landscape to build in. A pathetic remnant of former Benedictine glory.... I brought along for you the brochure put out by the monastic resort town of Alpirsbach. It's a fine example of the new touristified spirit informing the old Benedictine sites. And since we've been busy for a while now quoting texts, I'll do the same for this one:

Alpirsbach can be most succinctly and aptly described in terms of its past as a monastery and its present as a health resort. This is firstly because it owes its origin to the founding of the Benedictine Abbey in 1095 and secondly because the founders of such abbeys always selected sites that were especially noted for the charm of the landscape and the health of their climate.

Situated in a shielded and sunny location along the Black Forest Road in the Upper Kinzig Valley, this little town of 4000 inhabitants offers all the conveniences for which health resorts in the Black Forest are famous and is therefore rightly celebrated as a jewel of the central region of the Black Forest. Surrounded by a wreath of ozone-rich pine forests and favored by the extraordinary sunlight of the Central Mountain Range at a height of 435 to 750 meters above sea level, Alpirsbach is the ideal place to escape from the hectic everyday worries of the big city. It will afford both your heart and nerves some much-needed rest and recuperation. The air is refreshingly tart and fragrant. Well-cared for and clearly designated paths with many restful benches provide inviting opportunities for delightful walks, pleasant repose and splendid views of the beauty of the Black Forest.

Notable highlights of the cultural program include evenings of chamber music performed by famous German and foreign orchestras in the cloister of the Abbey. They provide the visitor with a unique experience and have earned Alpirsbach the reputation of being a "little Salzburg."

Your health needs are met by four general medical practitioners, two dentists, the Municipal Hospital, the Abbey Pharmacy and three sanatoriums.

164

I have found a great many things, my dear Abbot, in the
Rule of St. Benedict: instructions about keeping silent; about the
holy mass; about the duties of the Abbot and of the monks in
charge of guests, kitchen, novices and the gate; as well as guide-
lines and precepts about how to dress and eat. And I have also
found instructions that sound rather odd and, in the present-day
context, a little comic, like the following one about the way the
monks were supposed to sleep *(XXII, Quomodo dormiant mon-
achi)*, where it is written: *They sleep fully dressed with belt and rope
tied securely around their waists. While sleeping they should not carry
their knives on their persons, lest they inadvertently hurt themselves.*
I found this and a great many other instructions in Saint
Benedict's *Rule*, but I didn't find much about choosing suitable
places where the monks were supposed to settle and build, and I
found only a very few suggestions about the arrangement and
architecture of the buildings. Perhaps it's actually due to the
absence of specific instructions that Benedictine architecture flour-
ished so fully and variously. As a rule the abbots merely exploited the lack of rules... Hence my reason for praising the flexibility of the *Regula Benedicti*.

And it's clear that Benedict didn't have much use for hermits.
Maybe he was really aiming at a grand, representative style of
architecture? He was an Italian after all. Be that as it may, if we're
to conform to the conception that people nowadays have of Benedictine abbeys, then Benedict's *Rule* would have to be rewritten
in the style of the tourist brochure from Alpirsbach to read
something like this: *Brothers, take care to settle in the Central
Mountain Range where, avoiding extreme heights and inhospitable
sites, you will enjoy a pleasant climate. Be sure not to found your
abbey in places threatened by floods and/or earthquakes. The air
should be fragrant, tart and rich in ozone, blessed by the specially
mild sunlight characteristic of the Central Mountain Range. Around
the abbey, set up a network of well cared-for paths and restful benches.
The abbey itself should be constructed in such a way that summer
musical festivals can be conveniently staged in the cloister. The abbey
tavern should be friendly and cosy. Take special care to ensure good*

service there, as well as attractive surroundings and high quality food and drink. Also be sure that the abbey pharmacy is well stocked with a variety of medications.

No doubt that's what many people think the *Rule* should say. But the *Rule* says nothing of the sort. Only in Chapter 66, under the gatekeeper's job description, is there a passing reference to the location and arrangement of the abbey buildings: *Whenever possible the Abbey should be set up in such a way that everything necessary to its proper functioning may be found within its walls, namely water, a mill, gardens and the various workshops. In this way the monks need never run errands outside the walls of the Abbey, which is not beneficial to their souls anyway.* That's all. Benedict doesn't elaborate further on this subject. Other monastic *Rules* sometimes remind their readers about Christ's saying that people should not trouble themselves unduly about their daily needs, since the lilies of the field pay no heed to anything and are none-theless arrayed a thousandfold more magnificently than Solomon in all his glory.

To be sure the Benedictines seem never to have been wholly convinced by this *verbum ipsissimum*, for aside from the *Rule* and the Bible they developed some quite precise conceptions about what their domestic routine should be like. They not only provided for and paid attention to the details of church construction but they did likewise for the buildings they lived in. What would Western architecture be like without the contribution the Benedictines made to it! It's simply impossible to overlook their devotion to comfort and cosiness. Life is so pleasurable in some of these monasteries that it's easy to forget that one is a mere guest and pilgrim dwelling on earth. One would like to be able to rent accomodations here on a permanent basis. A suite in St. Paul's or in Melk – who wouldn't like that, my dear Abbot? Then one could forget about dying...

In itself Benedict's *Rule* is surely no great work of art, my dear Abbot, and it is certainly not as impressive as the architecture of the Upper Austrian and Bavarian Benedictine monasteries. These constitute an achievement that is due far more to the omission than to the prescription of rules by the *Rule*. The *Rule* is plainly and simply no work of art, but only a work of asceticism and religion. Hence it is only interested in – and of interest only because of – its subject matter. Unfortunately, reading it also provides one with no aesthetic pleasure. There are more attractive *Rule*s in existence, but I don't know if there are any better ones. I would characterize Benedict's style as ranging from wooden to leathery. In terms of its influence – an influence restricted entirely to its contents – the *Rule* has fostered not only the impressive flowering of Benedictinism in the West but also its modifications. It was solely due to these modifications that Benedictinism first exercised an appeal in different countries; it was only by virtue of the *Rule*'s permissiveness and its loopholes that it became possible for it to take root in different countries. Benedict made it possible for this special Benedictinism to flourish because he did not expressly forbid it. For it did not take the monks very long to learn how to use, adapt and interpret the *Rule*.

Wherever the sainted *Rule*-giver remains silent and issues no specific instructions, the so-called *Consuetudines* devised by pragmatists take over. The *Consuetudines* may be defined as the routine rights and duties of monks as formulated in the spirit of Benedictinism during the later period. The *Consuetudines* are essentially customary usage distilled from the compelling force of necessity and the normative power of the facts of life. The *Consuetudines* are interpretations and codifications of the ways in which the *Rule* has been applied. In a certain sense they merely represent a continuation of the *Rule*; they are extensions of the *Rule*. But the *Consuetudines* are also apocryphal. They sometimes bear the same relation to Benedict's *Rule* that the canonical gospels do to the later apocrypha. Quite often in these latter texts only the Biblical tone is imitated and simulated, whereas the spirit is utterly alien. My impression of the *Consuetudines* is much the same; I'm aware of certain parallels here. In relation to the *Rule* the *Consuetudines* frequently are more like so-called *contrafacta* or variations; they sanction everyday practices that have developed over time. It's not a rare occasion to suddenly stop and ask oneself: is that part of the *Rule*? Is that actually written in the *Rule*? It's no different with the Bible in general. The things that ingenious exegetes and casuists have tried to extract from the Book of Books! That's why you can prove anything by quoting from the Bible, even opposing and contradictory statements.

It's probably like that with all great legislative treatises; it's the fate of all significant books. Just think of what the Communists did with Karl Marx; just think of the capital they got out of his *Capital*. The Communists have the strangest *Consuetudines* and habits. What they claim to be true and what really is true are often diametrically opposed. It strikes me like some government passing a law prohibiting capital punishment and at the same time issuing bylaws according to which the ways of carrying out an execution are prescribed. One often hears it said that this or that law is no longer up-to-date, that this or that law has outlived its time. I'm perplexed whenever I hear anybody say that this or that law is no longer up-to-date, or that it has outlived its time. Then I say that, if that's the case, one shouldn't have allowed it to outlive its time. Nowadays people usually consider morality a matter of statistics. But morality, my dear Abbot, makes its own independent claims. The bad habit of confusing statistics with morality, of equating what is permitted with what is pleasurable, must come from America, my dear Abbot. In America people are asked in public opinion polls what they think of this or that, and if so and so many say they think so and so, then not only the pollsters but also the U.S. Congress say they must be right, so let's sanction and legalize it. The legislative process, my dear Abbot, only knows how to yield. The legislative process should wield, but instead it can only yield.

Now we only need philosophy to complete this sorry picture. Philosophy was once the *ancilla theologiae*, the handmaiden of theology, but today it is the whore of sociology and statistics; it is philosophy that has constructed a lovely house of theory to conceal an ethical dungheap. The superstructure covering this substructure is called *Pragmatism*. Such *Pragmatism* is the exact opposite, the absolute opposite, of what was once upon a time understood in the West as *Philosophy*. It is anti-philosophy in its purest and most barbarous form; it is the absence of culture. It's possible that some day somebody may turn up and ask: How far have you managed to get with your Western philosophy? Well, in the American sense of success, Western thought may not have been successful. We may not have succeeded in the sense of their "*business*;" we may even perish or we may perhaps already have perished. But with dignity. And perishing with dignity is, as is well known, preferable to living without dignity. This too is a perception that we owe to Philosophical Idealism. The Pragmatists are successful, for, as the Americans like to say, "*nothing succeeds more than success.*" Nothing, my dear Abbot, is worse than such success. My dear Abbot, the greatest catastrophe for the Old World was, as I have already remarked, the discovery of the New World.

I admit, my dear Abbot, that many of the *Consuetudines* do not contradict the *Rule*, but conform to the spirit and letter of the *Regula*. Benedict simply overlooked a great many things. For example, despite its reference to unfavorable climactic conditions, his *Rule* is purely Mediterranean as far as clothing is concerned. He does not waste a single word on how the monks are supposed to stay warm in winter; he doesn't mention a stove or any other means of regulating the temperature. But you can be sure that this problem was not solved by having the Benedictines settle, in accordance with the tourist brochure from Alpirsbach, in climactically favorable sites. That's why a tradition was developed in Benedictine monasteries, as well as in monasteries belonging to other orders, of heating one of the rooms. That's where the monks would take refuge every now and then, before going back to work. Only the winter-refectory was kept warm; the study-rooms and churches were allowed to remain at a temperature ranging from cool to cold. And later on, seeing as how under such conditions some monks naturally fell ill, a sickroom was also kept heated. I won't go so far in my adulation of tradition – in my *laudatio temporis acti* – as to praise this state of affairs or to describe it as particularly agreeable or comfortable. Of course, during the winter conditions in the monastery were a little uncomfortable. But on the other hand I am unable to approve of the diametrically opposite attitude either, namely the senseless waste of energy that we see running rampant today.

It ought to be enough for people living in big houses to heat only one room and keep the temperature in the other rooms at a lower level. That would also be a way of making sure that people would see each other more often. People would get together in one room and talk to each other in the way the monks used to do in the winter refectory, though perhaps they would also fight with each other. Nevertheless, even communication of this sort would be preferable to the terrible alienation and isolation people suffer from these days. No doubt one result of being thrust together spatially would be that people would quarrel and fight with each other, but they would also fight it out with each other. And no matter what you think of people fighting it out with each other, the end result is that they stick to each other. Wasting energy, however, is a sin much practiced these days. In governmental buildings and in offices the heat is turned up to such a degree that the people who work there have to wage a continual war against excessive warmth and against the tired feeling resulting from that warmth. They can hardly get around to doing their own work, since they are kept fully occupied with opening windows, regulating the temperature by means of taking off or putting on their jackets, and so on. Throughout winter a war against excessive heat is raging continually in government offices. The ease with which central heating and, above all, municipal heating can be can turned on and up has utterly destroyed everybody's awareness of the preciousness of warmth. Students in schools – some of whom have never even seen a furnace and never watched a stoker at work – have lost all conception of, and feeling for, energy and warmth. They possess no native sense of what temperature is, just as they can no longer connect cows with milk, or else they suffer from the delusion that milk comes out of cows' horns. They think temperature just exists all by itself, automatically as it were. Everything happens automatically and by itself – fully automatically. They automatically throw open the windows in the schools.

Thank God, lately the Government has realized that soon it won't be able to afford such extravagance anymore but will have to take its foot off the pedal and economize on gas if it doesn't want its whole budget to go up in smoke. I'm not convinced, however, that closing the schools in winter by introducing a so-called "energy vacation" is the absolutely best way to achieve that goal. It just shows how schools are esteemed and evaluated in what people like to call the real world. Evidently, the politicians were out to find a place where they could be least blamed for doing damage and that idea naturally led them right to the schools. Whether the students were going to be taught anything or not was in their view a relatively minor matter. Some educational pessimists even think schools do more damage than good to children. I myself do not share this view. It would certainly be worthwhile heating a good school – I'm talking about a good school, mind you. Heating a bad school would, of course, be bad. Perhaps the politicians also took it into account when they decided to close the schools during winter that nowadays we're not suffering from a scarcity of high-school graduates but from a surplus. Perhaps they hoped to discover some indirect means to dam up the current flood of unemployed college graduates by shutting down the school system in winter. Or perhaps they were only trying to dampen a little the students' enthusiasm for learning. Unfortunately it really is the case that there are plenty of applicants for professional jobs but none for the job of garbage collector. My dear Abbot, you may recall that the Municipal Heating Plant is always looking for stokers but simply can't manage to find any. So it's natural to suspect that the decision not to heat the schools was part of a plot by the Directors of the Municipal Heating Plant to make sure that they'll finally get people to work for them. I don't know if my theory is really so far-fetched as you claim it is.

The kind of damage that excessive heating causes is also evident in the criminal case that we're now faced with in Freimünster. I think a contributing factor here was that the porter's lodge was overheated on the day in question. This heat so affected the porter's circulation, which had already been weakened by an excessive consumption of alcoholic beverages, that he became drowsy and failed to observe how the man from Regensburg and his rucksack strolled past him through the gate right under his ruddy nose. How is it possible, O Sainted Benedict, for anybody to be *vigilax* or *watchful*, as your *Rule* requires gatekeepers to be, if they're being roasted and fried alive in their lodges?

Benedict knew nothing about central heating as it exists today in Freimünster. According to old accounts, the only rooms that used to be heated in the Abbey were, as we've seen, the refectory and the so-called *cella infirmorum*, or hospital. It was cold in the *oratorium*, *dormitorium*, *bibliotheca*, as well as in the *cella hospitum*, *cella novitiorum*, and *cella ostiarii*. In some particularly strict monasteries, no rooms at all were kept heated except for the *coquina* or kitchen. Only much later was a so-called *calefactorium* or hot room allowed in these strict monasteries. But the *parlatorium*, the so-called reception room, was not heated until the 19th century. You can imagine that conversations carried on under such cool circumstances must always have been very brief. It would be a good idea to re-introduce this old custom into the Parliament, which is the present-day secularized equivalent of the *parlatorium*. In that way political palavers might be kept in check.

Not even in castles, my dear Abbot, did people in former times allow themselves the luxury of heat. Only the camera *caminata*, the so-called women's room, was provided, as the Latin name suggests, with a chimney or, rather, with a fireplace. That's not to say, however, that these fireplaces were always in use. Heat in the Middle Ages, my dear Abbot, was exclusively the privilege of women. Only women were warm, and of course also the men who happened to be visiting the women in their heated rooms. They were warm too. I can even imagine that many a knight probably undertook to visit these heated rooms for the sake of warmth, namely in such cases when the warmth was more attractive than the lady. For the sake of warmth, some knights were no doubt willing to have the woman thrown in as well. Their hearts were warmed more by the prospect of warmth in the ladies' chamber than by their mistresses. I'm only assuming all this, my dear Abbot; I've not read anything about it. Not even Neidhart von Reuenthal writes about it; and if anybody might be expected to treat a subject like this honestly, he's the one. If the lady was beautiful, then of course entering the lady's chamber in winter was a double treat.

Before the introduction of heated refectories and of specially heated rooms in the monasteries, winters were a torture and a trial for all concerned. After all, that was in keeping with the ascetic program. Nature was the best and cheapest taskmaster. A hard winter in a strict monastery was always a time of intense suffering for the monks, especially when the Abbot himself was either particularly insensitive to cold or especially hostile to heating for moral and religious reasons. There is a reliable account of how in Maulbronn – the famous Cistercian monastery, later dissolved – more than half of the monks died during one winter. Elsewhere too the winters decimated the faithful. I can well imagine what meaning the Feast of Mary, Bringer of Light, on February 2nd, had at that time. Or, for that matter, what meaning springtime in general had – the coming of the so-called "outside" period, when people were, as it were, sprung. A sigh of relief went through the oratories. Stones fell from their hearts, stones the size of the so-called "peters" stored behind the rood screen in the Gethsemane Chapel in Freimünster. When spring came to the medieval monasteries there would be a census of the monks; after the winter the Abbot would order an inventory to be made. The Superior would then count the heads of his loved ones. And lo! A few would be missing. "Oh, Lord," the Guardian prayed, "you placed these men in my charge. It has pleased you to call them back this winter." The monasteries suffered from cold, my dear Abbot, but they did not suffer from any scarcity of fuel. There must have been more than enough fuel if you consider the immense size of the abbey forest holdings. In other words, the cold in the monasteries was not economic in origin, but religious and theological. If you happened to see someone's body shivering and his teeth chattering from the cold, you might have thought that he was praying his rosary. But I've also heard people cursing, my dear Abbot, cursing loudly, mostly during the War. I've heard them cursing loudly because of the cold.

Nowadays, my dear Abbot, we're no longer capable of understanding many aspects of life in the old abbeys. I don't just mean in terms of the cold. Our principal difficulty here derives from the fact that we are so overwhelmed by the tremendous impact of the architecture that we often don't get around to thinking about the spirituality contained by these impressive structures. We're so blinded by the multitude of facades that we don't notice what's behind those facades. We get lost in mere sightseeing. But what is the value of the most stunning sight – say, that of the Cathedral organ in Passau or the Bruckner organ in Saint Florian – without the music hidden in the machinery of those organs? After all, the Bruckner organ is no mere pianola... And, after all, an abbey like Melk was and is no mere Potemkin Village. The abbeys were once living houses, my dear Abbot. Let's not forget that. I hope they'll keep on living or that they'll come back to life. I would be absolutely delighted if the mistake made in the 18th century by the Viennese Emperor Joseph were to be undone or nullified this very day or at some other, more distant date in the future. But, alas, I know full well that my wish won't be fulfilled so easily or so quickly.

Our ignorance of the ways of the old abbeys is evident even in the way we talk about them, especially in our choice of words. During my travels from abbey to abbey in Southern Germany and Austria, I often met people who asked me if this or that abbey was, as they put it, *still in operation*. They didn't ask me if there still were monks inhabiting this or that place, or if prayers were still being said in this or that place, but they only asked me if this or that abbey was *still in operation*. But the industrial word *operation* makes no sense in the context of monastic reality, and not even in the context of the Benedictine commandment to work. The word *operation* pertains neither to the *oratorium* nor to the *laboratorium* of the monks. It's the Swabian factories that are *operating*, my dear Abbot. Swabia is full of operators. And Switzerland too. But it is precisely this operator mentality that accounts for so many monasteries in those places being *no longer in operation*. Monastic industriousness was never industrial. Nowadays, however, South German monasteries are being used to stage plays. The people who are in charge of cultural affairs there have decided that putting on plays is the best way to use the secularized monasteries that are *no longer in operation*. Consequently the mayors and the other people responsible for staging summer festivals in the secularized monasteries can now boast that their abbeys have gained a new usefulness.

I've run across festival plays and all sorts of artistic activities in various secularized Benedictine monasteries. In courtyards and cloisters where once monks customarily walked in meditation, either alone or in groups, now the boisterous Don Gil of the green pants prances about during summer evenings on a regular basis. Meanwhile, in some other ex-monastery, Urfaust is wildly applauded for getting a poor girl named Margaret with child and subsequently ditching her. The producers of these summertime cultural festivities even go so far as to stage operettas. Whenever there's mention of religious matters in these performances, then it's done by having some character send up an inquiry to find out if they've forgotten him, along with a further request that an angel, not otherwise occupied, be dispatched to fetch him. Or else someone is induced to sing a song about how the Cathedral priest presided at his wedding. Not to mention the organ concerts in the abbey churches or the serenades, where more or less boring ceremonial music is performed in an attempt to do justice to the so-called sanctity and dignity of the place. Here, as with all of these kinds of cultural events, it's never the program that really matters. It's the social occasion that attracts the people, the notorious desire to see-and-be-seen.

In connection with this discussion of art and culture, my dear Abbot, I would now like to return to a subject that I've touched on before, namely Austro-Bavarian folk art and folk music. In this context, I would like to make some fundamental observations about the relation between high culture (which the gentlemen from the abbey festivals claim to be serving) and everyday popular culture. For it's clear, my dear Abbot, that yodeling and singing rhyming verses are held in very low esteem by various proponents of so-called serious or classical music. When these highly cultured people hear anything of a popular sort, they usually feel miserable. They make faces as if they were being tortured and they stop up their ears with their fingers.

My dear Abbot, Austro-Bavarian folk music should not be held in contempt. After all, not even Anton Bruckner, our greatest Upper Austrian composer, thought he was too good to perform Austrian and Bavarian folk music for years on his country fiddle in dance halls and country inns. That was long before he became Cathedral organist in Linz or before he was appointed in 1868 to the Professorship of Basso Continuo, Counterpoint and Organ, the successor of his teacher Simon Sechter at the Conservatory in Vienna. It was also before he became Reader for Harmonic Theory and Counterpoint at the University in 1875 and, finally, before he was elevated to the post of Official Court Organist in 1878. And although he was a celebrated organist and symphonic composer, he remembered his Austro-Bavarian musical origins and incorporated them into the scherzos of his symphonies. You can imagine how that made the Viennese critics' eyes pop and their ears twitch. Besides, the Viennese thought that Bruckner's music was simply unplayable. The Viennese had grown accustomed to a kind of background music that reflected their urbane, effete and enfeebled nature; they were being fed a low-calorie diet from kitchens where music is always overdone; they were utterly [b]analized by superficial, musical foolishness and decadent ornamentation. As a result, they simply did not know what to make of that Upper Austrian phenomenon of nature named Anton Bruckner. And the Viennese did not merely try to trip him up by slipping one cudgel between his legs; they tried to trip him up with whole forests of cudgels.

Vienna became for Anton Bruckner one continuous whipping and stumbling block. That Bruckner nevertheless did not stumble and fall is due solely to his rural Upper Austrian toughness. It seems an absolute miracle to me now that the great man from Ansfeld nevertheless retained his sensitivity under these trying circumstances.

Bruckner's music bears the same relation to Viennese music of this period – to the bulk of the music composed in Vienna at the time – that the Ländler or the Bavarian dances bear to the waltz. The waltz, my dear Abbot, or especially the Viennese waltz, is, to be precise, more of a shuffle than a dance. The waltz is fast but it is also slowfooted, just as the Viennese dialect is slow-tongued. The greatest physical challenge it affords is in the turnings, the twistings. But all the wheeling (and dealing) of the Viennese waltz makes you feel dizzy. After dancing a waltz many dancers – good dancers too, men as well as women – feel sick. After a Viennese waltz you can always see a few male and female dancers leaving the floor in a panic. The Ländler, on the other hand, or the Bavarian is a natural dance. It's lively and healthy, though like everything that's living it also entails dangers and risks. What with the characteristic stomping of the feet, there's actually something threatening about it. Whoever is foolish enough to leave his foot near where the dancer of a Ländler is about to perform his "stomp," will be the unintended recipient of a lump on his toe or a nasty black and blue mark. If you don't hear any cries of pain while watching a Ländler being performed, then it's because those cries have been drowned out by the boisterous shouts of joy. Here it's possible to observe the essential ambivalence of all pleasure, namely that pleasure also involves pain.

And above all, my dear Abbot, dancing the Bavarian means lifting your feet. Just look at the paintings of Pieter Breughel, the so-called Peasant Breughel. I'm always telling my Viennese friends, "Gentlemen, why don't you go into the Museum of Art History in Vienna and look at the painting entitled 'A Peasant Wedding?' Or take his 'Peasant Dance' to heart. For in the painting of the 'Peasant Dance' you can see how the peasants in Flanders used to dance round about the year 1568, and you can also see how to this day they still dance in Flanders or in Upper Austria and in every other agrarian community conscious of its traditions. More than anything else you'll see how the farmers lift their feet when they dance. They don't slide their feet across the floor, which wouldn't have been possible anyway in open country. They literally throw their feet up into the air. You can also dance a Ländler," so I told the Viennese, my dear Abbot, "on uneven ground; you can even dance a Ländler high up in the mountains. Like all other peasant and folk dances, it's a kind of all-terrain dance. Our ancestors didn't just dance under the Linden trees, they danced through the fields. Their dancing signified a playful mastery and subjugation of space. To dance the Viennese waltz, on the other hand, you need a smooth wooden floor. You need a parquet floor, preferably a parquet floor that's been waxed. And," I went on to say, "the music composed by that native of Upper Austria, Anton Bruckner, is informed by a spirit similar to that of the peasant and folk dances. Bruckner's music is a sublimation and intensification of the kind of musical outlook expressed in this rural popular music, but it's not an over-refinement of it. Like the peasant dances, Bruckner's music is pithy. To compose music of this caliber," I told the Viennese, "is not like taking a walk in the park."

When Anton Bruckner celebrated his 70th birthday in 1894, he received congratulations and best wishes from all corners of the world. Among the birthday letters there was also one from his sister in Vöcklabruck, a simple woman who was married to a gardener. In this letter, written with sisterly concern, she appeals to him not to overdo it while composing, thereby endangering his health. *Dear Anton: For God's sake, don't overdo it while you're composing.* It would be very foolish of us to make fun of the way she expresses herself, for, in fact, by writing in this way she reveals not only her own deep family feeling but also a real grasp of what's involved in the process of composition. To compose in the way that Bruckner did, my dear Abbot, is no piece of cake. It's strenuous and exhausting work. Bruckner, like Michelangelo, never spared himself. Michelangelo didn't just produce knick-knacks and miniatures or porcelain figurines, but rather moved masses; and so too Bruckner slaved away at large-scale works. For his music was not composed while on summer vacation on the shores of the Wörthersee or Lake Garda, but in the aggressive urban setting of Vienna, that is, in surroundings that were inimical to someone from Upper Austria. And Vienna was Bruckner's Carrara.

And continuing with my analogy to sculpture, my dear Abbot, I told the Viennese: "When I consider Bruckner's Seventh Symphony and place it beside many contemporaneous works by other composers, then I feel as if I were looking at Michelangelo's Moses among a crowd of garden-dwarf sculptures. Bruckner wasn't easy on himself. And precisely because he wasn't easy on himself, the Viennese critics weren't easy on him either. After all, it's their habit to make life difficult for people who aren't easy on themselves, and who, for the sake of a great artistic career, shoulder a heavy burden. With such people, the Viennese critics add to their burdens and make their lives even more difficult. Viewed from this perspective, Bruckner erred while living in Vienna; he worked hard and was consistently creative. The reviewers resented it. If he had attended the parties hosted by the culturally fashionable high-flyers in Vienna, and if he had flattered the critics and editors, then he could have cut his work-load in half and, for the rest, just produced junk. Even so, he would have gotten nothing but praise and been showered with favorable reviews."

For what, my dear Abbot, is the best way to ensure a favorable press? Not, of course, just by doing mostly good work, but rather by having mostly good connections. That's how it was then, and it's not much different today. Then as now, people expected their artists and their art to be complaisant rather than anything else. Artists and art were supposed to be congenial. Artists were supposed to go in an out of the editorial offices of newspapers, and art itself was supposed to be easily accessible too.

Naturally, in a world where journalism takes priority, Bruckner didn't have an easy time of it, especially since he was neither given to sucking-up to, nor to giving suck to, a generation of pop-music loving vipers. Even so the Viennese didn't succeed in finishing him off. *Non confundar in aeternum, non confundar in aeternum...* A so-called good press is often, my dear Abbot, the result of corruption, of moral or artistic – or moral *and* artistic – corruption and weakness. It's also wonderfully revealing of Bruckner's lack of guile and of his unfamiliarity with the cultural scene that he asked the Emperor to support him against the Viennese critics. He should have known that above all the Emperor was Viennese himself. Anton Bruckner was to be spared nothing. It was not a pretty sight, nor did he take joy in it...

Once, however, my dear Abbot, my Viennese friends became very unfriendly. Contradicting my claim that Bruckner had disagreed and clashed with the prominent composers and critics of his time, they called him submissive and servile, a man who lusted abjectly after approval and recognition. After all, the Viennese said, he himself admitted that he had prostrated himself before Wagner and confessed to worshipping him. And then they went on to dig up and display all sorts of other similar stuff out of the rich and much recycled hoard of Bruckner anecdotes. But then I responded by explaining how all of this was to be properly understood, namely as follows: "Irrespective of certain petty human failings that might lead to a false impression that he was servile, as well as some slight personal vanities and compromises that, viewed in the right context, consisted of nothing more than conventional polite behavior, he made no concessions whatever in his work – and his work, after all, is what really matters. He made no concessions whatever to the defective perceptions and inadequate mental capacities of his contemporaries and fellow musicians. As far as his art was concerned, he remained true and uncompromising throughout his life. He made no allowance for the untrained musical memory of those listeners who can't remember anything beyond a triad." I told the Viennese that in order to understand Bruckner one needs not only a reasonably good short-term memory but also a well-developed long-term memory. *It's almost incredible, the number of times he makes the orchestra come to a full stop*, writes the reviewer of the "Viennese Evening Post" on the 17th of December 1877. And a little before that: *An unbridled and uncultivated Naturalism is at work in this stupefying music. No crudity is too great, no logical leap too daunting, and the composer perpetrates the most unheard-of things with truly childish naiveté. Mr. Bruckner murders mother and father in the conviction that that's how it should be.* If you read the accounts of Bruckner's appalling failure at the premiere of the 3rd Symphony on the 16th of December 1877, you're left with the distinct impression that the reviewers were complaining bitterly about being forced to watch some terrorist attack.

The critics felt badly treated. Instead of harmony and melody, they were treated to titanism and monumentality. Like the shepherds in Greek mythology, they were seized with an attack of panic terror. This music was an attack and an outrage. But aside from the horror that this music made the critics feel, it's also possible to observe another reaction that habitually follows unprecedented aesthetic experiences of this magnitude, namely mockery. Thus, according to Theodor Rätting, although a few students applauded, they were outnumbered by a *mob of hissing and laughing people; and the high-priests of fashionable musical society maliciously chuckled to themselves. This would provide splendid matter for witty conversation at the sophisticated dinners being kept warm for them back home.* My dear Abbot, if you consider Bruckner's early years in Vienna, then you might be tempted to conclude that, as far as his critics were concerned, they provided more than anything else a welcome occasion for pointedly satirical remarks. For years this composer from the Upper Austrian provinces was imposed upon and ridiculed.

Remorse, my dear Abbot, came too late. After Anton Bruckner's death, several people were very sorry about having treated him so harshly. Even Johannes Brahms is said to have been at the funeral mass and is supposed to have wept into his long beard. But Bruckner did not want to be buried in Vienna.

He wanted to go back to Upper Austria. *I would like for my mortal remains to be laid to rest in a metal coffin and placed in the crypt of the Church of the Regulated Lateran Canonical Abbey of St. Florian. Specifically, the coffin is not to be placed under ground but is to be set out in the open area directly under the great Abbey organ. To this end I have already, while yet living, secured the consent of the most honorable Prelate of said Abbey. My corpse is therefore to be embalmed, and Professor Paltauf has agreed to undertake this labor of love. I herewith authorize all the necessary procedures to be carried out as required by law (Cadaver, Class I), so that the transfer to, and interment in my chosen last resting place, St. Florian in Upper Austria, may be effected as I have requested.* And so Bruckner returned whence he came. And the circle was closed in a musical sense too. It is reliably reported that especially during his last days he would often play Austrian folk music in the Overseer's Apartment of the Belvedere Palace where he lived; and, with fingers shaking, he even performed on the piano for his doctor.

Oh, my dear Abbot, how unfortunate it is that it's always easier to let the dead live and prosper than the living. Now that Bruckner is dead, people come from all over to St. Florian and incline their heads respectfully before his sarcophagus. Not long ago they even opened his coffin, apparently out of concern for his esteemed well-being, and also to check up on how the Master was feeling. But then the papers published the astonishing news that the Commission of Experts was itself rather astonished at the excellent condition, the excellent health, of the contents. In this way, Bruckner still remains a mystery to posterity – and not only with respect to his music. In the newspaper it quite literally said "Commission of Experts," without specifying more closely what kind of experts these people were. I assume that they must have been a group of musical experts from Vienna who, on the basis of this inspection – this introspection – of the coffin, had expected and hoped to derive further insight into the difficult problems of counterpoint.

Or perhaps into the art of the fugue, my dear Abbot? It's my view that your colleague in St. Florian should not have yielded to their curiosity. Your Abbey Architect, Karl Friedrich, also voiced his disapproval of this undertaking, and I have great respect for his views in matters relating to Bruckner.

A Bruckner Renaissance, a Mahler Renaissance – our age is full of renaissances. But Bruckner and Mahler, my dear Abbot, have no need for renaissances. They're alive enough as it is. However, I always find it laughable when ill-informed busy-bodies try their hands at renaissances consisting of nothing but still births. There are lots of attempts these days to bring to life things that were never artistically alive in the first place. These kinds of renaissances are being systematically planned. Of course it's really people from the worlds of business and industry that are behind it. A blind man can see that it's business people who are lurking behind all these renaissances. And all these renaissances and nostalgia-fests are of interest to them only insofar as they can make money out of them. My dear Abbot, in all this renaissance business, I can't make out any interest other than monetary interest. The end result is always a business deal. The bottom line is always the line standing in front of the box office. Bruckner and the tinkle of coins, Mahler and the cash register – that's the bell that has to keep on ringing. It's grotesque, my dear Abbot. However, a masquerade like this always becomes gro- tesque whenever wheeler-dealers get busy resuscitating dead bodies. For there's nothing so tasteless and vulgar that a few re- fined and subtle souls can't be found to consider it charming, yes, even significant and magnificent. You only have to develop people's taste for the tasteless. Nothing, absolutely nothing, is safe from being resurrected these days.

My dear Abbot, I don't agree. I'm not in accord with all this. But it's not because of my profession that I don't agree; it's not my nature – neither my first nor my second nature – not to be *d'accord*. If I complain, if I'm always complaining, and if I'm always complaining about *something*, then there's a reason for it, even if this complaining habit of mine earned me the nickname of *Jeremiah* from the Viennese. The Viennese thought they were doing me God knows what sort of injury by applying this nickname to me. They thought being a Jeremiah was synonymous with being an obnoxious pest, or nay-sayer, or whiner. That's why I felt it incumbent upon me to enlighten them about Jeremiah. And also to provide them with some clarification about the art of complaint.

"You shouldn't confuse complaint with mere complaining," I said. "Complaint, Gentlemen," I said, "is a noble art. That's equally true for the formal and technical aspects as for the substantive and thematic ones. As for the first," I said, "of course the complaint only becomes an art when it is an art, which should not be taken to mean that it has to be recited as if it were composed in meter. And as for the second: a good complaint complains only about what's worthy of complaint. I, Gentlemen, complain like Jeremiah only about what's *worthy* of complaint. For me it's only worth complaining about things that are *worthy* of complaint. Similarly, I lay claim to possessing the gift of discrimination: I don't just complain about any old thing but only about such things as are worthy and important enough to be complained about. I only complain about things that have to be complained about if one is to forestall and prevent disaster. You, Gentlemen," I said, "complain about me and complain that, in conducting my investigation, I long ago lost track of the stolen Chalice. You complain that I'm always digressing, and my digressions were all I was ever interested in. This is an example of baseless complaint; this is a memorable example of untenable and unjustifiable accusation. For, as was proved in the end, my way of investigating, of interrogating, of following up leads, and of seeing connections turned out to be successful, despite or rather because of my apparent penchant for taking round-about routes. I also took the liberty of making several detours, or what you referred to as detours, even after I had already uncovered the decisive clue, but that was precisely how I managed to lull the thief into thinking he was safe, how I prevented him from realizing that I already had my eye trained on him. And then finally I struck the decisive blow. I turned out to be right. My success confirmed that I was right."

"And in this respect, Gentlemen, I do in fact resemble the great prophet Jeremiah. For Jeremiah also turned out to be right. People laughed at his *Lamentationes*, at his numerous songs of complaint. People mocked him for being a gloom-and-doom sayer and a pessimist, but people not only mocked and ridiculed him, they also tried to prevent him from speaking prophetically. They forbad him to speak at all; they threw him in jail; they threatened to put him to death. But Jeremiah did not let himself be swayed or led astray. And then in 586 the time was ripe, Gentlemen. When Jerusalem fell in 586, these people's eyes suddenly opened wide. But Jeremiah said: 'I told you so! If only you'd listened to me!' 'Yes, if only we had listened to you,' the people then replied."

"I'm no prophet," I told the Viennese. "I'm only a simple country policeman who makes use of his brains. But to recognize that your Viennese way of doing things leads nowhere – to do that you really don't have to be a prophet. You only have to have a sober head screwed on right and possess some Upper Austrian common sense. You do me too much honor by referring to me by the nickname, *Jeremiah*. Unfortunately, I'm no prophet. You don't get to be a prophet," I said to the Viennese, "just because you want to be one. You can't just decide to be a prophet as you might decide, say, to be a chess-player. Prophecy is a calling; prophecy is still a calling in the old root sense of the word. You're called to be a prophet. In the Book of Jeremiah it says: *Before I formed thee in the belly I knew thee; and before thou camest forth out of the womb I sanctified thee, and I ordained thee a prophet unto the nations.* This call terrifies Jeremiah: *Ah, Lord God! Behold, I cannot speak: for I am a child.* And the reply of the Lord: *Say not, I am a child: for thou shalt go to all that I send thee, and whatever I command thee thou shalt speak. Be not afraid of their faces: for I am with thee to deliver thee.* And further it is written in the Book of Jeremiah: *Then the Lord put forth his hand, and touched my mouth. Behold, I have put my words in thy mouth. See, I have this day set thee over the nations and over the kingdoms, to root out, and to pull down, and to destroy, and to throw down, to build, and to plant.* That, Gentlemen, is how a prophet – a real and true prophet – receives the call. To be sure, there are plenty of self-proclaimed prophets, namely of the sort who open their mouths wide but only speak for and in behalf of themselves; nevertheless they try to give the impression that they're concerned with the general well-being of people, and with the nation and society. False prophets will arise, as the Bible says in connection with foretelling the Last Judgment. If that's the case, my dear Abbot, then it's scheduled to take place soon.

The agenda of every prophet is succinctly summarized in Jeremiah's vision of being called: *to root out and to pull down, to destroy and to throw down, to build, and to plant.* If I may say so myself with all due modesty, that was exactly what I hoped to do too. My first thought was and is for destruction; only my second for construction. If you want to create something new, something good and healthy – something constructive, in other words – you first have to clear the way, or, as the Book of Jeremiah says: you have to *root out* and *pull down*, *destroy* and *throw down*; you have to make room. It's a rule that applies equally to the construction business as to police investigations or intellectual history. There are always far too many outworn and worthless ideas that need to be annihilated and extirpated in people's brains to make room for some fine, new, good idea. It's the same with intellectual history as it is with mechanical engineering and solid-state physics, where the first principle of these disciplines posits that no two things can occupy the same space at the same time. That's the Law of the Impermeability of Matter. Therefore people's brains first have to be cleaned out and purged as the Augean Stables had at one time to be cleaned out and purged, to make room for the development of something better. Only in the brains of the insane is there room for two disparate ideas to coexist at the same time. Clear heads, on the other hand, are strictly given to monoculture. But some ideas and thoughts, my dear Abbot, have so polluted and poisoned people's brains, that this organ must be deemed to have been destroyed too. You know how it is with grey cells: once they've been ruined by alcohol or drugs, they can't regenerate anymore. They're dead; they're cooked, nothing more than a dish of brains scrambled with eggs.

It's often the case, my dear Abbot, that a simple cleaning isn't enough. The stable needs to be disinfected too. The old smells can be very persistent and penetrating, rather like a stable in which goats have been kept. A place like this has to be deodorized first. It's a problem of deodorizing when you want to turn a goatshed into a living room. And that's how it is with ideas too, the difference being of course that you won't make it any different by applying cologne, even whole truckloads of the stuff. For example, in order to overcome the indolent minimalism and the exaggerated egalitarianism that have muddled people's brains with misguided and misconceived Socialism and Communism, you'll need more than a deodorant. You'll need to rethink everything. Here you'll need to resort to old-style *metanoia*, to radical rethinking and alteration. That's a painful process. You have to root out these thoughts, as it says in the Book of Jeremiah. You have to root them out in the way that teeth used to be ripped out of people's mouths, back when dentists were still called "tooth crunchers." In other words, before it became fashionable to have your teeth extracted. There are ideas that wreak havoc in people's brains like the Devil, ideas that therefore have to be driven out. In such grave instances the brain has to be disinfected with smoke and sulfur in the way cider barrels are, so as to prevent the new cider from taking on the smell of the barrel and becoming undrinkable.

As for the subject of prophecy, the prophet's business is often confused with fortune-telling and crystal-gazing, with reading people's palms and such-like hocus-pocus. A prophet, however, is no ordinary futurologist or prognostician or researcher into the future. He foretells the future only in a certain narrowly defined sense, namely religiously and morally. Above all he points his finger at festering wounds; he reveals unsuspected sources of illness and hidden damage. This kind of diagnosis provides clues to the possible consequences of weak spots. Naturally such anamnesis also has a prophylactic and prognostic dimension. Nowadays there are a great many false prophets – in the area of the arts too – who predict, portend and pre-figure quite self-evident truths and who therefore consider themselves prophets. To predict that a human being is going to die is, I must say, no great prophetic achievement. Death, unfortunately, is inescapable; seen from this perspective, death is unfortunately a trivial matter. Death is no great achievement; death, my dear Abbot, is no big deal.

Jeremiah's prophecies never had anything of a private nature about them. They were public; they were concerned with the life of the community. Jeremiah's prophecies had nothing to do with soothsaying or with astrology, with oracles and auguries, with Pythian and Sibylline prophecy, nor with anything else of the sort. He was filled with divine inspiration. Truly, his office was not an easy one when he was compelled to utter these words: *And I will make Jerusalem heaps and a den of dragons; and I will make the cities of Judah desolate, without an inhabitant.* To be compelled to prophesy like this was risky and dangerous: *Prophesy not in the name of the Lord, that thou die not by our hand.* But Jeremiah did not let himself be intimidated, and said: *Behold, I will feed them, even this people, with wormwood, and give them water of gall to drink.* Naturally, Jeremiah was not beloved of his contemporaries. And not only Jeremiah but no other prophet has ever succeeded in making himself beloved by virtue of his prophetic services. The fate of those who warn and prophesy is very much like that of bringers of bad news in ancient times. As is well known, such messengers were put to death. The bearers and harbingers were made to atone for the unpleasantness of their tidings – actually a rather simple procedure. After all, there is a proverb – one which is forever being misunderstood – that says that a prophet is not honored in his own country. That should not be taken to mean that the prophet is being deprived of some sort of honor, such as honorary citizenship, or an honorary nomination or medal, or something silly like that. After all, it would never cross the mind of a prophet worthy of the name to expect such ridiculous honors. No, it's rather that the proverb makes clear that people refuse to believe what the prophet tells them. They despise what he tells them; they pay no attention to it; they ignore it.

The people who are really good at not paying attention, my dear Abbot, are the Viennese. That's something that's impressed me again and again in the course of my investigation. I only really understood for the first time, while working with the Viennese on this case, why long before my time another prophet – a real one and a man of God – why the Augustinian barefooted Mendicant, Johann Ulrich Megerle (or Abraham a Sancta Clara, as he was called), literally had to talk the soul out of his body in order to be heard and understood. When I think about Father Abraham's life, I feel almost as if Vienna must have attracted him magically, since Vienna must be the greatest imaginable challenge for someone who set out, as he himself writes that he did, *to conquer the vices of the world by means of the Word.* That's exactly the outlook on life that makes great medical doctors go into places where epidemics are raging. Abraham a Sancta Clara was similarly attracted to the then Capital of Empire and Vice. And so he left his village of Kreenheinstetten in the Parish of Messkirch in Baden, where he had heard his father's customers cursing in the family inn, "At the Sign of the Grape," and where he had learned how to curse himself. He went to Vienna, where he put his talent to good use in numerous speeches and publications, but especially in this one: *Vienna, Take Heed, or a Detailed Description of Death's Harrowing the Famous Capital City and Imperial Residence of Austria During the Year Sixteen Hundred and Seventy Nine. Together with Some Instruction Beneficial to Both Truth and Conscience, Compiled at This Very Time Within the Afflicted City.*

A sermon by Abraham a Sancta Clara, my dear Abbot – that's something, I think, that nobody these days would venture to undertake anymore, certainly not your Father Adalbert, whom you inflict on us every Sunday. And nowadays nobody would dare either to speak anymore about the Viennese in the way this Augustinian barefooted Mendicant did. Father Abraham wasn't just a barefooted Mendicant; he also spoke like one. Nobody since that time has employed unvarnished speech of such power and clarity and directness. I'm also aggrieved at how people in the Federal Provinces are more and more afraid to say anything about the Capital City. And although I certainly do not mean to put in a word for Vienna-bashing – a tradition, to be sure, of some standing in Upper Austria – I do find it humiliating for all of us when, as happened recently, the Chiefmost Viennese told his Upper Austrian party pal to keep his mouth shut, just because he wanted to make some remark on the subject of Vienna. And the Upper Austrian toed the line. Now it's reached the point where we can't even say that we haven't said anything. If, for example, some accident happens in Vienna, or some catastrophe, if, for example, it happens, as it often does, that something collapses, then it is no longer permitted for anyone in the provinces to say: "This or that thing collapsed in Vienna." The simple reason for this is that if anybody says that this or that collapsed in Vienna, then the Federal Government in Vienna says: "No more money for you!" The Chiefmost Viennese told his Upper Austrian fellow party member: "These days not even the Conservative Party says anything anymore about Vienna."

In Vienna, my dear Abbot, something actually did collapse recently. You remember, my dear Abbot, a bridge collapsed in Vienna. Thank God the bridge collapsed at night. God has a foible for fools. As the Viennese experts concluded afterwards, everything was in good and proper working order; only the bridge, only and uniquely the bridge, was not in proper working order. Everything was in proper working order, according to the Official Report that was longer than the bridge. The periodic check-ups were in order; the city councillors were and are in order; only the bridge was not in order. *Tough luck* for the bridge. My dear Abbot, I find it touching that year after year one of the classes from your High School is allowed to make an excursion to Vienna. I also think that the current campaign about *Austria's Youth Gets to Know Vienna* is quite good, or at least it's well-meant. To be sure, sometimes I think to myself when I see another class in the railway station climbing bright-eyed and bushy-tailed into the train: "Austria's youth is getting to know Vienna..." Oh, little ones, you'll get to know it soon enough. Oh, my dear Abbot, where is the writer who will tell the Viennese what he thinks of them as Abraham a Sancta Clara did. Just think what Father Abraham would have made of an event like the collapse of the bridge. I haven't heard anything Abrahamian about it. I've heard a few little songs – also more well-meant than good – but not a word of the kind that Abraham a Sancta Clara would have spoken. Naturally, there was no reason to expect anything from the Viennese themselves on this subject, my dear Abbot, but where were the great writers from the provinces? Nothing was to be heard from them, not from a single one of them, nothing even from Alois Brandstetter or whatever their names are. But this would have been a great opportunity for B. I'm convinced, my dear Abbot, that the plague could break out in Vienna and today's provincial writers wouldn't waste their bad breath on the subject. The writers from the provinces keep staring fascinatedly at Vienna, quiet and well-behaved like churchmice for fear of forfeiting some literary prize or subsidy.

In 1680 the man from Baden addressed the Viennese as follows (I'm quoting and so can't make any changes): *Maggotbags, Dungheaps, Shitbarrels, Puspourers, Dirtclumps, Junkyards, Lying-louts, Pigholes, Stinkpants, Cesspools, Scabskins.* And then he went on to make the following entry into the Viennese family album: *You, human filth, when you consider the crud emanating from your mouth, your nose, your ears and all your other bodily apertures, then you couldn't hope to meet a more loathsome dungheap than yourself.* My dear Abbot, this isn't just kidding around. You can go to jail nowadays for saying things like that. This kind of verbal injury, when uttered in the direction of Vienna, would certainly not get you an Austrian State Prize, and definitely not a nomination to be Court Preacher. Such words would result in a legal action for defamation. However, since all the writers from the provinces have failed to rise to the occasion with respect to the recent bridge accident, despite the fact that there are some passionate devotees of disaster among them, I will have to make up for the omission myself by providing a brief description of it composed in the style of Abraham a Sancta Clara. Naturally, my dear Abbot, you can't apply international literary standards to me, a mere Police Inspector named Dr. Franz Einberger. I'm neither Jeremiah nor Abraham: *The imperial residential city of Austria, this fortified bastion of granite, this city great in power, honor, and history has borne from time immemorial the name Vienna, a name which, in its German form "Wien," begins with a W, as in "Wail," and in English rhymes with "Whine." Now with weeping eyes and heavy heart I must point out and bring to mind that whosoever wishes henceforth to indite "Wien" must do so with great and ever greater wailing and whining in Wien, at Wien, and of Wien. Wherein this place now doth betide full many an evil sign and wonder, so that there be no wonder at such evil signs befalling. A bridge therein did once lead across the River Danube, which bridge did bear and suffer upon its back many a whiner and Wiener, translating them to further shores. But no blessing was there on this bridge, but only Wiener and whiner folk, which back and forth did flow, albeit when queried on the further side, wherefore they did traverse, gave no reply but only said they wished to cross, as likewise did those on the nearer shore, saying only that they too wished to cross. An unceasing movement was there crossing hither and again thither. Such is the senseless way of the world, which like unto Wien doth with a W, as in "wail" or "whine," begin. Thereupon one splendid day this bridge at night did groundless, so it seemed, grind into the underground. Whereupon in Wien they sought to find the guilty one. Yet did the Burgomaster not only master the situation, he mastered too the incensed burgers. However, only with difficulty did he persuade them, on their part, to desist from insisting, in the case of this case, on the propriety of putting distance between the responsible parties and the municipal instance. So it came about that, while the ruins of the bridge were located, no guilty party was. Nor was it possible to gain more information from the Official Report, which had been commissioned and was duly completed. No more was to be learned from this Report than they managed long ago to squeeze out of the Saint from Pomuk, otherwise known as Nepomuk, honored as the Patron of Bridges and Martyr to the Confidentiality of the Confession. Hence his image standing on many bridges shows him holding his stony finger to his stony mouth. That is the reason why no one in Vienna fell from the bridge, as Nepomuk fell in Prague into the River Moldavia in the Year 1393. No one fell because in the formerly imperial, now republican, city of Vienna in Austria, this fortified bastion of granite, the bridge itself fell, thereby leaving everyone crestfallen.*

Vienna, take heed, it is a veritable miracle that it should be possible for many things occurring within your walls to have bad consequences but nevertheless leave behind no impression whatever. Vienna, take heed. And so on, my dear Abbot.

Our national capital really shouldn't have Clemens Maria Hofbauer as its patron saint, but rather the Saint from Pomuk. Or maybe Saint Jude, the so-called helper *in extremity*, who is invoked in hopeless cases and who has an altar in the Church of St. Michael. To be sure, even all of the 14 emergency helpers put together – as depicted in the Church of the Fourteen Saints in Franconia – couldn't manage to rescue a city like this one. There simply aren't as many guardian angels around as would be needed by just this city alone. Vienna, oh ye olde Vienna, city of my nightmares, all by yourself you would need a whole heavenful of guardian spirits and angels. Or to vary the familiar sentimental ditty a little: "Holy Sloppiness, your mommy hails from Vienna!" In former times, people used to say that a monastery or any kind of ecclesiastical structure was enough to sanctify a city. You'd have to show me the building, my dear Abbot, that would redeem a city like this one. Not all of the remaining provinces of Austria, including the Holy Province of Tyrol, could make that happen. The Scots, with their Abbey in Vienna, can't manage it all by themselves. As for the Tyrolians, I'm more and more inclined to believe that they too can't afford to export any more prayers. Even their religious balance of payments is gradually turning negative. Even the conservative black Tyrolians are slowly writing in socialist red ink into the Lord's books. Nowadays Tyrol is ruled by crass materialism. For some time now, the Tyrolians have not been praying as much as they used to; and when they do pray, it's mostly for good weather and for the blessings of tourism. Actually, what with Wilten, Fiecht and Stams, monasticism was never widely established in Tyrol, compared, say, with Upper Austria. But these days, my dear Abbot, you can learn how to ski-jump in the Cistercian Abbey of Stams. Ski-jumping, my dear Abbot! Since, to your credit, I assume that you don't really know what ski-jumping involves, I'll try to explain its rudiments to you briefly. For on this particular subject you won't be able to consult any helpful books in your library.

Ski-jumping is defined as the infantile attempt to slide down a mountain with two misshapen wooden boards fastened to your feet and then leave the ground for a short interval at the end of a jump. The aim of this exercise is to compute the distance between the point where you took off and where you landed. This distance is then compared with the distances of other ski-jumpers. Well, that'll make you sit up and take notice, eh, my dear Abbot? Nowadays, my dear Abbot, in Austria they even have so-called Skiing *High* Schools. Aside from the Ski-Jumping *High* School, they also have other Ski and Sports *High* Schools. Cultural and educational policy in this country is travelling along some mighty peculiar paths. In the so-called Ski-Jumping *High* School you can't learn Latin, Greek or Hebrew anymore, or Mathematics, Physics, Music, German, History, Geography or Religion either; you can only learn how to jump high and glide far on skis. That's why they're called *High* Schools and Ski-Jumping *High* Schools. I'm sure that we will soon also have Ski-Jumping Universities and Ski and Sports Universities for more advanced high-flyers. I'm surprised that they haven't founded a Ski-Jumping University in Innsbruck yet. "Who can watch this happening without whistling a quiet little tune to oneself?" Franz Kafka writes in a different context. And if you were to ask the pupils in the Abbey boarding school about their favorite role models and idols, then you'd probably be given the names of so-called ski-jumpers and other sports figures. You probably wouldn't hear the name of Benedict of Nursia mentioned, nor for that matter any other name taken from the Roman calendar. Nowadays the young look up to ski-jumpers, not to oldfashioned sky-jumpers.

Our age worships *peculiar* saints, my dear Abbot. I must tell you that, personally, I still prefer the peculiar saints of the Church, the so-called *sancti memorabiles*, and consider them more worthy of respect than the modern saints of ski and sport. (In this connection I won't even talk about the Real Saints. Because for me the Real Saints are sacred.) The miracles which our modern "saints" perform consist of record performances in stupidity and vulgarity. The Austrian Ski Miracle is really something wondrous, just as the Economic Miracle once was. The only people involved in this whole business whom I consider admirable are the ski equipment manufacturers. And, further: what the Austrians are willing to put up with, that too is almost miraculous.

I'm reminded here of an incident in the legend of St. Gangolf, who was a Frankish nobleman and a vassal of Pippin at the beginning of the 8th century. It's a kind of burlesque, actually more of a minstrel's anti-legend than anything else. The Holy Martyr Gangolf was killed by his wife's lover, a cleric, after the former caught the latter red-handed, as it were. Now, according to the legend, his wife heard that miracles were occurring at her former husband's grave shortly after his death when pilgrims went there to pray for his help. When she heard that, she broke out in roars of laughter and said: "That's something even I can't swallow! Before I believe that, my a – will perform a miracle." Whereupon God punished her for her blasphemy by inflicting on her the identical death that he had earlier devised for Arius, the false teacher who had spread heresies about Him. Of the latter it is said: "He emptied out his soul with the slops on the dungheap." If today, my dear Abbot, everyone that's given to teaching false doctrine, scorning the true saints and worshipping heathen gods or idols, was punished with an Arian-type death – Mrs. Gangolf's death too, that is – then the dungheaps and garbage dumps of this world would become dangerously overcrowded.

Even though people don't actually die on them, these trash heaps and garbage dumps are, however, deeply connected with death, with mental and spiritual death, with the demise of reason. They are the wondrous monuments and cemetaries of consumerism – of consumerism and not of abstinence and asceticism. You don't really have to be endowed with the stupendous medieval gift of symbolical, allegorical and typological understanding in order to grasp the symbolical significance of our modern mountains of trash and rivers of sewage. But they are not only symbolical; alas, they are also real. They don't stand for something else, as in the Thomistic definition of the symbol; rather, they stand for themselves. They *are* what they *mean* and *signify*. I fear these mountains and heaps of garbage are none other than those mountains that even faith is unable move. For they are, quite literally, made of materials that will outlast chalk, sandstone, quartz, mica and shale. In fact, some of these materials are utterly incorruptible and indestructible. Mt. Grossglockner in the Alps will sooner fall victim to erosion than one of these little plastic bottles will suffer decay. It's bad, not to be able to rot. Our age has simply lost a healthy relationship with the temporal phenomenon of duration. What in former times endured a long time, now only endures a short time; and what in former times benefitted mankind by decaying and by being rapidly transformed into something else, nowadays doesn't decay at all anymore and isn't changed in a thousand years. For example, my dear Abbot, in former times a marriage was a permanent arrangement; generally speaking, it endured a whole lifetime. Nowadays a marriage lasts an average of five years, but a plastic bottle that's used for shampoo lasts five hundred thousand years. In former times friendships, too, or memberships in churches and other kinds of organizations lasted a lifetime; they endured over generations. Nowadays people are proud of their so-called *mobility*; they try their hands at one profession after another, they alternate among all conceivable churches and sects only in order to wind up believing nothing at all. They run through great numbers of friends and acquaintances, both male and female, as if they were shoppers in a supermarket, and in the end they're left without the slightest hold on or the least link to either a reliable person or a reasonable idea. These people have nothing to provide them with a sense of security or place of refuge; they are homeless, uprooted, alone. Now it's too late. For, after all, the attempt to try out everything has to come to a natural stop somewhere, just as it does when you try out various brands of cars.

People choose their philosophies and outlooks on life – mostly it's popular philosophy and outlooks based on hindsight – the way they choose hats in a hat store. All of a sudden they're donning some trivial myth; then they top it off with rationality, that is, pseudo-rationality. Then again they get all dolled up in nostalgia or some pseudo-revolutionary fad, etc. My dear Abbot, this is not my idea of fulfilling one's life. An unstable and fickle life like that has not been fulfilled or fully lived. It is full, to be sure, but full of mindlessness and lack of direction, full of experiments and lack of commitment. I'm almost tempted to say that one should even show more consistency in one's vices, not to mention one's virtues. Of course, that doesn't mean that I consider somebody specially virtuous who has spent his whole life remaining faithful to the bottle. It's unmitigated fickleness, my dear Abbot, that leads many people to trying out ever new experiments and fads. It often strikes me as if people were only looking for various ways and means of finding death; people are driven by an unconscious longing for death. That's how it is with some people. With others, however, it's only that they're so insanely fearful of disease and death that they become utterly sluggish, immobile and lazy. Some people rush headlong and at breakneck speed into death; others die of overdoses of cholesterol and heart attacks.

One ought to be able to explain to people what kind of duration makes sense and what kind doesn't – where, that is, duration is helpful and where it isn't. That's the problem. Unquestionably there are circumstances in one's life when mobility and readiness to change make sense; that's called dynamism, adaptability and flexibility. In other contexts, however, flexibilty and mobility should be evaluated differently. In business it may be necessary to look around for new markets, but not, I would say, in a marriage. And once a marriage is done for, then you won't be able to resuscitate it by performing push-ups in bed.

I'm always fascinated, my dear Abbot, by the Miss Lonelyhearts columns in the various illustrated magazines. That's where people who are seeking advice write letters describing the problems they're having in their marriages and with their partners. Mostly they're then told to try out new sexual positions or unusual sexual variations. In these advice columns, people's personal and interpersonal psychological problems are largely reduced to questions of gymnastics and physical exercise. Some poor guy complains about coldness and lack of understanding, and the biddy in the paper tells this misunderstood creature: "Why don't you try it next time from behind? Take your wife from the rear." Another correspondent feels isolated and abandoned, and the lady newspaper sexologist tells this alienated person to have a large mirror installed above his bed. A third person complains that his wife won't respond to him, and the relevant lady gutter journalist, the adviser from the newspaper, recommends that he get himself a waterbed so as to intensify every physical sensation. Yes, my dear Abbot, it would of course be wonderful if our miseries could be cured by means of push-ups and knee-bends, and if our solitude could be remedied with mirrors and waterbeds. But, alas, that can't be done by even the mightiest of knee-bends or by the sexiest lingerie, or by standing on one's head or by a plastic doll.

If I were forced to give advice, then I would advise people to undertake spiritual exercises. I would recommend going on religious retreats. And if I were the person leading these spiritual exercises, then I would do so in the sense of St. Ignatius of Loyola's little book of spiritual exercises, though with minor modifications. At night I would rouse everybody out of bed that was busy doing spiritual exercises or being spiritually exercised, and I would take them to the Freimünster garbage dump. There I would preach a mighty sermon about abstinence in the face of

this cultural disgrace, this monstrous manifestation of civilization
– this symbol of, this monument to human irrationality. I would
preach a sermon in the style of the early popular missionaries.
*Sermon of the dead Christ, as delivered from the heights of the
garbage dump, that there is no God.* I would talk about how people produce so much waste, how lots of people leave behind no
trace of their existence beyond waste and garbage, dregs and filth.
I would say that, in the case of many people, you can't expect
anything but urine and excrement. *Inter faeces et urinas nasci-
mur.* Urine, excrement, and plastic. No art, just artificiality.
Nothing constructive, just destructive. Then I would turn to the
topic of *car cemeteries* (perhaps at this point the moon would
shine forth from behind clouds that were racing across the night
sky and so provide an effective backdrop for my sermon). A car
cemetery, I would urge, is not ground sanctified unto God. It's
ground belonging to the devil, comparable to the cemeteries in
which suicides are buried. I would thunder like Jeremiah and
Abraham a Sancta Clara: "Oh, ye sons of men, do ye not see how
the filth ye leave behind is even despised by the lowest of
creatures: by the rats, the toads, the moles and the hedgehogs.
Even the snakes themselves are disgusted by your so-called
output."

But perhaps, my dear Abbot, I wouldn't talk like that at all.
Perhaps I would change my mind and simply read out loud a few
chapters from Martin Linius of Cochem, the great baroque popular writer from Wahusel near Bruchsal. He also preached and
frightened people out of their wits in Bavaria, Austria and Bo-
hemia. What's of particular interest in this context is that his
books contain some very precise and splendid descriptions of
hell. He speaks of the maggots and earwigs that populate hell.
Martin of Cochem is the greatest hell expert, the finest connoisseur of inferno that you can imagine. He was able to determine
with absolute precision from a reading of the scriptures – carried
out according to his own lights – as well from numerous secret
and private revelations, just how big, long, wide and high the
dwelling-place of the damned is. He also possessed detailed

information about the infernal stench and diabolic noise down there. So, in his *Life of Christ*, he treats the subject more or less as follows: *At the same time and in conjunction with the miserable damned sinners, the accursed devils will howl and commence shrieking in so unheard-of a manner that the whole prison-house of hell will fall to trembling. Some of the devils will roar like lions, others will howl like wolves; others bark like dogs; and others grunt like pigs. Others will screech like cats, and still others will rage in different ways, and all together they will make such an unspeakable hullabaloo that all heaven and earth will tremble. When so many hundred thousand millions of devils and humans are simultaneously howling and roaring at the tops of their voices, then it must inevitably come to pass that there will arise such a horrific din that no human mind can encompass it.*

Nowadays, of course, my dear Abbot, we're able to imagine much worse acoustic hells than this one. That's progress. The great Martin of Cochem is actually depicting for us the rather soothing phonetic situation characteristic of a zoo or a circus or even a large farm. And how easy it really is to make a pig, for example, calm down. That's something I learned from personal experience on my parents' farm in Andach. Sometimes I would step out into our noisy pigsty and strike the gate of one of the stalls with a broomstick. All at once the pigs would become as quiet as churchmice. Suddenly they would be very quiet and almost reverentially attentive – and curious too about what was going to happen next. Then gradually they would resume their grunting, at first quietly and then more loudly, until at last they were going at full blast again. That's the same effect you'll get with people in restaurants, when, for example, somebody strikes his spoon against a glass, or when, as they do in the movies, somebody fires a shot in some bar or dive. After a sensory signal like that, the noise level rises, at first gradually and slowly, then in successive stages swelling back again to a crescendo, with everybody shouting and drowning out all the others with their noise.

Nowadays, my dear Abbot – and that's what I really wanted to suggest by making this excursus into the realm of acoustics –

you are hardly going to be able to use pigs to make anybody's flesh creep. Not lions or wolves either. Since we've become acquainted with the noise of a Jumbo – that is, of a jumbo jet – yes, since we've discovered what it sounds like when two of these cast-iron colossi collide and crash, we almost feel a kind of nostalgia for a real-life lion or an elephant. Anybody who owns a house near a spot where a superhighway goes up a hill, or who settles down close to a shooting gallery, will have a good idea of what a hell of sensory impressions and sensory perceptions is like. The devil, I'm convinced, must work with a pneumatic drill. He drives a moped with a hole in the exhaust pipe, always going uphill. He uses unmuffled compressors and sonic booms. The devil breaks through sound barriers. Actually for us Cochem's hell is really almost attractive. Somebody who is hard of hearing or even deaf would really find it quite pleasant. For, of course, my dear Abbot, all of this old stuff doesn't have the same effect on us anymore that it did then, or if anything, it's like the haunted house at a fair. For us today the baroque conception of hell is no- thing more than a ghost story, a kind of stage-magic produced with smoke and mirrors. Our age has become so perfect at pro- ducing and depicting catastrophes that, by comparison, Martin of Cochem seems like a pastoral dreamer.

Cochem's hell is a place full of nooks and crannies, a spot where you can find corners to shelter you from the wind, where it might even be possible for a condemned soul to hide away for a while and recuperate. If you find yourself damned in a hell like this, you don't have to be continuously riled up or excited. You can leave for damnation in much the same way you would for the morning shift at work. For all its horror, you can even imagine having a kind of right to a vacation in the baroque version of hell. It may contain other open spaces where it might even be possible to organize the damned into labor unions. In a certain sense Martin of Cochem's hell is only a very big heating plant. Of course, that doesn't mean that it isn't very unpleasant in some ways. More than anything else, I can imagine that it must be really awful to have to slide down kilometer-long, razor-sharp knives on one's bare behind.

And yet, my dear Abbot, for us the imaginary baroque version of hell is almost soothing compared to the infernos that have turned into reality or at any rate have now become thinkable. To my mind, even the many historical atrocities and horrors that have actually happened – in Church history too – are relatively harmless by comparison with the hideous crimes that are being committed today or at least have now become possible. Though they may not have happened yet, they've already been scheduled and planned to happen. Nowadays the devil works with the most up-to-date methods, with electroshock, with electricity and gas; he works chemically and bacteriologically and psychologically. To be sure, the tried-and-true mechanical methods of torture are still being employed too. But it's been quite a while since hell was a mere problem in mechanics and thermodynamics, as it still was during the baroque period. Cochem's hell is the hell of classical physics. Cochem still conceives of hell along Ptolomaic lines. But unfortunately we, my dear Abbot, are living in a post-Copernican world, though it terrifies me to think so.

Incidentally, my dear Abbot, Dante Alighieri also depicts a Ptolomaic world in his *Divine Comedy*. There you will also find a description of Gehenna, and you will meet all those fine folks in hell who you would never have imagined actually lived there. Also, among them, men of the Church, my dear Abbot, even Popes, even Abbots, something that one would scarcely have expected. On the other hand, you will meet gentlemen and ladies in Paradise for whom you would have chosen a different address. Dante allocated his people quite arbitrarily and according to his own moral whims. By now he must have received more accurate information on the subject.

My dear Abbot, Martin of Cochem also devoted an impressive chapter to the subject of "The Abbey and Hell," yes, even to the subject of "The Abbey as Hell." He writes: *Take heed of the following example which is told to us by the Cistercian Chronicle: It happened that a worldly youth entered the above-mentioned Order and then decided to leave it because it was overly strict, when lo! his dead mother appeared to him in his sleep, saying: "My son, why do you want to leave the Order, of which there can be no doubt that it is a certain way leading into Heaven?" The son replied: "Because I cannot endure the strictness of the Order." Then the mother said: "Oh you miserable wretch, if you can't endure a short and easy penance on earth, how then will you be able to endure the eternal pain of hell?" The son replied: "Methinks there can be no hell worse than this Order."*

Thereupon the mother took him by the hand and led him away against his will, saying: "Come, I will show you what hell is like." While they were still at some distance from hell, the novice heard such a monstrous grunting of sows and such a horrific yelling that he thought to himself that the whole world was coming to an end. He was also so mightily terrified by all this fearful howling and shouting that he fell unto the ground and concluded that he must needs lose his powers of sight and hearing. Wherefore he said unto his mother: "Oh Mother, do not lead me any further, lest my head and heart burst from the noise of such fierce howling." Then the mother said: "If you promise me that you will stay in the Order, then I will lead you back."

And now, my dear Abbot, I have to interrupt briefly and prepare you for the curious conclusion of this story, one which I don't know exactly how to interpret myself. I have a feeling that Martin of Cochem realized that the way the mother behaved wasn't exactly fair. When you're dead, you don't really act this way. Without putting too fine a point on it, the mother's behavior amounted to the vilest kind of blackmail. That's really no way of persuading a young person to stay in a monastery. I also know that if you, my dear Abbot, had been told by some youth during the admission process that he'd had a dream like this one, you would either not have admitted him at all or else you would have advised him to get rid of his nocturnal trauma first. In any case, the following ending to the story strikes me as a cop-out. To my mind, it's no more than a very poor substitute for a real conclusion. But now back to Father Martin:

After he had made the promise, the mother led him back, but by this time he had grown so ill and faint that he did not regain consciousness until the mother arranged for several angels to journey thither, who thereupon brought him back to life with their sweet song.

Just what the worldly youth then set about doing is not revealed, but it isn't difficult to imagine his probable end. Even for Martin of Cochem the result was so obvious and inevitable that he didn't bother to waste any more words on it.

In many descriptions of hell, my dear Abbot, there's a separate compartment reserved for people who have committed crimes against the Church – for thieves who stole Church property, for pilferers from the collection-bag or the alms box, for blasphemers and for all those wretches who took God's name in vain. Generally speaking, it's a very uncomfortable sort of place where the heat is turned up specially high. "It's in this particular compartment," I told the Federal Police from Vienna, "that someday you'll also find the thief of the Arnulf Chalice. Then you'll know who took the valuable Chalice from the Abbey of Our Dear Lady in Freimünster. I'm afraid," I told the Viennese, "that now you're feeling pretty good about the way things have gone, and that you won't lose any sleep if the case is left cleared up and resolved like this. You've got your eyes trained on some otherworldly solution," I said. "I can't help thinking that's how you feel when I watch you doing your work. But, as for the Chalice," I told the Viennese, "that's something you won't be able to take into custody on the other side. It's unlikely the thief will still have it in his possession; he will have left it behind. On the other hand, as for me," so I told the Viennese, "I personally never thought of this case as belonging to a specifically religious category. I never dreamt of investigating the case by following your infernal criminalistic methods. I always wanted to solve it in the here and now, though never without taking the religious and religious-historical context into proper consideration. I never dreamt of fusing theology with criminology the way you apparently did, judging by the hopeless way you went about it. I wanted to drag the thief, as well as the

Chalice he'd stolen, out into the open – out into the light of day. I didn't want to have to rely on God to solve the case in his own way."

Afterword

"When truths are spoken without first being refracted through the medium of irony, satire or parody, they often don't find the form that's appropriate to them – naiveté instead of intelligent judgment."
Fifth of Wilhelm Gössmann's ten commandments.

Alois Brandstetter was born on December 5th, 1938, in the small town of Pichl in the Austrian (then German) Province of Upper Austria, where his father owned and operated an old-fashioned water-powered flour mill and where the family raised vegetables and a few animals for domestic consumption. Brandstetter, the youngest of seven children in this rural and very traditional Catholic family, was sent away as a boy to live and study at the venerable *Petrinum*, a prestigious Catholic preparatory school, or seminary, in the nearby Provincial capital, Linz. His parents evidently intended him for the priesthood but, at the age of thirteen, he was expelled from the school, an event which not only frustrated those intentions and deeply embarrassed his family, but was also crucial to his subsequent development as a writer. From one moment to the next, like Paul but in reverse, it left the young Brandstetter skeptical about and even hostile to the Church (but also obsessed by it), a reaction which, in much attenuated form, is still evident in some of the characters depicted and views expressed nearly thirty years later in *The Abbey* (1976), his second novel and first great literary success. The tragic figure of his gifted, suicidal classmate Isidor Seitenstettner, briefly but memorably described by the semi-autobiographical narrator of the novel, Franz Einberger, is perhaps to be interpreted as an oblique reference to Brandstetter's own youthful spiritual and emotional crisis.

This momentous and traumatic experience of being expelled

from a community that had seemed to nourish him and where he had felt himself cherished and secure may also have led Brandstetter to adopt a critical attitude towards authority in general and to sympathize, as he (or, rather, his persona, Einberger) does in *The Abbey*, with "outsiders" like the Architect Karl Friedrich and the Nativity Art expert Ernst Radinger, or with nonconformist monks like Robert Inder, the dreamy, perpetual-motion theorist, and Theodore, the despiser of Viennese and other conventional authority. It is discernible too in Einberger's fierce espousal of unorthodox artists and scientists like Stifter, Mendel and Bruckner, who during the early stages of their careers (or even during their entire lifetimes, as in the case of Mendel) were also considered to have been failures. And yet even in Einberger's critical stance *vis à vis* the Church and authority – or in Stifter's, Mendel's or Bruckner's analogous stances, for that matter – there remains a staunch refusal to join the chorus of faddish collective opposition. Here too Einberger, along with his heroes, remains alone, an outsider even among the herd of orthodox "outsiders."

Not that Brandstetter's fascination with these figures, and similar ones in his other novels, is to be wholly ascribed to the anti-authoritarian impulse awakened by his own youthful disappointment in the Church. For in Brandstetter's fiction there is also a powerful sense of regional identity, a sense that, as in the case of Mendel's genetic experiments with peas, it is better and certainly more effective to carry out a close examination of something relatively small, like an Upper Austrian Abbey or the apparently insignificant theft of a chalice, than to waste one's breath and the reader's time in grand but unconvincing speculations about the universe. It should be noted, however, that this is not the same thing as saying that provinciality and universality are mutually exclusive in the realm of art. For as Brandstetter, who is anything but naive or provincial in conceiving or speaking about his own work, remarks: "Of course I'm a regional writer. Only I believe there's a special kind of regionalism. Günter Grass, for example, has written about Danzig and yet managed to provide his readers with world-literature; and he's even been translated into all the principal languages of the world. But there's also a variety of regional literature that, for whatever reason, hasn't been translated and perhaps isn't particularly easy to translate. For to translate this kind of regional literature you have to provide the whole context, the whole tone of the thing, along with the plays on words."[1] Like Joyce, another Catholic writer who was also a peculiar kind of regionalist, hard to translate and fond of playing with words, Brandstetter uses his regionalism, his *provincial* identity as a way of suggesting that all identity ultimately is provincial in the sense of being rooted in a very localized, even family environment, and that, further, particularly in the modern age, "centralized" identity is homogenized identity, is lack of real identity. To be authentic means to be provincial, means to acknowledge one's origins in a particular place not easily confused, as in the case of most modern urbanized environments, with most other places. That is also why (in part at least) Brandstetter and his personae are so much given to attacks on Vienna or, more painfully in the case of readers of this translation, the United States.

This deep interest in origins is something that is not only evident in Brandstetter the creative writer; it is also present from the very outset in Brandstetter the literary essayist and Brandstetter the professor of medieval German language and literature. Brandstetter, who now teaches at the University of Klagenfurt (Austria) and previously taught at the University of Saarbrücken (Germany), successfully pursued a career in the academic world before he ever began to publish fiction. Indeed, professionally speaking, writing fiction is still something of a sideline for him, though he does occasionally combine the two activities (business and pleasure, as it were) in popular books dealing with interesting developments in language or with words and their etymologies. The subject of his doctoral dissertation at the University of Vienna is symptomatic of this overarching interest in his own regional and linguistic roots, dealing as it does with the dialect of his native Pichl, an idiom no doubt identical with the dialect spoken in Einberger's fictive home village of Andach.

Another, less immediately related but nevertheless important aspect of Brandstetter's sense of regional identity is his interest in the past and in the ways in which the past (the political, economic, social, as well as cultural past) leaves its mark upon the present. *The Abbey* is resonant with events that happened long ago – the foundation of the Abbey itself more than a millennium earlier by Duke Arnulf of Bavaria or the bloody Peasant Wars of the seventeenth century occurring nearby, for example – but it also evokes the more immediate past in the destruction of the great Benedictine Abbey of Monte Cassino during the Second World War or in the indoctrination of German and Austrian scientists and academics generally by the Nazis during the thirties and forties. Some of this "resonance" is perhaps inevitably lost in translation, for allusions like that to a "people without land" in Einberger's description of the crowded High Mass in Andach or his comparison of modern bus pilgrimages with "the last great migration of the Germanic peoples" will be wasted on most English-speaking readers who lack the necessary historical context (not having grown up into the Second World War or in post-war Austria or Germany) and so won't catch the ironic Nazi echo in the first phrase or the bitter pun on the enforced post-war evacuation of millions of eastern Germans in the second.

Brandstetter's belief in the intrinsic importance of the past and in its relevance to the present also underlies his first major scholarly publication in 1971, a detailed stylistic analysis of the ways in which later prose versions transformed earlier medieval German courtly epics but did not for that reason, as previous critics had customarily argued, corrupt them. This massive, structuralist study – originally a so-called *Habilitation*, written to satisfy the German university requirement that candidates for professorships must complete a definitive study of some aspect of their discipline – still remains Brandstetter's single most impressive academic publication. Aside from its own considerable merits, it provides useful insights into Brandstetter's subsequent practice as a writer of fiction, especially in cases like *The Abbey*

where he "transforms" one genre into another, without, however, in the process "corrupting" either. It helps to explain, for
example, why *The Abbey* adopts and yet undermines (or transforms) the genre of the detective novel, or why digressions play
so important a role in the apparently inconclusive narrative, and
why they interrupt, delay and even obscure the principal "action"
or plot. For, as he points out, the real function of digressions in
medieval courtly epics was to reveal the absolutely sovereign
power (or, literally, the authority) of an author able to dispose of
his characters and story in whatever way he chose. In this way,
too, the ostensible plot of the story was shown to be a simple
artifice in whose reality neither author nor audience could
wholly or unselfconsciously believe. Thus the reader was *alienated* – Brandstetter deliberately uses the word made famous by
Brecht, *Verfremdung* – or distanced from the story, with the
result that the so-called digressions really become the central
concern of the fiction.[2]

The point here, however, or the main point at least as far as
the present-day novelist Brandstetter is concerned, is not to strut
his stuff before the helpless (and apparently hapless) reader in
order to display his mastery of narrative and audience; nor is it,
I think, to convince critics (though he has certainly succeeded in
doing so in a couple of instances) that he is some kind of up-to-
date, with-it, post-modernist writer. The main point, rather, is to
engage in a playful interchange with the reader, a game where the
fun lies in recognizing how, and in speculating why, generic and
plot expectations are continually being frustrated. It is a literary
game that, as Brandstetter knows full well, is by no means new.
In the German novelistic tradition it reaches back at least as far
as Jean Paul and E. T. A. Hoffmann, and in the English even
further to Henry Fielding and, especially, to Laurence Sterne –
with both of these national traditions deriving ultimately from
the example of Cervantes' great novel, *Don Quixote*. To be sure,
the rules have changed considerably since these great masters first
played it. Most notably, the author himself has disappeared from
his fiction, to be replaced by what has variously come to be called

a persona, or a dramatized or focalized narrator, that is, a character who tells the story and who is often or even usually himself an "actor" in it. All the novels that Brandstetter has published so far are narrated in this way, though even here part of the "game" (and hence a part of the reader's enjoyment) is to watch carefully as the "real" face of the author intermittently appears and then vanishes behind the mask of his story-teller.

Different too is the virtual disappearance of action or plot in the usual sense. Already in his Habilitation study, Brandstetter had argued that it is easier to discern and define descriptive passages in narrative than it is to do so for passages of action. As a way of resolving this dilemma he proposed therefore simply to define action negatively as consisting of those parts of a narrative that are not descriptive. Action, so he maintained, was nothing more than a mere "'filler' between the static parts."[3] It is this implied disregard or even contempt for action and plot that has also led Brandstetter to describe himself – a little defensively, perhaps – as "a writer of cultivated boredom or of what people who need 'action' in books consider boredom."[4] It is evident too in his admiration for the great Austrian novelist, Adalbert Stifter, who in recent years has come under fire for being far and away the most boring novelist in the German language. (Though some would argue that Stifter faces some pretty stiff competition here.) Of Stifter, Brandstetter remarks in his *Kleine Menschenkunde* (1987) that he is in his opinion "the prototype of a story-teller; his [novella] *Indian Summer* is the archetype of all stories."[5] Franz Einberger, one should recall in this connection, is also a fervent admirer of Stifter who feels called upon to justify his own digressive and static mode of investigation (along with his mode of reporting on that investigation) when attacked by his Viennese colleagues for showing a lack of "action."

Story-telling, then, is for Brandstetter something that is only marginally connected with "action" or plot in the traditional sense. While it is an element that is never entirely absent from his fiction, it is also never unambiguously or naively pre- sent. Like E. M. Forster and José Ortega y Gasset before him, the narrative line is for Brandstetter clearly a "lower" and more primitive element of story-telling, or, as Forster puts it memorably in *Aspects of the Novel* (1927), it is a regrettably essential aspect of the novel that is "immensely old – goes back to neolithic times, perhaps to paleolithic. Neanderthal man listened to stories, if one may judge by the shape of his skull. The primitive audience was an audience of shock-heads, gaping round the campfire, fatigued with contending against the mammoth or the woolly rhinoceros, and only kept awake by suspense. What would happen next?"[6] For Forster, the elements or aspects of narrative that are truly central to all post-Neanderthalian narrative are plot (in the sense of causality rather than straightforward narration) and, most emphatically, character, whereas for Ortega the primary interest of modern(ist) fiction lies in the sophisticated interplay between the author and an audience of initiated readers.

While these are to differing degrees also significant aspects of Brandstetter's own narrative practice, his primary emphasis is not on complex causality, character, or hidden meanings. Franz Einberger, for example, is the only character in *The Abbey* who can be said to possess even a minimally three-dimensional shape (to use Forster's terminology again); for the rest, the Abbot never puts in an appearance in his own right, and the monks and lay employees of the Abbey reflect a fairly narrow spectrum of character and interest, being all eccentrics and monomaniacs of one sort or another. Indeed, riding and even galloping about on their hobby-horses (and then talking at length about having done so) are the principal activities (not to say "actions") of just about every character in Brandstetter's novels, definitely not excluding his narrators.

Nor is Brandstetter's real interest (either his own or his intended reader's) to be found in the concealment and discovery of hidden meanings. To be sure, as Brandstetter himself admits, he is very much an intertextual author, agreeing emphatically with his eminent Austrian colleague, Ernst Jandl, that "every text is a text about another text," and referring his readers explicitly to Peter Wapnewski's description of him as a "Master of

Analogy."[7] And certainly, as will become apparent later, *The Abbey* does contain a "hidden" dimension that has hitherto eluded the scrutiny of its (admittedly not very numerous) critics. Still, what really seems central to Brandstetter's fiction is something that, in the broadest sense, may be called its humorous dimension. This includes, aside from the "game" between author and reader already referred to, a kind of gentle whimsy that is evident in, say, the description of how the priest used to be "helped" into his vestments before Mass in Andach. It also includes puns, wordplay and linguistic exuberance of every (not always translatable) sort; parody or pastiche, as when Einberger rewrites parts of Benedict's *Rule* in the manner of a tourist brochure or when he delivers a tirade in the style of Abraham a Sancta Clara about the collapse of a bridge in Vienna; bawdy humor, as in his discussion of what qualifications a genuine Austro-Bavarian waitress must literally fulfill; exaggeration (especially in terms of insults) carried to a ridiculously exaggerated extreme, as in Katherina Schindler's berating Richard Kronawitter for his alleged stupidity and brutality in causing a minor traffic accident; and, most obviously, in the multitude of apparently random digressions that seem to be connected only by the almost maniacally associative mind of Franz Einberger (also very much a "master of analogy" in this respect). It is this last trait of Einberger's mind (and Brandstetter's mind behind Einberger's, of course), that makes *The Abbey* seem at times almost like the shaggiest of all shaggydog stories. Associated – sometimes very subtly and quite sanely associated – with all of these more or less amusing elements of Brandstetter's fiction is a pervasive tone of irony that makes it difficult for the reader to decide just how to respond to any given passage. That is, the reader is made to feel that she must consider everything as perhaps affected or infected by irony, or perhaps not. The resulting, rather disquieting feeling is like walking on uncharted ground that may give way at any moment.

It should be clear by now that Brandstetter is a highly self-conscious and complex writer, fully informed of the entire repertoire of narrative technique and ready to pull out all the stops in putting that repertoire to use. However, given all this theoretical and practical expertise, it is astonishing how inadequately the critics have so far responded to his work – the academic critics, that is, for on the whole Brandstetter's work has received a favorable and sometimes (as in the case of *The Abbey*) an enthusiastic popular press. And certainly his work has succeeded in reaching a wide, non-academic readership which has remained loyal to him over the years. One of the standard German literary reference works, the *Literatur Lexikon*, for example, refers to his books as "popular" and "much read."[8] Even so, the one published critical book that is entirely devoted to Brandstetter's work originated as a doctoral dissertation at the University of Osnabrück in Germany. Characteristically, its author, Sigmund Geisler, begins by complaining of the virtual absence of academic criticism on Brandstetter, despite his being among the most prolific German-language novelists of the last couple of decades. Though unable to discover any obvious reason for such neglect, Geisler suggests that one factor may be the difficulty critics have encountered in attempting to classify his work, or, conversely, that they are too preoccupied with classifying (i.e., pigeonholing) it by comparing it to the work of Austrian contemporaries like H. C. Artmann or, especially, Thomas Bernhard. Finally, Geisler observes that some academic critics may have been put off by Brandstetter's preference for regional subjects or even for so-called *Heimatliteratur* or sentimentalized rural subject-matter.[9]

Of these suggestions, the last is clearly the most persuasive, for there can be no doubt that the mature Brandstetter is widely perceived as a spokesman for traditional rural, Catholic values. Even a sympathetic commentator like Jutta Landa describes Brandstetter's characteristic socio-political stance as basically conservative and possibly reactionary. In her view, his work endorses the values of tradition and the existing social order. "Nature and honest work are glorified," she concludes, "and a humanistic tradition is strongly defended."[10] Given this perception of Brandstetter, it seems obvious that his work cannot be expected to exercise much appeal on the general run of academic readers.

This group, after all, is, or usually likes to think of itself as being, progressive and anti-traditional. Brandstetter as fogey (or even bogey) is an image, however, that is widely and often uncritically accepted in the German-speaking academic community – also accepted, for that matter, by the political right, where of course it is accounted to his credit – though, in my view, it is partly mistaken or at any rate does not reflect the whole truth about the very complex writer Brandstetter is.

This is not to say that Brandstetter *really* is some sort of closet liberal. He certainly isn't anything of the sort, just as he certainly is not a mouthpiece for the social and/or ecclesiastical *status quo*, as anyone who has read *The Abbey* with any care must realize. So, while Brandstetter consciously places himself within an Upper Austrian regionalist tradition which accepts the conservative and traditional Stifter as its model – a Stifter, let us recall, who also belongs to *World Literature* – and while he has explicitly referred to himself as writing in an idyllic rather than realistic vein,[11] Brandstetter is anything but a nostalgic sentimentalist who is always merrily remembering the supposedly good old days. He knows, and repeatedly shows in sometimes grisly detail, how many of those old days (whether under the Nazis, the Habsburgs or even Saint Benedictine himself) were not specially good. People in positions of power and politicians of all shades do not come off well in his books – and nobody at all comes off entirely unscathed. Even God is faulted for tolerating and fostering stupidity in the Church.

The main point to grasp here is that Brandstetter is above all a *satirist*. As such, he is continually confronting the ideal (and also the *idyll*) with the real, and showing how poorly the two match. The satire is especially acute in areas where the distance between the ideal and the real tends to be great, as it is, for example, in the Church, in politics, or in the university – all objects of Brandstetter's satiric wrath. As a satirist, Brandstetter must also appeal to some accepted moral standard. In *The Abbey* this is the function performed, on the whole, by the Benedictine's *Rule*. That the *Rule* endorses hierarchical authority and hard work (both physical and spiritual) fits in well with Brandstetter's largely traditional value system, though it should be recalled that the *Rule* also endorses honesty, charity and communality (i.e., love in the sense of *agape*). It also expresses, as Einberger notes, some grave reservations about the Abbot's power and the undue influence exercised in spiritual matters by the rich. Nor does the *Rule* itself altogether escape the narrator's ironic scrutiny, especially in areas relating to discipline.

Though undoubtedly dear to Franz Einberger, the institution of the Abbey is not sentimentalized by him as a place of unqualified grace. On the contrary, precisely because it is so dear to him, he subjects it and its inhabitants to the minutest and most critical investigation, an investigation from which not even (or especially not) the Abbot is exempt. The novel, in fact, is – as its title suggests – much more intensely concerned with determining the current moral state of the Abbey and of the society whose values that Abbey symbolizes than it is with investigating the theft of a famous chalice. In the final analysis, Einberger belongs more to the moral police – to the Universal Vice Squad, as it were – than he does to the Upper Austrian Provincial *Gendarmerie*. His real search is not for the thief of the Arnulf Chalice but for the causes of the festering moral wound of which the theft is merely a symptom.

The Abbey, then, is a very amusing book and Alois Brandstetter is a very amusing writer, but he is not, as the saying goes, "merely amusing." Without ever pulling long faces or engaging in humorless (and boring?), monomaniacal rantings and ravings in the manner of Thomas Bernhard – which admittedly can sometimes wind up by being extraordinarily funny – Brandstetter is a very serious writer. He belongs to that strain in the Austrian literary tradition which he himself describes as sinister and macabre, displaying a strong tendency towards black humor. This is also a tradition which, as in the notable case of Thomas Bernhard, replaces the notion of a sentimentalized "Heimat" with that of an ironized "Unheimat" – that is, it replaces the cosiness of home with the uncosiness of unhome.[12] To be sure, Brandstetter does not actually assign himself to this group; he views himself rather as playing the relatively harmless role of "Merry Alois" alongside that of the terrible "Son of Thunder," Thomas Bernhard. He is perhaps right in not claiming kinship with such infernal colleagues, for no matter how outraged he or his characters may be, they never go off the deep end. Reading Brandstetter one never gets the uncomfortable feeling that one has suddenly wandered off (or been shoved) into a lunatic asylum where everyone is shouting madly at each other. No matter how black Brandstetter's humor, there is always, as it were, light at the end of the esophagus.

Still, if Brandstetter remains safely on this side of the abyss, he is not afraid of peering occasionally over the edge. Andach, for example, may not exactly represent the uncosiness of unhome but it doesn't represent the cosiness of home either. There is a kind of surreal madness about the place, inhabited as it is by various ex-students who have "lost their memory" and "disstudied" themselves into mental aporia. Then there is the slapstick comedy of dressing the village priest in the sacristy, or the weird musical rivalry of young boys engaging in bouts of singing-along and singing-above. Even the father who seeks to temper the air-pressure in his water-mill by filling a variety of bags with air seems to participate in this aura of genial lunacy. Given such eccentric behavior, it seems hardly right to call Brandstetter a writer of "Heimat" fiction or even someone who idealizes/ idyllizes rural Austria. He is far more of an anti-idyllist than he is an idyllist. It's not hard to agree, therefore, with an assessment of his fiction that differs radically from that made by virtually all of his critics, namely his own: "My novels are surrealistic and, in the strictest sense, shouldn't really be classified as novels at all. They are, rather, long monologues, testamentary reports."[13]

With this verdict from the author's own mouth we now arrive at Einberger, the longwinded testamentarian and expert monologuist. To begin with, the first and most important thing to remember about Einberger, is that he isn't Brandstetter. While at times he may and probably does express attitudes or reflect experiences shared with Brandstetter (like Brandstetter, for example, Einberger's father was a miller; and both come from small Upper Austrian villages), even in such cases his views and experiences must be related primarily to Einberger the character rather than to Brandstetter the author. As Brandstetter himself points out in an interview, Einberger often says things "that are absolutely contradictory and that one could never endorse oneself. It's a game intended to provoke others or to spur oneself on. For whenever one exaggerates or practices irony in literary contexts it always means deviating from something that one really knows better; and whoever writes ironically or satirically is deliberately acting wrongheadedly in order to get people to talk about a subject and about the right way of dealing with it."[14]

Einberger, in other words, is part and parcel of Brandstetter's irony. This is made evident at several points in the "narrative," though, generally speaking, the very fact of the existence of his immense, rambling, chaotic "report" to the Abbot ought to alert readers to the presence of irony. So, for example, at the close of his Deputy Erwin Hatzenbühler's longwinded accident report, Einberger observes that "naturally" he would have written a report like this quite differently, "namely shorter" and much more to the point. This is an assertion that is hardly borne out by the evidence of Einberger's own report, a report whose prolixity and apparent irrelevance make Hatzenbühler's seem like a model of succinctness. Similarly, Einberger censures the mealymouthed sermons that are preached in the Abbey Church, arguing that what needs to be said in them is never said, that "the needful word is never spoken." Here again, Einberger's advice to others applies doubly to himself, for, though he certainly cannot be faulted for being mealymouthed, he also never speaks the needful word about who committed the crime of stealing the Arnulf Chalice or why. This despite the fact that the theft is the ostensible subject of his report. And his claim that he is not prejudiced against Vienna but rather loves it with a kind of tough love is deservedly dismissed with contempt by his Viennese colleagues.

This is not to say that Einberger is either a fool or a madman.

After all, he does seem to have solved the crime using methods exemplified in and by his report, though initially ridiculed for doing so by the Federal Police. His name itself points to the ambiguous role played by him in the novel. In German, "ein Berger" could mean either someone from the mountains, a designation that would presumably reinforce his regional identity versus the Viennese who come from one of the principal "Cities of the Plain;" or it could mean "a saviour," "a rescuer," especially of something hidden away, referring perhaps to his role as the sole successful investigator of the crime. Even more ambiguously "ein Berger" could also be taken to mean a person who hides or conceals something himself, though usually for good reason. This last sense of the name might allude to Einberger's frustrating but steadfast refusal to identify specifically the name of the criminal, beyond revealing that he comes from Regensburg (more on this later).

Nor should we think of Einberger as an unlikely narrator because of his extensive knowledge of Latin, the Bible, the Benedictine *Rule*, Old High German, ancient and modern history, milling techniques, Goethe, Stifter, Baroque sermons, contemporary book production and marketing, architecture (ecclesiastical and otherwise), art history, psychology, theology, linguistics (especially structural linguistics), folk dancing, classical music and Mendelian genetics. After all, he is a former pupil of the Abbey School who had once seriously considered entering the priesthood before going off to Vienna to study law. A number of the subjects in which he is versed (e.g., Latin, music, theology, Mendel, Goethe, Stifter, art history) he would have picked up while at the school and, for the rest, one simply has to assume that (like Sherlock Holmes before him) he is a good detective because he possesses a curious mind well stocked with apparently useless (but in reality very useful) information.

Like Holmes, Einberger is also good at masking his real intentions. He is not above manipulating witnesses and evidence, for example, as when he attempts to distract the Federal Police from discrediting the testimony provided by Father Robert Inder. And some part of his apparently random digressive method turns out to have been a conscious stratagem on his part to deceive the thief. As he says himself in this connection: "... my way of investigating, of interrogating, of following up leads, and of making connections turned out to be successful, despite or rather because of my apparent penchant for taking round-about routes. I also took the liberty of making several detours, or what you referred to as detours, even after I had already uncovered the decisive clue, but that was precisely how I managed to lull the thief into thinking he was safe, how I prevented him from realizing that I already had my eye trained on him. And then finally I struck the decisive blow. I turned out to be right. My success confirmed that I had been right." (p. 183)

The Abbey, then, is a novel of ironic and ironized consciousness, where the reader's principal interest is in tracing that consciousness (i.e., Einberger's) through an extraordinary variety of byways to what seems like a deliberately inconclusive conclusion. When, near the close of the novel, Einberger tells the Abbot that he's at a loss about how to interpret the "curious conclusion" of the tale from Martin of Cochem that he's just been retelling, it seems clear that he is also (and Brandstetter behind him) referring to the anti-climactic close of his own report and of *The Abbey*. This is apparently part of the "game" between writer/narrator and reader/listener which we are intended to savor. Such savoring, however, is not what happens with all of the readers of this book. Sigmund Geisler, for example, finds Brandstetter's (ab)use of the genre of the detective novel contradictory and annoying. He questions how, on the one hand, the case can be solved (as Einberger claims it is) and, on the other, the thief is only to be apprehended in the beyond. There's no explanation or justification for such blatant contradiction, except Brandstetter's apparent desire to mock those naive readers who still "need" answers to superficial questions like "who done it?".[15]

It's certainly true that there are some problems with Einberger's (Brandstetter's?) use of the genre of the detective novel or even of the "genre" of the monologue. To begin with, though

Einberger at one point specifically refers to his performance as being the "official report" regarding the theft of the Arnulf Chalice, it's unclear why the report is being made to the Abbot rather than, say, to his superiors in the Police. Secondly, there is at times an awkward sense – even on Einberger's part – that much of what he has to say is already known by the Abbot and by the inhabitants of the Abbey generally; but if so, are we then to read the report as being primarily a massive ego-trip on Einberger's part? And, thirdly, what is the *form* of the report? Is it a "letter" as some critics contend? This seems unlikely, for Einberger specifically refers to *reading out* Hatzenbühler's report to the Abbot. If that's true – and there seems to be no reason to doubt it – then it would appear that Einberger's report is being delivered *viva voce* to the astonishingly patient (and unresponsive) Abbot. Also, the genre of the official report, even when stretched to accommodate examples of Einberger's unorthodox investigative methodology, can hardly remain realistic when Einberger begins quoting racy rhyming verses or trying his hand at sermons in the style of Abraham a Sancta Clara.

What to make of all this? One answer might be that we are not supposed to look so carefully at possible narrative inconsistencies, since as Brandstetter has said elsewhere he tries to avoid excessive revision in his books and is willing to accept inconsistencies and even contradictions rather than risk losing spontaneity.[16] On the other hand, Brandstetter explicitly admits to doing extensive research on his books before starting out to write them, mentioning *The Abbey* specifically by name in this connection.[17] So where is the truth here? And should we care? I think we should, for even though (or because) we may not find satisfactory answers to all our questions and objections, we can get enough such answers to suggest that continued patience (even like unto the Abbot's) may be warranted.

Take the matter of the crime, for instance. What do we know about this crime and its perpetrator? We know that the crime has: 1) been solved; 2) that the identity of criminal is known; 3) that he comes from Regensburg; 4) that the Chalice was taken through the main gate in a rucksack; and 5) that it was an inside job, committed by someone who is still connected with the Abbey. We are, however, never informed of the specific motive of the criminal nor of his name; we are also not told why his connection with Regensburg is significant. Here, it seems, along with a series of apparent red herrings, we are also fed some rather specific and potentially useful information. For, logically, if the crime was committed by someone within the Abbey, it must have been committed by someone who, at the very least, has been introduced to us in the course of the narrative. Two such characters seem especially relevant: Father Inder, the prime suspect of the Federal Police and the only character who claims to have actually seen the thief; and Father Ambrosius, the Archivist, whose malicious destructiveness of valuable manuscripts makes him a likely candidate for committing other wilful crimes.

One further character also comes into question, namely the Abbot himself. Not only does Einberger accuse the Abbot of laxity in not enforcing a stricter regimen at the main gate, he also accuses him of a general failure to enforce discipline in the Abbey. Einberger also points out that in the Abbot's sermon about the theft, the presence of the thief in the Church is, if only figuratively, assumed; therefore, it may be that the Abbot was either aware of the thief's identity or was himself the thief. Certainly part of Einberger's intention in "reading the *Rule*" to the Abbot is to make him aware of how far he has diverged from it. In this sense, Einberger's "report" is not so much a report on what he himself has done but an indictment of what the Abbot has failed to do. It is also surely significant that he specifically includes the Abbot in the list of people who are implicated and at one point even suggests, though only indirectly, that he should resign. Regardless, however, of whether the Abbot is guilty of the specific crime of stealing the Chalice, he unquestionably shares in the criminal's guilt, for it is he, as Abbot, who bears the ultimate responsibility for whatever happens in the Abbey. Though in the end it remains unclear if this is the entire extent of his guilt, it is surely suggestive that, like the stolen Chalice, the Abbot is at one and the same time "absent" from and yet very *present* in the narrative. The mysterious reference to Regensburg may also have some significance here, since the Abbot is specifically said to have come to Freimünster from a "home" abbey located somewhere in Bavaria.

What is certain, however, is that the founder of the Abbey, Duke Arnulf of Bavaria, resided in Regensburg and is buried in the Cathedral there. Regensburg, therefore, would appear to possess a kind of right to take back what it had once given, especially if its gift no longer serves as a warrant for the kind of conduct that it was originally meant to ensure and that it still symbolizes. It is in this sense – as a symbol – that the Chalice and its theft are, I think, finally to be understood; and it is only in this larger and more profound sense that the question of who, specifically, the thief was becomes largely irrelevant. For, though no critic hitherto seems to have thought it worthwhile to make the point, the Arnulf Chalice is of course also the Holy Grail. Like the Grail, it has gone "missing," and, like it again, a search has been instituted to find it. Here that search is not conducted by the Arthurian Knights of the Round Table but rather by the Federal Police assisted by Dr. Franz Einberger. The latter's apparent "simplicity," however, qualifies him as a likely Percivale and helps to explain why it is he, rather than the Viennese, who manages to find the culprit. He knows full well, also, that as with the wasted realm of the Fisher King, the spiritual health of Abbot and Abbey is gravely endangered. As he points out to the Abbot, he is much troubled by all "those people who, inhabiting the houses of the spirit, suffer breakdowns of their spiritual and emotional health. It's quite obvious that especially in this kind of community the rate of collapse and incapacitation is very high. And if these people don't actually attract anybody's notice in your Abbey, the foundation stone for attracting such notice elsewhere later on has been laid here." Freimünster, then, is an Abbey suffering from moral and spiritual illness; it needs to be restored to health, to be "saved."

Is it actually saved in the end? The answer to this important question is almost certainly negative. The Arnulf Chalice or Grail is never recovered, for while Einberger the "saviour" is both a Knight and a Detective of sufficient, if not surpassing, purity to ask the right questions and get the right answers, we, however, are not sufficiently pure, and neither is the society in which we live. It is a "case," like that of the legendary Grail, which, in the final analysis, can only be solved "on the other side."[18]

Peter Firchow

Notes

[1] Evelyn S. & Peter E. Firchow, "Interview mit Alois Brandstetter," *Modern Austrian Literature*, 29 (1996), 36. The translations from the German here and elsewhere in the essay are mine.

[2] Alois Brandstetter, *Prosaauflösung. Studien zur Rezeption der höfischen Epik im frühneuhochdeutschen Prosaroman*. (Frankfurt: Athenäum Verlag, 1971), pp. 140-41.

[3] *Ibid.*, p. 37.

[4] Jutta Landa, "Ein Dichter der kultivierten Langeweile? Ein Gespräch mit Alois Brandstetter," *Modern Austrian Literature*, 25 (1992), 72.

[5] Alois Brandstetter, *Kleine Menschenkunde* (Salzburg: Residenz Verlag, 1987), p. 81.

[6] E. M. Forster, *Aspects of the Novel* (New York: Harcourt, Brace, Jovanovich, n.d.), p. 26.

[7] Firchow, "Interview," 26.

[8] Walther Killy, ed., *Literatur Lexikon*, vol. 2 (München: Bertelsmann, 1989), p. 162.

[9] Sigmund Geisler, *Der Erzähler Alois Brandstetter*. (St. Ingbert: Werner J. Röhrig Verlag, 1992), pp. 9-10.

[10] Jutta Landa, "*Vom Schnee der vergangenen Jahre*: The politics of Memory in Alois Brandstetter's Works," *Modern Austrian Literature*, 23 (1990), 205-06.

[11] Landa, "Dichter," 72.

[12] Alois Brandstetter, "Nachwort," in Alois Brandstetter, ed., *Österreichische Erzählungen des 20. Jahrhunderts*. (Salzburg: Residenz Verlag, 1984), pp.429-30.

[13] Quoted in Hans-Jürgen Schrader, "Nachwort," in Alois Brandstetter, *Landessäure. Starke Stücke und schöne Geschichten*, ed. Hans-Jürgen Schrader (Stuttgart: Reclam, 1986), p.89.

[14] Firchow, "Interview," 25-26.

[15] Geisler, p.15n.

[16] Landa, "*Schnee*," 78. There is, however, one unmistakable error made by Brandstetter which concerns the 1200 year anniversary of the foundation of Freimünster Abbey by Duke Arnulf of Bavaria. Celebrating such an anniversary would suggest that the Abbey was founded in 776 A. D., a date which is hardly possible because Arnulf died in 937 A. D. That it must be this particular Arnulf (sometimes called "Arnulf the Wicked" for having secularized various Benedictine monasteries in Bavaria) who is responsible for the foundation is clear from references to him as Duke of Bavaria and as belonging to the family of the Agilulfingers. If this were not the case, the Emperor Arnulf, last of the reigning Carolingians might also have come into question. He too is buried in Regensburg, though his dates make it equally impossible for him to have founded Freimünster (he died in 899). See *Lexikon für Theologie und Kirche*, vol. 1 (Freiburg: Herder Verlag, 1957), pp. 899-900. Brandstetter, who is presumably aware of the problems with his chronology here, may have wished to retain the founding date nevertheless because the 1200th anniversary of the Abbey of Kremsmünster occurred at this time. Kremsmünster, as he has acknowledged repeatedly (including in the Foreword to this translation) is the model for Freimünster.

[17] Brandstetter, *Menschenkunde*, p. 84

[18] It may also be relevant to note here that, according to one of the theories about the origins of the Grail legend, it first came to be known in the Benedictine Abbey of Fécamp in northern France.

ARIADNE PRESS
New Translations

Against the Grain
New Anthology of Contemporary
Austrian Prose
Selected by Adolf Opel

New Anthology of Contemporary
Austrian Folk Plays
Edited by Richard H. Lawson

The Massive File
on Zwetschkenbaum
By Albert Drach
Translated by Harvey I. Dunkle

Springtime on the Via Condotti
By Gustav Ernst
Translated by Todd C. Hanlin

Chasing after the Wind
Four Stories
By Barbara Frischmuth
Translated by Gerald Chapple
and James B. Lawson

Walk about the Villages
A Dramatic Poem
By Peter Handke
Translated by Michael Roloff

The Tragic Demise of a Faithful
Court Official
By F.von Herzmanovsky-Orlando
Translated by David A. Veeder

The House of the Linsky Sisters
By Florian Kalbeck
Translated by Michael Mitchell

Woman's Face of Resistance
By Marie-Thérèse Kerschbaumer
Translated by Lowell A. Bangerter

Ornament and Crime
Selected Essays
Selected by Adolf Opel
Translated by Michael Mitchell

Hollywood Haven
Homes and Haunts of the
European Emigrés and Exiles
in Los Angeles
By Cornelius Schnauber
Translated by Barbara Schoenberg

Ice on the Bridge
By Erich Wolfgang Skwara
Translated by Michael Roloff

Price and Plays
By Henry Gregor
[Prince Starhemberg]
Translated by Harvey I. Dunkle

Constanze Mozart
An Unimportant Woman
By Renate Welsh
Translated by Beth Bjorklund

Flowers for Jean Genet
By Josef Winkler
Translated by Michael Roloff

The Serf
By Josef Winkler
Translated by Michael Mitchell